"A rich and witty story w............ at its heart. . . . Quinn-Kong's story of an influencer mom sued by her resentful daughter is of the moment, but its exploration of female power and privilege is timeless."

—Amanda Eyre Ward, *New York Times* bestselling author of *Lovers and Liars*

"Quinn-Kong superbly crafts a tale about the price of online influence while making us root for both a mother and daughter on opposite sides of an issue you're sure to debate with your friends. A thought-provoking page-turner of a debut that is oh so timely!"

—Nancy Johnson, author of *The Kindest Lie*

"*Hate Follow* is a riveting, thought-provoking read about what parents owe their children in the internet era—and indeed what privacy even means in the dopamine-fueled age of social media. I am an instant and ardent fan."

—Katie Gutierrez, bestselling author of *More Than You'll Ever Know*

"Wildly timely, deeply relatable, *Hate Follow* had me rooting for every character even when it seemed impossible that they could all win."

—KJ Dell'Antonia, *New York Times* bestselling author of *The Chicken Sisters*

"I raced through this juicy, funny, insightful novel about a mom who makes a killing by oversharing her kids' lives online and the teenage daughter intent on stopping her. Erin Quinn-Kong examines all the fraught elements of this arrangement without ever casting judgment on her characters."

—J. Courtney Sullivan, *New York Times* bestselling author of *Friends and Strangers*

"An absolute binge-worthy delight! I couldn't tear myself away from Erin Quinn-Kong's razor-sharp novel. . . . Riveting, timely, meticulously plotted and deliciously entertaining, *Hate Follow* is a must-read!"

—May Cobb, author of *The Hunting Wives*

"Erin Quinn-Kong has written an irresistibly juicy story, so timely it feels downright prescient. . . . But the heart of the novel is the real empathy Quinn-Kong has for all her characters. Even when you love to hate them, you'll still be rooting for their happiness."

—Alex Kiester, author of *The Truth About Ben and June*

"*Hate Follow* is such an important and timely book. Without judgment, and with nuance and care, Erin Quinn-Kong highlights the pitfalls and repercussions of sharing so much of our lives, and our children's lives, online. . . . You will fly through this book and empathize with each of the fully drawn characters as they weigh the moral issue tearing their family apart."

—Amy Neff, author of *The Days I Loved You Most*

HATE FOLLOW

HATE FOLLOW

A NOVEL

ERIN QUINN-KONG

WM

WILLIAM MORROW

An Imprint of HarperCollins*Publishers*

This is a work of fiction. Names, characters, places, and incidents are products of the author's imagination or are used fictitiously and are not to be construed as real. Any resemblance to actual events, locales, organizations, or persons, living or dead, is entirely coincidental.

HarperCollins books may be purchased for educational, business, or sales promotional use. For information, please email the Special Markets Department at SPsales@harpercollins.com.

FIRST EDITION

Interior text design by Diahann Sturge-Campbell

Computer with phone illustration © vladwel/Stock.Adobe.com

Library of Congress Cataloging-in-Publication Data has been applied for.

ISBN 978-0-06-337973-2

24 25 26 27 28 LBC 5 4 3 2 1

For my parents, who believed I could
write a book long before I did.

And for my children, who inspired me
to put words on the page.

CHAPTER 1
WHITNEY

Everything looked perfect.

Surveying her home's expansive living area, Whitney Golden was proud of the lavish winter wonderland she'd created. There were not one, not two, but three Christmas trees—one decorated in dazzling shades of gold; another all white, from the lights to the star on top; and the third, set up on the back patio overlooking the pool, with old-fashioned glass ornaments that reminded her of a Norman Rockwell painting. Personalized plaid stockings adorned the mantel above the blazing fireplace, poinsettia-dotted garland and white twinkle lights lined the staircase banister, and the dining table was set for a festive dinner party. This was the Christmas scene Whitney had dreamed of as a little girl, and it was exactly right for the variety of holiday photos she had planned for that afternoon. The thought of shooting all the photos she needed to create content for the rest of the year made her giddy.

As "All I Want for Christmas Is You" blared from the speakers, squeals of delight came from her ten-year-old twin daughters, Chloe and Charlotte, and three-year-old son, Mason, who were in the kitchen with their aunt Rosie—

Whitney's youngest sister, who was living with them while attending college in town. Judging by the scent of chocolate in the air, Rosie had made cookies. Whitney hoped the kids didn't stain the outfits she'd picked out for them.

She looked at her watch. Where was Mia? School had been out for an hour, and it took only twenty minutes to walk home from the high school. They couldn't start the family photos until she arrived. Whitney's Instagram followers—all one million of them—loved family shots.

"Whitney, we're ready for you," the photographer called from the back porch, where he'd set up the first scene. Sweat shimmered on his forehead. They might have been creating winter content, but the October sun was beating down and it was a steamy eighty degrees in Austin, Texas.

"I'll be right there." Whitney grabbed her phone off the coffee table. No texts or missed calls from Mia. Whitney had planned the shoot meticulously to include her oldest, and she hated making everyone wait.

At least her boyfriend of six months, Ace, was right where he should be, standing across the room at the bar, where she'd placed a trio of holiday nutcrackers surrounded by tinsel. He was sipping his signature cocktail, a bourbon on the rocks. She'd kill for a drink right now. A heavy pour of red wine, and probably one of those cookies, would be her reward after the shoot was over.

A smile lit up her face when they made eye contact. Ace's presence was part of the reason she wanted this shoot to go perfectly. After months of teasing her followers with strategic shots of a tall, dirty-blond mystery man—a glimpse of his chiseled jawline here, a photo of them hugging from behind there—she was ready to hard launch him as her boyfriend on all her social channels. The plan was to get a few shots of just the two of them against a neutral background, so she could post the reveal whenever they were ready—preferably before the holiday rush started.

The air in the room shifted as the front door creaked open. "Mia?" she called.

A sigh confirmed it was, in fact, her daughter.

Whitney headed toward the foyer, excited to see what her firstborn thought of the holiday decor. But when she came around the corner, her fifteen-year-old looked anything but enthused.

"What are you wearing?" Mia's eyes were wide.

I could ask you the same thing, Whitney thought, taking in her daughter's baggy T-shirt, denim cutoffs, and hoodie tied around her waist. But she had to admit Mia possessed the fresh-faced glow she could never recapture as a thirty-seven-year-old mom of four, no matter how many serums she slathered on her face.

Whitney looked down at her hunter-green lace midi dress with elbow-length lace sleeves, paired with crimson pointed heels and perfectly matched lipstick—one of several outfits she had planned for today's shoot. Her assistant, Gabby, was currently steaming each piece of clothing in the breakfast nook so everything was crisp and ready for her to pull on.

She put her hands on her hips and preened. "You don't like it?"

"A bit much for a random Thursday in October, isn't it?" A frown touched Mia's lips.

Smiling, Whitney flicked her long, wavy auburn hair, which was mostly extensions, off her shoulders. "No, silly. Today's the Christmas shoot, remember?" Her daughter scowled in response.

Uh-oh. Mia wasn't happy. That seemed to be the case more and more. While Whitney would have once called her daughter an old soul, Mia had really been leaning into the teenage thing lately.

"C'mon. It'll be fun." She put her arm around her daughter's shoulders. "What do you think of the decorations?"

Instead of replying, Mia shook off her arm and stepped away. Whitney's stomach dropped. She could practically see the storm cloud hovering over Mia's head. Her eldest daughter was not going to make things easy. And Whitney needed her to make this easy, because they had a lot of photos to shoot in a short amount of time.

Before Whitney could say anything else, Tawny, her friend of nearly twenty years and trusty hair-and-makeup artist, came around the corner. Clad in her signature business-on-the-top, party-on-the-bottom look—black button-down shirt, flawless makeup, and her hair in short black finger waves paired with ripped jeans and tie-dye-printed Crocs—she did a little jig when she saw Mia. "How ya doing, girly?" Tawny pulled the teen in for a quick hug.

Mia's face lit up in her first smile in weeks before falling. "Tired." Her turquoise eyes were dark and sad, and the exhaustion on her face was evident.

A part of Whitney's heart squeezed. She knew Mia had been up late studying for her biology test.

"How did the test go?" Whitney asked. "Did your extra cramming session help?"

But before Mia could reply, the photographer invaded their group. "Can we get started?" He sounded irritated.

"One minute!" She turned to her daughter. "Your dress is upstairs. It's gorgeous—your favorite color. We only need a few family shots, okay?"

Mia looked at her with contempt, something she'd perfected recently. "No. I'm going to take a nap."

Whitney forced a smile, hoping Mia wouldn't cause a scene. "Oh, don't be a grouch. It'll only take a few minutes."

Resolute anger flared on Mia's face. "You and I both know it'll take hours to get the 'perfect shot'"—she used her fingers to make air quotes. "Not. Today."

"Listen," Whitney hissed. She hated being unprofessional, and Mia was backing her into a corner. "I'm not making a request. Go up and get dressed, and then come down for hair and makeup."

Her daughter's eyes flashed. "Seriously? I'm not your employee."

Whitney threw her hands into the air. "Why are you being like this?" She hated the whiny tinge in her own voice. "You used to love these shoots."

She thought back to the last family shoot they'd had, on Labor Day weekend. Mia had started out looking sullen and refused to wear makeup, but after a bit, she'd been laughing and posing for the camera with her siblings. Whitney chalked up her daughter's recent moodiness to starting high school. She'd always struggled with change.

Mia scoffed. "Yeah, Mom. You know me *so* well."

Whitney saw the fury on her daughter's face. Tawny must have seen it too, because she stepped between them. "Okay, okay. Let's all relax a bit."

The commotion had caught the attention of everyone in the large room, including the photographer. He shook his head at his assistant, who looked almost as young as Mia.

Ace headed their way, a typical carefree grin on his face. "Everything all right over here?"

"Mia doesn't want to do the shoot." She massaged her temples, where a dull ache had started.

"C'mon, Mia," Ace said. "Your red hair will look awesome in these shots." Mia's long, thick, copper-colored hair was so stunning that strangers on the street stopped her to comment on it—much to her dismay.

Mia didn't bother to conceal her eye roll.

Crossing her arms, Whitney glared at her daughter. "No need to be rude." She paused, deciding what move to make. "If you don't do this, you're grounded for three weeks."

Mia's laugh was hollow. "We both know you're not home enough to actually enforce that." Before Whitney could reply, Mia turned and sprinted up the stairs, pounding down the hallway before slamming her bedroom door.

Whitney rubbed her forehead and tears filled her eyes. She was tired too. And now she had a throbbing headache.

Ace snaked his arm around her waist. "Don't worry, babe. We'll get some nice photos without her."

She groaned. "Trust me, it's not that simple. Everyone will ask in the comments, 'Where's Mia? Where's Mia?' And then they'll start making up theories about why she's not in the holiday photos. Or they'll say I'm a bad mom for not including her."

"It's not the end of the world." Tawny gently took her by the arm and steered her into the makeshift makeup chair they'd fashioned in one corner of the living room. "Let's give your face a touch-up and brainstorm reasons to tell your followers why Mia isn't in the photos."

"While you do that, I'm going to check out those cookies." Ace arched his eyebrows at them. "Can I bring you ladies anything?"

"Maybe later. Thanks." Whitney smiled as she watched him saunter to the kitchen.

Dabbing a tissue under her eyes, she looked at Tawny in the mirror. "So much for the fun shoot I thought we were going to have." She sniffed. "I don't get her anymore."

Tawny tilted her head. "She's fifteen. Don't you remember how hard that age is?"

Whitney thought back to her own freshman year in high school in the Texas Panhandle. She never saw her parents, who both worked sixteen hours a day, yet barely made ends meet. After she finished classes every day, she walked to the elementary school to pick up her four younger siblings, and then made sure they were fed—some days all they had were bologna sandwiches and canned corn—bathed, and finished their homework before bed. She'd been a good student, like Mia, but she'd never gotten a chance to shine because she was too busy raising her siblings. Being in a photo shoot sounded like heaven compared to that.

She shuddered, pushing the memories away. "Posing for a few photos is not a big deal."

Tawny quickly freshened up Whitney's lipstick. "I remember high school like it was yesterday. It's a complicated time for everyone, especially when your mother is a gorgeous influencer."

Whitney's cheeks heated. Tawny was merely trying to butter her up, but she appreciated the compliment.

Tawny placed her warm hands on her shoulders. "Give her a break. She's had a hard life too."

Tears pricked Whitney's eyes yet again. Her gaze wandered to the mantel, where there was a photo of her, Mia, and the twins with her husband, Michael. She knew her eldest daughter was still grappling with her father passing away unexpectedly nearly four years before. Sometimes that felt like a lifetime ago.

Wait. What was today's date?

"Oh my god." Whitney covered her mouth with her hand. "The anniversary of Michael's death was on Tuesday. There's been so much going on with work I completely forgot. I'm such a jerk." She started to get up from the chair. "I have to talk to Mia."

Just then the photographer appeared next to Tawny in the mirror—and he looked downright pissed. "We've got to get moving." He tapped his watch. "I was booked for three hours, and almost an hour is gone."

Looking toward the stairs, Whitney felt her heart tug. She really needed to speak with Mia, to tell her she was sorry for forgetting the day that changed their lives forever. But it was clear from the look on the photographer's face that he wasn't going to wait a moment longer.

She blew out a deep breath. She should let Mia nap. After the shoot, she'd have a good, long talk with her daughter.

"I'm ready," Whitney said, squaring her shoulders. "We're doing the shoot with only the little kids today."

"Got it. Let's go." The photographer hustled back to his camera, which was ready and waiting on a tripod.

"Hey, kiddos!" She put on her sunshine mom voice as she called out to Chloe, Charlotte, and Mason, who were playing in the living room with Ace and Rosie. "Who wants presents?" She'd learned long ago that the key to keeping kids happy at photo shoots was new toys. Each child had three gifts under the tree ready to be opened, including Mia.

She laughed as Mason barreled toward her, with Rosie close behind. The solid toddler was like a tiny Mack truck. But before he could reach her, Mason tripped over his feet, his momentum tipping him forward until his forehead smacked the floor. Whitney's heart sank when he let out a wail.

Everything else fell away as she ran to him, swooping him into her arms in one quick movement. "Oh, sweetie." She scanned his face. No blood, no cuts. Only a red mark on his forehead. "That was quite a fall." She rubbed his back as he sobbed in her arms. "I think this calls for a Popsicle and an ice pack, don't you?"

Mason, his face the color of a beet, took a deep, shuddering breath and nodded. "Orange Popsicle."

She kissed his cheek. "You got it, bud."

As she turned toward the kitchen with Mason on her hip, the photographer stepped in front of them. "Can we start? It's getting late."

Holding up a hand, she scowled at him. "We need five minutes. All right? Then we will knock it out."

With a curt nod, the photographer huffed back to his camera.

Rolling her eyes, Whitney made a mental note to never hire him again. What did he want her to do? Leave her baby in a puddle on the floor?

After Mason had his Popsicle and was happily sucking away, she transferred him to Rosie's arms. Her sister blew a raspberry on Mason's cheek, making him shriek with laughter. She squeezed Rosie's arm, thankful yet again that she was there. Her brilliant, warm, computer science–major sister always made everything better.

With that situation taken care of, Whitney went looking for the twins. She found them playing a card game on the coffee table. They were pros at entertaining themselves among the chaos.

Decked out in sequined gray dresses with magenta headbands holding back their long strawberry-blond hair, they were barefoot, glittery rainbow nail polish sparkling on their toes. She loved the casual touch. "You two look awesome. Ready to see your gifts and take some photos?"

Chloe's and Charlotte's faces lit up as they jumped to their feet. At least they loved getting their pictures taken.

"Let's do this." She reached out to take Chloe's hand, and her daughter immediately grasped palms with Charlotte, the two forever connected.

Hand in hand in hand, they headed to the Christmas tree to get their shots, with Ace, Rosie, and Mason close behind.

* * *

Two and a half hours later, they'd blasted through five different photo setups and everyone besides Tawny had packed up and left. Ace had headed home to get ready for a flight the next morning, Rosie was feeding the kids dinner, and Whitney had poured herself that glass of wine.

"Want one?" she asked her best friend.

"Nah. I need to get home." Tawny rolled her makeup case toward the door, stopping to give her friend a hug. "Great shoot today. You're a far cry from the eighteen-year-old country bumpkin I used to know."

Whitney snorted. "That is true." When she'd first met Tawny, she'd just arrived in Austin after graduating high school and hightailing it out of the small town she'd lived in her whole life. While plenty of her peers were going on to college, Whitney had been thrilled to get a job waitressing at a sports bar near the University of Texas at Austin. Tawny had been her coworker. Seven years her senior with killer cornrows and flawless makeup, she had taken Whitney under her wing and taught her how to thrift shop and helped her open a bank account. Whitney had worshipped her. She still did.

Tawny nodded toward the staircase, which led to Mia's room. "Everything gonna be okay with you two?"

"Oh, yeah." Whitney gave her a sad smile. "I feel awful I forgot Michael's anniversary." She grimaced. "And I had no idea how hard it would be to mother a teenager. You can't make things all better with a kiss and a Popsicle."

Tawny smiled, kindness in her brown eyes, then chuckled.

"It gets harder. And easier." Tawny had two kids of her own, a senior in high school and a sophomore in college. "I know it's frustrating, but you have to start trying to understand Mia and her emotions now if you want to be close when she's older."

Close. Whitney remembered when Mia was little and had to be touching her at all times. While she cooked dinner, when she tried to fold laundry, even when she had to pee. Back then she would have given anything for some space, and now she had to worry they'd never be close again?

Tawny turned the doorknob, bringing Whitney out of her daydream. "I'll see you soon, okay?"

Whitney gave Tawny one last hug before closing the door behind her. She turned toward the staircase and took a deep breath, steeling herself to apologize to her daughter for forgetting about the date of her father's death and their annual ritual of talking about their cherished memories of him over breakfast for dinner—his favorite meal. *I'm so sorry I forgot, Michael*, she thought, squeezing her eyes shut and rubbing her thumb along the inside of her wrist, their secret signal when they wanted to leave a party or needed out of an annoying conversation. Now it was her reminder of his gentle touch.

Her heart raced as she climbed the stairs.

"Knock, knock." She softly tapped her knuckles on Mia's door. No response. "Mia? Are you awake?" She waited a beat before pushing the door open. Inside, Whitney found an empty bed and no sign of her supposedly napping daughter.

Turning back toward the door, she shook her head in disbelief. Mia had snuck out.

October 12 - 7:36 p.m.
Smug Takes: Did you see the outfit Whitney posted in her holiday photo shoot preview? A dark green lace dress with red heels—woof.

October 12 - 7:42 p.m.
Retail Therapy & Rainbows: Yeah, that look was not cute.

October 12 - 8:05 p.m.
Moose Willis: And it probably cost thousands of dollars. I hate to say it, but I really miss the old, authentic Whitney.

October 12 - 8:17 p.m.
Big Hick Energy: Me too! Also, I couldn't help but notice Mia was nowhere to be found in that behind-the-scenes footage on Stories. She is so over getting a camera shoved in her face 24/7.

CHAPTER 2
MIA

The good part about living in a house always filled with people was that escaping unnoticed was a breeze.

After the scene with her mother downstairs, Mia had seethed on her bed, trying to ignore the berry-colored party dress her mom had hung on the closet door for her to wear during the photo shoot. With a lace top and taffeta bottom, the dress was pretty but totally not her style anymore. She would have preferred black and simple. Not that her mother cared.

Sometimes, she hated this house and the people inside it. Well, her mother and that cheesy guy she was dating. She adored her little brother and her Aunt Rosie. And her twin sisters were pretty great, though it bothered her they loved getting dolled up and photographed for Instagram. Mia pulled a pillow over her face and screamed.

Even her bedroom annoyed her. It had been decorated by an interior designer her mother had hired. Everything was very pretty, styled in shades of cream with purple and green accents her mother called lavender and mint. She'd told them she loved it—anything less than gushing would have disappointed her mom—but what Mia really wanted to do was plaster her walls with Harry Styles posters, Broadway ticket stubs, and vision boards. Instead, she got framed art and color-coordinated bookshelves.

Mia covered her ears, trying to block out the loud music and shrieks of delight coming from downstairs. She was never going to fall asleep here. She fished her phone out of her pocket before rolling onto her stomach and shooting off a text message to her best friend, Camila: Can I come over? My family is driving me bonkers.

Camila replied in an instant. For sure. My mom's making churros.

She'd been eating Camila's mom's churros since they had met in kindergarten. Omw! she messaged her.

Launching off the bed, Mia picked up her backpack and shoved in a T-shirt, underwear, and a clean pair of jeans. She knew Camila's parents would ask her to stay for dinner, and sometimes that turned into her spending the night after doing homework with Camila. She loved staying over in their cozy, quiet home, with no assistants or photographers or siblings. It was the only place she ever really relaxed anymore.

Easing open her bedroom door, she crept down the hallway. Mia paused on the stairs and held her breath when the blaring Christmas music changed songs. Once it picked up again, she tiptoed down the last few steps before slipping out the front door.

The short mile from her house to Camila's suddenly seemed like it stretched on for ages. She shook her head and kicked at a rock. What a crap day. She'd gotten another C on a biology test—and that was after she'd pulled an all-nighter. Then there was the stupid photo shoot and the fight with her mom. Mia couldn't believe her mother hadn't even said anything about the anniversary of her dad's death. No one in the family had, though she guessed Chloe and Charlotte got a pass since they had been so young when it happened. And her mom had still been pregnant with Mason. Sometimes she wondered if she was the only person who even cared about their dad anymore.

The afternoon sunshine made her sweat. Mia stopped to drop her backpack on the sidewalk. She untied her favorite dark green Northwestern hoodie from around her waist and stuffed it in her bag. It was her dad's alma mater and where she planned to go to undergrad. If she could keep her grades up. While some kids might not care about the C in bio, school used to be the one straightforward thing in her life. And now it too was a struggle. High school was kicking her butt. How was she going to be a cardiologist if she couldn't figure this stuff out?

She swung her backpack onto her shoulders and started to pound down the sidewalk again.

Finally rounding the last corner to Camila's tree-lined street, Mia brightened when she saw the Garcias' blue bungalow. She loved this little house a hundred times more than the one her own family moved into a year ago. With a brown brick exterior, black shutters, and stately white pillars, Mia's family's house—okay, mansion—looked like something out of an architecture magazine. It even had a small balcony over the front door, which seemed unnecessary, but her mother loved it. "Think of the photo ops!" she'd trilled when they first toured the property.

Camila's house was small and cozy. Like a real family lived

there, not one who posed like they were a perfect family for Instagram.

Shame coursed through Mia as she remembered the scene she'd caused at home. She sighed. Maybe she should have done the shoot. It would have made her mother so happy. But she couldn't stomach it today. It was too much on top of her biology test and the unmentioned anniversary.

As she scurried up the walkway, she ached for the way her family used to be. Before her dad died. Before her mother became the city's biggest influencer, started worrying about how she looked all the time, and bought a grand house. At least they'd stayed near their old neighborhood. Mia wouldn't have been able to stand it if her mother had made her move schools and leave Camila. Not after everything she'd been through.

Mia didn't bother to knock. The Garcias thought of her as their second child, and she considered them her second family. As she pushed open the front door, the smell of fried dough and sugar wafted over her. She took a deep breath, feeling her body and brain calm immediately. It was like getting wrapped up in the world's biggest bear hug.

"I'm here!" she called, crossing through the open living room as she headed toward the kitchen.

"Hey." Camila looked up from her seat at the kitchen counter. She was wearing an Austin City Limits crop top, baggy joggers, and bright orange sneakers. Her long, dark hair was thrown up into a messy bun and gold hoops shimmered from her ears. Mia wished she could be as effortlessly stylish.

"What are you working on?" she asked, sitting on the stool next to Camila.

"Ugh. English. I do not know what to write for this essay." Camila scowled, grabbing a churro off the plate in front of her and dipping it into some chocolate sauce. "I'm eating my feelings. Help yourself."

"Thanks." Mia picked up a warm churro. Camila's mother cooked for her more than her own mother these days.

"Hi, Pepita." Camila's mom, Eva, rounded the corner from the laundry room with a fresh load of folded whites. Mia grinned when she heard her nickname—in the second grade, she'd played a pumpkin seed in the school play, and Eva still said it was one of the cutest things she'd ever seen. "How are things?"

"Hey, Eva." When they'd started high school a few months before, Camila's mom insisted Mia call her by her first name. It quickly became second nature.

Mia filled them in on her crappy day. "And my mom's pissed at me because I wouldn't pose for her stupid Christmas shoot."

"Ooh! Christmas shoot?" Camila squealed. "Tell her I'll do it. Though my curvy Latina *lewk* probably wouldn't match the vibe of the rest of the family."

Mia giggled as she shook her head at her friend. "Too bad we can't switch families," she said, as she had so many times before. "I'll stay here and eat churros."

That's why they were such a good pair. Camila was a confident dancer who liked nothing more than being the center of attention, while Mia's whole goal in life was to avoid any missteps that could cause her to stand out. If you googled the word "gawky" you'd probably find her picture.

Eva gave her a smile from the stove, where she'd started

stirring something in a big pot. It looked like soup. "Was the shoot that bad?"

Mia scrunched her nose. "No. But I hate that she always assumes I'll do it. She never *asks* if I want to. And I have my own stuff going on." Mia didn't tell them her mother had forgotten about the anniversary of her dad's death. She wasn't sure why. Probably because it would make her emotional, and she hated getting emotional. And because she didn't want them to think bad things about her mom—even if her mom deserved it.

Eva leaned against the counter as she considered Mia's words. "Sounds like you need to talk to your mom. Tell her how you feel. You girls are getting older now. You should get a say in how you spend your time."

"Does that mean I don't have to do my chores anymore?" Camila asked mid-chew. "'Cause I definitely don't want to spend my time cleaning toilets."

"Ha. Nice try, mija." Eva reached over the counter to pinch her daughter's cheek. "Chores are still mandatory in this house."

Camila wrinkled her nose. "Burn."

Eva picked up the laundry basket. "Stay for dinner?"

Mia nodded gratefully. "Thanks."

"Text your mom to let her know." She headed toward the bedrooms at the back of the house. "I'm going to put the clothes away and maybe lie down for a bit. I think one of the kiddos may have given me something. Little germ gremlins." Eva worked at the neighborhood preschool, so she picked up every virus going around.

Camila and Mia snorted as she left the room. "Why can't

I have a mom like yours? She's so awesome," Mia said. Eva was everything Whitney wasn't: round and soft, sweet and caring, a good cook.

"She's pretty great." Camila shrugged. "Though I wouldn't mind if she got all the free makeup and clothes that your mom does."

Mia groaned and gave her a gentle shove.

Camila stuck her finger into the leftover chocolate sauce on her plate and licked it. "Just saying."

A few hours later, Mia was finishing a delicious dinner of pozole with Camila, Eva, and Camila's dad, Omar. They'd had a lively conversation where everyone went around the table and shared their highs and lows for the day. It was so nice. So normal. Whenever she was home for dinner these days, it was usually her, the kids, and Rosie. She loved her aunt, but she missed her mom. Her mother and Ace went to a media event, to a party, or on a date several nights a week. And when she was home, her mom was always busy with the kids, especially Mason, who was a terror at dinnertime. Her mom rarely asked her about school or what was going on in her life. Mia swore she could disappear and no one would notice.

After helping clean up and leaving Eva and Omar to watch whatever court drama was on, the girls headed upstairs to do homework.

They sat side by side on the unmade bed, laptops open. Camila worked on her dreaded English essay, and Mia focused on her algebra homework. She struggled through a few problems, but her mind kept drifting back to her fight with her mom. Mia checked her phone to see if her mother had texted since she had let her know she was staying over for dinner.

Tell Eva and Omar thank you. And I'm sorry I let the anniversary of dad's death pass without a mention. There is no excuse for forgetting. (Though I wish you wouldn't have snuck out.)

Mia's throat tightened. Her mother had remembered, after all. She dabbed at her eyes with the sleeve of her sweatshirt.

"You okay?" Camila asked.

"I'm fine. Texting with my mom."

When she didn't elaborate, Camila turned back to her essay. After ten years of friendship, Camila knew Mia would talk when she was ready.

Mia started to type again: It's okay. Sorry about today.

She paused. Was she sorry, though? Her mother always expected her to take photos for the blog. But had she ever actually asked if Mia wanted to? She clicked the back button on the phone. Delete, delete, delete.

She tried again: Hope the shoot went well. Sorry about the fight . . . But then deleted that too. It felt weird to even mention the shoot. Shouldn't her mother be the one making sure she was okay after their fight? Wasn't that, like, a parent's entire job? She looked over at Camila. She doubted her friend ever agonized over texting her mom like this.

Mia turned back to her algebra homework. The xs and ys in the equations swam in front of her. This wasn't complex stuff, but her brain was not functioning. She needed sleep.

"I'm toast. Can I stay tonight?" Mia knew she didn't have to ask, but it still felt like the polite thing to do.

Camila nodded, not even glancing up from her computer. "Of course."

"You're the best." Mia nudged her knee gently against Camila's. She knew how lucky she was to have such a good friend. Camila looked up and stuck her tongue out at her.

Laughing, Mia picked up her phone again. She needed to text her mom something. Her eyelids started to droop as she snuggled into her best friend's soft pillow. Before she nodded off, Mia typed, Exhausted. Staying with C tonight, and hit send.

The phone lit up as she rolled over and placed it on Camila's nightstand. It was her mom: OK. Good night, xo

CHAPTER 3
WHITNEY

By eight thirty in the morning, Whitney had worked out with her trainer, scrubbed her face with a new exfoliating wash—a gift from a brand that wanted her to review it—and gotten dressed in a pair of boyfriend-style jeans she'd promised her followers she'd try out. She'd made everyone breakfast and hugged the girls goodbye—Rosie dropped them off at school before heading to her own classes at UT—and then she'd taken Mason to day care.

It was their normal routine, but one person was absent. Even though Mia wasn't much of a morning person, Whitney missed her presence, grunting one-word answers to questions while scarfing down a bagel. She wished they'd been able to talk the night before, but she also knew sometimes Mia needed space.

Whitney forced thoughts of their fight to the back of her mind as she perched at the kitchen table with her assistant, Gabby. They were going over the next week's schedule for her blog and social media accounts.

"Thanks for all your help at the shoot yesterday." Whitney took a sip from her second cup of coffee. Usually, she allowed herself only one cup (with two tablespoons of fat-free half-and-half—yes, she measured), but she felt particularly unfocused today so she let herself have a second. TGIF and all that. "I'm relieved we have the images done before all the holiday madness starts. Now we only have to focus on the words."

"It was a great shoot," Gabby replied, pushing her pink glasses up on her nose and sweeping her dark bangs off her forehead like she meant business. "And I can't wait for the meeting with Amazon Fashion next week to discuss your capsule collection. Did you want me to do anything in particular to prepare?"

Whitney sat up straighter. This clothing line was one of her biggest career achievements to date—along with her makeup collection with Sephora, which sold out in two hours. "Would you pull pictures of some of the other influencers' clothing lines? I'd really like to avoid the pastel color palettes and sweet floral prints they all seem to pick. I want jewel tones and bold prints."

While Whitney hadn't designed the clothes—someone else did that—she got to select the silhouettes, colors, prints, and fabrics. She was pumped her name was on the label, and she got a percentage of every piece sold.

"Will do." Gabby flipped open her laptop and added an action item to her long to-do list. "And I saw that you loaded the social media content for the next two weeks. That's awesome."

Whitney smiled. "Thanks." Some influencers of her stature relied on teams of people to help them create their content. But she prided herself on writing every word that was posted on Instagram and TikTok or appeared in her weekly newsletter and on her blog. She had a knack for writing posts that struck the perfect balance of self-deprecating, authentic, and revealing that her followers craved. She'd even gotten into making video content the last few years, thanks to copious pressure from her manager, Taylor. Whitney's presence on TikTok was much smaller than on Instagram, but she enjoyed posting cute videos of the twins dancing or a life hack or parenting tip. It added a whole new dimension to her content.

Gabby continued with her list. "On Monday, we have three sponsored posts to shoot: Colorful Calendars daily planners, Blacksmith leather backpacks, and Skinny Mini cocktail mix. And on Tuesday you're scheduled to do an Instagram try-on at Nordstrom, so I'll go over those ad campaign requirements and make sure we have everything covered."

"Perfect." Whitney had lucked out when she found Gabby. A graduate of Texas State's print journalism program, the twenty-four-year-old was smart, creative, and incredibly diligent. Whitney had been burned by assistants before—ones who'd been rude to clients or made glaring mistakes on contracts—so she planned to hold on to the calm and professional Gabby for as long as she could.

Everyone thought being an influencer was a mindless job mostly involving photo shoots and writing pithy Instagram captions. While Whitney did do those things, most people didn't realize companies were paying her in the high five figures to create promotional campaigns with them. And each one came with specific requirements and details, including how many social media posts, blogs, Reels, TikToks, and Stories to create, which products to feature, and exactly what to say about each one—all while making it seem as natural as possible. It was a lot to juggle. She was grateful Gabby was there to make sure she didn't miss anything critical.

The only other person she worked with was Taylor, who handled all of her sponsorships and contract negotiations. Whitney had nicknamed Taylor "Scary Spice." She was the type of person who would compliment your lipstick one minute and rail at a barista for getting her coffee order wrong the next.

Whitney looked at her watch. She was scheduled to have a call with Taylor in an hour, and she had some writing to do first. "Anything else?"

"Nope. I'm going to run to the craft store to look for Halloween projects for the blog." Gabby gathered up her phone, papers, and water bottle. "I'll be back before lunch. Oh, and remember to photograph your breakfast for next week's What I Eat in a Day post. I know your followers will love that."

Whitney groaned. "I forgot." She pictured the two doughnuts she'd shoved down her throat an hour ago while standing over the kitchen sink. But she couldn't tell her followers that. "I had yogurt and berries, so I can easily re-create it. And I'm also going to post an Ask Me Anything box later."

"Excellent. They go crazy for those." Gabby headed toward the front door. "Shoot me a text if you need anything while I'm gone."

"Will do!" Whitney tried to match her assistant's chipperness, but she wasn't successful. In the back of her mind, she was still thinking about the argument with Mia—and how she'd forgotten the anniversary of Michael's death.

As the front door clicked shut behind Gabby, Whitney

headed toward her office. Strolling over to the bookshelf, she ran her finger along the spines until she found what she was looking for. Plucking the photo book from its spot, she plopped down in her desk chair and opened it up. Her throat tightened as she took in the pictures on the pages. Michael, her sweet, serious husband. She'd started making annual photo books the year they got married. This one was for what ended up being his last Father's Day. She'd filled the pages with all her favorite pictures of Michael and the kids—the day Mia was born, Michael's eyes soft with love as he gazed at her tiny face; introducing Mia to her new baby sisters; the first time the twins tried guacamole at their neighborhood Tex-Mex spot. Seeing their precious memories laid out in front of her made her miss their old life something fierce. She'd met Michael at twenty, still young and naive. He'd been two years older, so smart and serious and sure of himself. He'd made her feel safe.

She turned the page and saw it: her favorite picture of Michael. He was holding the twins, who were about six months old, one on each knee, as Mia hung on his back, her arms practically strangling his neck. All four had enormous grins on their faces. The joy was palpable.

Opening her phone, she scrolled through the gallery until she saw the same image. Clicking on it, she uploaded it to her Instagram page and started typing.

My sweet Michael, gone four years this week. Though right now, looking at this picture of him and his girls, I can practically feel him next to me. Life has continued, but he is missed today and always.

Seconds after Whitney uploaded the Instagram post, comments started to appear from her followers.

> What a lovely tribute. I know he's looking down on you and your beautiful children.

> I lost my husband to an aggressive form of cancer ten years ago, and I still think about him every day. Thank you for making me feel seen.

> I admire your strength. May your beautiful memories with Michael bring you comfort.

Whitney's vision blurred as she read the tender and heartfelt comments. She loved the people who followed her. And no matter what people thought about influencers, she knew the online community she had created mattered.

Wiping her eyes, she looked at her watch. Only twenty minutes until her call with Taylor, and she desperately needed to go through her email inbox before they chatted. She'd let herself read one more comment, and then she'd put her phone down and open her laptop.

A chill ran up her arms as she read the latest comment, from a woman named Jane Mumford:

> I don't know if this is the right time to tell you this, but last weekend my husband mentioned his left arm was tingling. I remembered your husband's heart attack, so I made him go straight to the ER. He had a blockage in his artery and had to have surgery immediately! Thank you for saving his life.

She couldn't stop herself from typing a reply: Jane! That just gave me chills. I am thrilled your husband is okay and really appreciate you sharing. xo

Leaning back in her chair, Whitney shook her head as warmth spread through her chest. She had saved someone's life. Never in her wildest dreams would she have imagined that.

Whitney thought back to eight years before, to the random night she sat down at her computer and started pouring her heart out to the anonymous void of the internet about being a struggling mom to two-year-old twins who wouldn't sit still and a seven-year-old who asked her a million questions each day. Back then few moms were writing about the hardships of parenting like they do now. She'd confessed that she hadn't slept for a year after the twins were born and it almost broke her; how she desperately wanted to get the spark back in her marriage, but by the end of a long day at home with three kids, all she wanted to do was sit on the couch, eat chips, and watch Netflix; and how sometimes she missed when it was just her, Michael, and Mia—before the twins arrived. The three of them had been so close, and Whitney had found so much joy in raising her little girl. She loved all her kids equally, but there was something special about your first kid and the one-on-one time you got with them.

She'd had no idea the blog would take off the way it did, but she'd quickly amassed a devoted following of other moms who just got her. And then when Michael died and her life imploded, Whitney had wanted to write about it. *Needed* to write about it. And not only had her community embraced her words but they'd understood. And then the sponsors started knocking, and she'd realized she could make enough money for her and the kids to live comfortably. There aren't a lot of careers that allow you to stay home with your kids while making good money. Absurd money, really.

And now look—she'd saved someone's life. How amazing was that?

Her phone rang. She hoped it was Mia calling to ask her a question or maybe even to chat. But she didn't recognize the number.

"Hello?"

"Hey, sis! How the hell are ya?" It was her brother. The one who was almost thirty years old yet couldn't seem to hold a job—or his liquor.

"Hi, Brendan." She stood and started pacing. Brendan only called when he needed something. And something was usually money. "What's up?"

Her brother cleared his throat. Whitney could hear yelling and banging in the background. "Well, ah . . ."

"Spit it out, please. I have a call in a few minutes."

"I kind of got arrested last night."

Whitney stopped pacing and sat down hard on the arm of the sofa. "Oh, come on. You promised this wouldn't happen again."

"I know, I know." She pictured her little brother raking his hand through his curly hair, the same reddish-brown shade as hers. The same hair she used to love to brush after she bathed him when he was a toddler. He still had the same round cheeks and mischievous mahogany eyes he did back then. And he still tried to get away with everything.

"But it wasn't my fault this time. I was helping out a friend, and there was a misunderstanding with the cops."

"Sure there was." Even though her brother was almost four hundred miles away, she knew he could tell from her tone she was not amused. "Have you tried Stephanie or Tom?" Their sister, who was married to a cotton farmer and pregnant with a baby girl, and their high school PE teacher brother, who had his own young family, still lived in their hometown along with Brendan. Whitney was the only one who had left.

"No. You know neither one has any money."

Suddenly parched, Whitney headed to the fridge to grab a drink. While getting a call from jail may be out of the norm for most families, when you had a brother like Brendan, this could be any old Friday. There was no need to beat around the bush. "How much do you need?" she asked, taking a sip of her LaCroix.

"Ten thousand dollars."

Whitney choked on her sparkling water. "What?" she sputtered. "Are you kidding me? What in the world did you do?"

"Last night was a disorderly conduct charge. But since it's my second, I need twenty-five hundred for bail. But the rest of the money is for, ah, some gambling debts."

Gambling. Just like dad. Acid started to burn in her stomach. She'd never forget the nights when she'd hear her mother screaming at her father for losing that week's grocery money at the blackjack table or betting their rent at the horse races. Every time, her father would cry and beg and promise he wouldn't do it again. And her mother would pick up more shifts, leaving Whitney to do everything at home. And then her father would do it all over again a few months later.

Looking up at the ceiling as her brother yammered on about poker tournaments and lawyer fees, Whitney couldn't believe history was repeating itself. This was why she stayed away from her family as much as possible. They always tried to suck her into their problems.

Besides, she didn't even know if she had an extra ten thousand dollars lying around. Numbers started flipping through her head.

Mortgage for the new house: $8,000/month
Austin's astronomical property taxes: $29,000/year
The family's health insurance: $2,500/month
Rosie's in-state college tuition and books: $15,000/year
Gabby's salary: $32,000/year
Mason's day care: $1,300/month
Credit card bills: $3,000/month—on the months she really
  watched their spending
Debt she didn't like to discuss: $2,000/month

Plus there was contributing to the four kids' college accounts, and all the normal bills: groceries, clothing, electricity, phone, and internet. Everything was on her. As the numbers added up in her mind, she could practically feel sandbags getting stacked on her shoulders.

"I don't know if I have it." Her voice was void of emotion.

"Oh, please, sis." Brendan's voice quickly went from calm to high-pitched. "I don't have anyone else to ask."

Neither did she. There was no one to ask.

Whitney had forgotten to add one of the other biggest expenses to her mental list: the rent for her mother's retirement community, which Whitney had been paying for since her dad died two years ago. She'd moved her mom there after she realized Sandy needed companionship—and help cooking and cleaning since advanced arthritis in her hands made it difficult for her to do most chores. Whitney was more than happy to help her mother, but the cost was like having a second mortgage. Still, there was never a good time for her to visit her hometown, so footing the bill helped alleviate her guilt.

Maybe she could use that in her favor. "Okay. I'll send the money—but only if you promise to visit Mom every Saturday for the rest of the year." Whitney knew her other siblings who lived in town visited their mother often, but Brendan barely managed once every two or three months. "And you have to call me when you're there and let me talk to her."

Now it was Brendan's turn to sigh. "Shit, sis. The rest of the year? That's like ten weeks."

"Then I'm paying you a thousand dollars per visit. What a deal."

Her brother groaned. "You're right." He paused. "Thanks, sis. This'll be the last time . . . promise."

"It better be." She doubted that, but one had to have hope in life. "Talk to you and Mom tomorrow."

"Oh, crap . . . tomorrow?" Brendan paused. "I think I may have plans."

"Do you want the money or not?"

"I do, I do." He sounded defeated.

"Then I'll speak to you and Mom tomorrow. Two o'clock, sharp."

"Okay, okay. Two o'clock. Bye, sis. And thanks again."

"You're welcome." She ended the call and sighed. Her brother knew she'd always bail him out; the pull of family obligation was too strong.

Sitting on the sofa, she rubbed her forehead, where an ache crackled. She needed to call her accountant to make sure she even had the money. More always seemed to be going out than coming in. Then she had to ask Taylor if she could wrangle her a few new sponsorship deals.

She hung her head in her hands. Worrying about money was so overwhelming. She'd been doing it all her life, except those years with Michael, when she'd been naive enough to stick her head in the sand and let him handle everything. Little did she know they were living beyond their means, and he'd made a bad investment he'd never told her about. They were in the hole—by a lot—and she'd had no idea.

When he died, it had taken her months to sort out where their money was and how much they'd owed to whom—all on top of her grief, raising three kids, and being pregnant with a fourth. Each day felt like she was swimming in the ocean, struggling to breathe, as wave upon wave crashed down over her. She'd vowed then and there to never financially rely on a man ever again.

Her thoughts were interrupted by her phone ringing. It was Taylor, right on time.

Time to get back to work.

October 13 – 9:56 a.m.
Waxing and Chillaxing: Whitney posted about her dead husband again. She must need some bills paid.

October 13 – 10:15 a.m.
Smug Takes: Yep. Her fan poodles always go crazy for those posts. Someone even said Whitney saved her husband's life! Give me a break.

October 13 – 10:17 a.m.
Thirst Trap: Anyone who uses a dead spouse for content deserves to be canceled.

October 13 – 10:19 a.m.
Smug Takes: There are A LOT of influencers who need to be canceled then.

October 13 – 10:20 a.m.
The Good Karen: She also mentioned a "secret project" on Stories. Any guesses what it is? I'm betting a fashion line with Amazon.

October 13 – 10:27 a.m.
Olivia Mild: Oh, it's totally an Amazon fashion line, exactly like all the other big influencers are doing these days. Much original.

CHAPTER 4

MIA

Mia stared out the window during social studies, her last class of the day. She had no idea what was being discussed or what she was supposed to be learning. The clock ticked down, second by second, minute by minute, and all she could think about was that she had to go home when the bell rang. And her mom was going to want to talk.

Mr. Tompkins told them he was going to show a video about the Declaration of Independence. At least it would eat up the rest of the class time.

As her teacher queued up the video, Mia felt something hit her shoulder. It was a balled-up piece of paper.

"Hey," someone stage-whispered behind her. It was Olivia Banks, the most popular girl in her class. And one of the meanest. She had a Cheshire cat–style smile on her face. "I saw your mom on Instagram." Mia's cheeks grew hot. Olivia never talked to her. Probably because Mia was so far below her on the social ladder.

"If she's an 'influencer'"— Olivia used air quotes, exactly like Mia had at her mother yesterday—"why do you dress so bad?"

All the people sitting around them snickered. Olivia

looked pleased with herself. She'd been a bully since elementary school.

Before Mia could think of a reply, Mr. Tompkins flipped the lights off and started the video. Mia sank down in her chair, pulling her Northwestern hoodie tighter around her. Her stomach burned. She'd never thought about kids at school following her mom on social media or reading her blog. Why would they? There was no way they wanted parenting tips or to dress like her mother.

Mia's blood ran cold. Oh no. Had her mom been posting embarrassing stuff about her?

While the person in the video droned on about the three purposes of the Declaration of Independence, all Mia could think about was wanting independence from her mother. She couldn't remember the last time she'd read her mom's blog or checked her Instagram. Usually, she tried to avoid both at all costs. But after Olivia's comment, she realized she was going to have to look and see what ammunition her classmates had against her.

The video finished right as the last bell of the day rang. All the kids in her class got up and headed for the door, excited to start their weekends. Olivia clustered by the door with her friends.

Taking a deep breath, Mia pushed past them, bracing herself for the inevitable snarky comment from Olivia.

"Say hi to your mom for me." All the girls around her giggled in harmony.

Head down, Mia ignored the laughter coming from Olivia and her minions. She and Camila called them the Filters, because they were always on their phones, taking selfies. Mia bet Olivia's photo gallery was filled with pictures of herself with unnaturally smooth skin and duck lips.

She avoided eye contact with anyone in the hallways, heading straight to her locker.

Wrenching her locker open, she noticed the photo of her and her mom at *Hamilton* from when the show came to Austin a few years ago. Her mother's manager had pulled some strings and gotten them front-row seats. It had been a great night. Had her mother posted about it on the internet too? Probably. Most likely that was why her manager had snagged them seats in the first place, for "content." This realization made the whole experience seem less special. Less real. Mia grabbed her biology book for the studying she planned to do all weekend and slammed her locker shut.

"Whoa." Camila strolled toward her. "You okay there?"

"I'm fine." She zipped up her backpack, not ready to tell Camila about Olivia's remarks yet. "Excited for the weekend."

"I hear ya." Camila opened her locker, which was plastered with pictures of her with Mia, and her with her parents, and dozens of shots of Jennifer Lopez. She was Camila's idol. Camila always said she wanted to be a triple threat, like J.Lo. The only problem was she couldn't sing. Or really act. But she could dance, and she was very enthusiastic. "Ready to head out?"

Mia nodded, falling into step with her best friend. It was an unspoken agreement that they were heading to Cam's house. Camila didn't have dance practice on Fridays, and Mia wasn't ready to face her mother yet. Not before she did some research.

Outside on the school's lawn, the freshmen and sopho-
mores were clustered in groups in the grass, either hanging
out or waiting for their parents to pick them up. All the cool,
older kids were headed for the parking lot, where they'd
jump into their fancy cars. Mia could hear people talking
about the upcoming UT football game and a big concert at
ACL Live that weekend, not that she planned to go to either.

"You know what I was thinking about?" Camila looked
excited as they turned off school property and toward her
house. "My birthday."

"In February?" That was four months away.

Camila nodded eagerly. "Yeah. My mom and dad said
they're going to throw me a quinceañera. Isn't that awesome?
It's gonna be small, not a blowout like some girls have, but
I'm so excited. I've been thinking about planning a choreo-
graphed dance. Would that be weird?"

Mia didn't know much about quinceañeras, besides what
Camila had told her about the Mexican tradition, but she
knew her friend was an amazing dancer. "Not at all."

As Camila continued to chatter about the party, Mia
wished she had her best friend's confidence. There was nothing she'd hate more than being in the spotlight for her fifteenth birthday, performing a dance for a crowd of people.
But she was happy her friend was happy.

For her own fifteenth birthday the month before, her
mom had wanted to throw her a party, but Mia had refused.
Instead, she, Camila, and her family had gone to her favorite
Tex-Mex restaurant for enchiladas. When the waiters had
come out at the end of the meal with a huge slice of tres
leches cake piled high with whipped cream and sung "Happy

Birthday," her mother and Camila had hooted and hollered. Mia had wished she could melt into her seat like queso.

"I really hope I can find a magenta sequined dress. Or maybe jade. I look really good in jewel tones." Camila was still talking about her birthday party as they walked into her house twenty minutes later.

They dropped their backpacks on the floor and took off their shoes. Mia waited for Eva to come around the corner with a big smile, as usual, but the house was quiet.

"Where's your mom?" Mia asked.

"I don't know." Camila frowned as she stepped into the living room. "Mom?"

"In here," Eva called from her bedroom.

Camila headed in that direction, but Mia stayed put. She didn't feel comfortable in her own mother's bedroom—not since Ace had started hanging around anyway—so she wasn't going to barge into her best friend's parents' room.

After a moment of soft discussion, Camila closed the door and came back out into the living room. "Mom's definitely got a cold. She's resting but said to get a snack. She'll come say hi later."

Grabbing yogurts, they headed toward the living room. "It's four o'clock," Camila said. "You know what that means."

"*The Drew Barrymore Show*," they said in unison.

They'd started watching the show when it premiered in 2020 and had never stopped. Even though Drew was older than their mothers, she was so *cool*. They loved watching her interview celebrities, discuss the news, and share her fashion and makeup tips. Today, Drew's guests were Addison Rae, who Camila said was a huge deal on TikTok, and Martha Stewart, who Mia's mother loved. They were going to make "spooky" Halloween cocktails. Shawn Mendes was the musical guest.

"Oooh, I like him." Camila sprawled out on the couch.

Mia sat down next to her and shrugged. "Eh. He's no Harry Styles."

Mia wasn't big on pop culture, preferring to get lost in novels, listen to music, or study. Unless you counted Lin-Manuel Miranda. He was a genius. And Harry, who was smoking hot and very talented.

After finishing her yogurt, Mia threw away the container, and then went over to her backpack and pulled out her laptop.

"Homework already?" Camila barely looked up from the TV.

"No." Mia sat in a chair diagonal from her friend. She didn't want Camila peeping at her screen. "Need to look something up real quick."

Opening a new window, Mia did something she hadn't done in ages: she typed in her mother's website, whitneygolden.com. She scanned the tabs at the top—Fashion, Lifestyle, Home Decor, Family—and clicked on the last one. The landing page contained a variety of parenting posts, including a picture of a grinning Mason wearing only a T-shirt and Superman underwear with the headline "Five Tips to Make Potty Training a Breeze." She cringed. Why would her mom post that photo? It was so . . . intimate. And it wasn't even true. Mason hated potty training and was still having lots of accidents.

"What?" Camila turned away from the talk show, where Martha Stewart was showing Drew how to make a Bloody Scary cocktail.

Mia shook her head, shifting to make sure her computer screen was out of view. "Nothing."

Her heart pounded like a snare drum the more she scrolled. She found a fall bucket-list post, where her mom had listed everything she wanted to do with the family that season, from apple picking to going to a pumpkin patch; a twin fashion post featuring adorable pictures of Chloe and Charlotte; and her mom's ruminations on starting to date again. *Ew*.

And there was more: blogs about birthday parties and family trips; gift guides that included details about her siblings' personalities; there was even a post that described how Whitney felt dropping Mia off at high school for the first time. Mia had had no idea about that one! At least her mom hadn't shared Mia's real first-day photos, where she was queasy and shaking with nerves. Instead, her mom had used pictures from a random family photo shoot from a few months ago. Mia remembered twirling with the twins, a big smile on her face. She'd never stopped to wonder if her mom would use those photos for anything other than family memories.

There was so much more than she ever realized her mother had shared about her, about their family.

She needed to start at the beginning. Mia scrolled down to the bottom of the screen and clicked the back button until she got to the very first post her mother had ever shared: "My Twins Are Two! The Good News: It Gets Easier." It was time-stamped eight years ago. Mia knew her mom had started blogging because she felt like not enough moms talked about the difficulties of having twins. Two babies who don't sleep, two times the crying and dirty diapers, two high chairs to clean, two babies who started walking (and destroying things) at the same time. But she didn't get a huge following until Mia's dad suddenly died.

Her dad's death. Mia's stomach dropped into her shoes. Had her mother posted about that? *Oh god, no.* Her hands shook as they hovered over the keyboard. Should she do this now? She looked over at Camila, who was busy salivating over Shawn Mendes's performance. Scroll, scroll, scroll. Her breath caught in her chest. There it was: "My Husband Died. And I Don't Know How to Go On."

Sitting back to take a breather, she was grateful Camila chose that moment to use the restroom. Mia clicked on the link to open the post, reading her mother's words about her father.

I can't believe I'm writing this, but my beloved Michael died three days ago. On Sunday, he kissed me in the kitchen before going for a jog. But he never came home. Someone saw him collapse on the sidewalk and called an ambulance. The ER doctor said he had a catastrophic heart attack. It killed him instantly.

And there's something I haven't told you: I'm eleven weeks pregnant. We took a few pictures on Saturday and were going to share them with friends and family and all of you next week. And now he'll never meet this baby. Or know if it was a boy or girl. If he or she has his eyes or his smile. We were supposed to be celebrating a new life, and now I have to say goodbye to my husband, my children's father. The grief is too much to bear.

I feel like I'm in a nightmare and can't wake up. How am I supposed to do all this without him? I have three kids, soon-to-be four, and no job. And Michael didn't have life insurance beyond the standard that his job offered—and that won't stretch very far. He was only thirty-five, and we decided saving up to buy a house was more important than additional life insurance. We thought we were being smart, cautious. How could we have known?

I thought we'd be together forever, we both did. I don't know how to go on without his hand to hold and his lips to kiss. Without him to work his magic with the kids and hug me when I'm stressed.

His funeral is this weekend. I know I'm supposed to wear black and cry dignified tears and shake hands and tell everyone "thank you for coming." But all I want to do is crawl into bed and sleep forever. Why did this happen? How can I get him back? Oh, Michael, please come back to me.

Tears fell freely onto Mia's keyboard as she read her mother's heartbreaking words. She tugged the sleeve of her hoodie down onto her hand, drying her face and wiping her nose before swiping at the droplets on the keyboard.

Mia didn't remember much from her dad's funeral, but she remembered how composed her mother looked. She'd been so strong, shaking hands with everyone who attended the funeral, exactly as she mentioned in the note to her readers. Mia had clung to her mom's black skirt until her grandmother had pulled her away. She'd clung to her grandma instead.

Lost in thought and staring at her mother's post, Mia noticed the word "funeral" was blue and underlined, as if a link to something else. She clicked on it and gasped. There was another post with picture after picture of her father's funeral—her family's private pain—on the internet for the world to see. The sound of her blood thundered in her ears, and her skin grew hot. *How could she do this?* Her adored father, who was the sweetest, most intelligent, most unassuming person she had ever met. There was no way he would have agreed to this—and she knew her mother knew that.

As she scrolled to the bottom of the page, she gasped again.

"What?" Camila asked, walking back into the living room holding a banana.

Mia didn't reply. Fat tears streamed down her face.

"What's wrong?" Camila sounded panicky.

Mia couldn't find the words to tell her friend about the awfulness, so she pointed at the computer screen. There was her dead father in his casket. And next to him, in a black velvet dress, her red hair pulled back in a French braid, was eleven-year-old Mia, howling with raw grief.

This time it was Camila's turn to gasp. "Holy shit."

Mia nodded, sniffling. *Holy shit indeed.*

Because her dad had died so suddenly—the doctor had called his kind of heart attack "a widow-maker"—his death hadn't felt real to her until she'd seen his lifeless body at the funeral. No one had told her about the open casket, so Mia had been completely taken by surprise. She'd broken down. It was like an out-of-body experience. She didn't even remember anyone taking photos that day, but no one on the internet knew that.

All Mia knew was she'd had nightmares about her father's pale, lifeless face for months after the funeral. And now her own mother was making her relive it all over again.

"Are you okay?" Camila put her arm around Mia's shoulders.

Taking deep breaths, trying to settle her rolling stomach, Mia slowly shook her head. And then she launched herself off the chair and ran to the bathroom down the hall to vomit.

After a few minutes of sitting on the cold tile floor, there was a soft knock at the door.

"Mia?" Camila asked.

Standing up, Mia washed her hands. "I'm okay." But the puffy-faced, red-eyed girl staring back at her in the mirror would beg to differ.

She opened the door and looked at her best friend, trying to hold back tears.

Camila pulled her into a hug. "I'm so sorry."

"I didn't even know those photos existed," Mia whispered.

"Don't you read her blog?" There was a hint of doubt in Camila's voice.

Mia stepped back. "No. I mean . . . I know she has a blog, obviously. But I don't even follow her on Instagram."

Camila looked at her with surprise. "You don't?"

"No. I unfollowed her after she started dating Ace." All the mysterious, staged pictures had been too much for her to stomach. Especially when she had been devastated that her mom was seeing someone seriously. "And you know I barely look at Instagram anyway."

Mia squinted at her best friend. "Do you follow her?"

"Yeah. But I follow everybody." Camila had something like two thousand followers on Instagram. "And I swear I never saw those photos. But I've seen other stuff about you. I never brought it up because I assumed you knew and didn't want to talk about it."

Mia's stomach lurched. Her best friend had been reading god knows what about her and she hadn't even known. She felt so violated. And stupid. How had she not kept tabs on this?

"I can't believe you don't follow your mom," Camila said.

"I mean, it's her job—that's it!" Mia threw her hands in the air. "How much do you know about what your dad does for his job?"

Camila's brow furrowed. "He's a paralegal."

"I know. But what does that mean? What does he do all day?"

"No idea."

"Exactly." She covered her face with her hands. "Why can't my mom have a normal job, like everyone else's parents?"

"What are you going to do?" Camila asked as they slowly walked back to the living room.

Mia hugged her arms over her chest and sat down on the couch. "I don't know." It was like her skin had been ripped from her body, exposing her organs, her cells, and her most private thoughts. "I can't believe those pictures have been up for four years."

Cam was quiet as Mia processed.

"Can I stay here again tonight? I can't go home."

Camila touched her arm. "You don't even have to ask."

* * *

MIA HAD BEEN tossing and turning for hours, pressing a pillow around her head to drown out the sounds of Camila softly snoring beside her. Every time she shut her eyes, she'd flash back to the pictures of her father's casket, his pale, unmoving expression, and her bright red, grief-stricken face sobbing next to him.

When she couldn't take her mind spinning out of control any longer, she quietly eased out of bed, grabbing her laptop and bringing it over to Camila's desk. With the blue light illuminating her face, she pulled up Google and typed in her mother's name. She couldn't bear to look at the blog again tonight, but she knew other publications had written about her mother. What else didn't she know?

She hit enter and her stomach dropped: there were 296,000 results. How was that even possible? Her mother was just a mom of four kids who blogged about parenthood and Target try-ons in Austin, Texas! Who could possibly care about her . . . three hundred thousand times over?

The first two hits were her mom's Instagram and Facebook pages. Mia clicked on her mom's Instagram account and the first thing she saw was a picture of her father with her and her sisters.

"What the heck?" she muttered, glancing over to make sure she hadn't woken Camila.

Her mom had posted that very morning, noting that her husband had passed away four years ago this week. She told her followers what a devoted husband and father Mia's dad had been. But her mother didn't tell them that she'd forgotten to acknowledge the *actual* anniversary of her husband's death to her own daughter.

Grinding her teeth together, Mia went back to the Google results. After the Instagram and Facebook pages there were

HATE FOLLOW   49

links to her mom's blog, TikTok, and Pinterest. Then came the stories that had been written about her mother, on parenting websites, lifestyle sites, grief sites. Mia sat back in her seat, rubbing her eyes in disbelief.

Opening another Google page, she inserted her own name into the search box—more than seventy thousand hits appeared. What? How was that possible? There were Instagram posts featuring letters her mom said she'd written to her on her last few birthdays. Interviews her mother had done for other publications where she mentioned her children by name. There was even a blog post of "house reveals" that included photos of Mia's bedroom. Another thing she hadn't known about.

Mia's chest was tight with rage as she chewed on what was left of one of her thumbnails. She'd been so young when her mother started blogging, she hadn't really understood what it meant. And then when she did understand it, she didn't want to deal with it, so she pretended it wasn't happening— and her mother had been posting about her all this time.

A wave of fatigue washed over her. She rested her elbows on the desk and scrubbed at her forehead. Maybe she could finally sleep now. Right as she was about to snap her laptop shut, her eye caught something on the screen: HateFollow.com.

Mia knew she shouldn't click on it—she really needed sleep—but she couldn't help herself. Her mouse drifted toward the link . . . click.

What she found was a forum listing categories of influencers: Instagram personalities, TikTok stars, YouTubers, momfluencers, dadfluencers (*That's a thing?* she wondered), food bloggers, fashion bloggers, beauty bloggers, healthy-living bloggers, DIY bloggers, and more. And within each category, she found lists of names: The Purple Fairy, Farmhouse Aesthetic, Minimalist Eats, FitChick42. Mia had never heard of any of these so-called influencers, but apparently they were important enough for strangers to comment on their lives and social media content—sometimes for hundreds of pages.

"I can't believe this," she whispered, wishing she could wake up Camila and show her the forums. She looked over at her friend, who was sleeping soundly and drooling on her pillow.

Turning back to her computer screen, she clicked on the "Momfluencers" forum inside the site. She started scrolling the list, expecting it to take a while to find any snark dedicated to her mother, but she was wrong: there was her mother's name on the first page, sixth from the top.

She could feel the blood rushing to her head as she clicked on the link with a shaky hand. Who were these strangers and what would they say about her mother? Her family?

The first post was from someone who called themselves The Good Karen: This is the last lady I'd take parenting advice from. Her oldest daughter always looks miserable, and I don't even think the four-year-old is potty-trained yet.

Mason's only three, Mia thought.

Then there was a remark from someone named Ew, Dorothy: Size 8? As if. Try again, Whitney.

Her mom was always dieting, but Mia thought she already looked great.

The third comment, from Moose Willis, was like a punch in the gut: She's going to post a full picture of her new boyfriend any minute now. Whitney's dead husband must be rolling in his grave.

Hot tears flooded Mia's vision again. Her dad was nothing more than a "dead husband" to these people. These strangers. She wiped her eyes and read one last post.

Olivia Mild said: Mia would be so pretty if she gained a few pounds and, you know, actually smiled.

That was enough. Slowly shutting her laptop lid, Mia stared into the pitch black. So apparently, her mother was too big and she was too thin. (She was only fifteen! And she would love to have some curves. It didn't matter how much she ate, she was still a stick.) How sad was it that strangers on the internet could tell how unhappy she was? Why couldn't her mother?

Her whole life, her whole existence, she'd worried about what people thought of her. Her mother, her friends, her classmates, her teachers. She used an infinite amount of brainpower analyzing how she looked, stupid things she'd said, how she walked, who she inadvertently offended. Turned out Mia had a whole other group of people judging her she hadn't been aware of: strangers on the internet. The biggest group of them all.

CHAPTER 5
WHITNEY

Are you coming home today?

Whitney watched her phone for a moment, waiting for those telltale dots to pop up, letting her know that Mia was texting her back. But nothing happened. She hadn't seen her since their fight two days ago. She knew her daughter hated confrontation, but forty-eight hours seemed like more than enough time for her to process and get some space. Now they needed to talk.

Whitney walked into the kitchen and placed her phone on the counter. She tapped her manicured nails on the marble. Maybe a snack would make her feel better. She opened the fridge and eyed the contents inside. Nothing was appealing except the bottle of pink wine that glistened from the bottom shelf. Should she have a glass? It wasn't even one thirty.

Shrugging her shoulders, she grabbed the bottle. Maybe it would help her relax. She poured a small glass and took a sip. *Oh, that's good.* She filled her glass to the top before putting the bottle back in the fridge.

Slipping the phone—still nothing from Mia—into the

pocket of her peach silk robe, she picked up her glass of wine and strolled out the glass doors into the backyard. This was supposed to be her relaxing Saturday afternoon. The twins were at a playdate, Rosie was studying with friends, and Mason had just gone down for a nap. Whitney had been so excited to lounge by the pool and have a date night with Ace, but now she felt out of sorts and jittery. She'd already done her workout—Tracy Anderson Method, like Gwyneth—and eaten lunch, and now she didn't know what to do with herself. Perched on the pristine white chaise lounge by the sparkling blue pool, she sipped her wine and gazed out at the backyard. This place was her haven. There was a lap pool surrounded by a clear glass child-proof fence with a shallow "beach" for the kids to play in; a hot tub for those few chilly Texas nights each year; and impeccable landscaping. It was the backyard of her dreams.

Right then her phone started ringing, making her heart jump. But it wasn't Mia; it was Brendan. He was a few minutes early for their call with their mother. Whitney had totally forgotten.

"Hey, sis!" Brendan said when she answered. "I have Mom here, ready to chat."

"Thanks, Brendan," Whitney said with a sigh as she heard her brother hand their mom the phone. "Hi, Mom. How are you today?"

"Hello, Whitney. I'm doing okay." Her mom's voice sounded far away and, to be honest, old.

Whitney's heart flipped. She needed to go home to see her mother, but it was always so depressing revisiting her past. "Have you gone to the clubhouse to do any of the activities lately? Bingo? Painting? Some of them sound really fun."

Her mother was quiet for a beat. "No. Not really."

"Have you made any new friends?" Whitney felt like she was talking to a preschooler at this point.

"No. I had one friend, Alice, and then she went and broke her hip. She lives with her daughter now. Must be nice. Most of the others are stinky."

Whitney simultaneously held in a chuckle while ignoring the daughter comment. "They're stinky?"

"Mm-hmm. All the men, the few of them there are, smell like tuna fish, and the women are swimming in perfume. It gives me a headache."

Whitney shook her head. She'd forgotten how much her mother complained. Nothing was ever good enough for old Sandy. "That's too bad. How are those meals I've been getting sent to you?" Since her arthritis made cooking difficult, Whitney had a meal delivery service drop off nutritious prepared meals a few times a week.

"They're okay," her mom huffed. "I like the chicken and dumplings, but they only bring those once a month."

"Something to look forward to." Whitney tried to sound cheerful.

"Speaking of, Stephanie is due any day now. We really missed you at the baby shower a few weeks ago."

Whitney cringed. "Sorry. Things are just so busy around here with work and the kids." She'd ended up guilt-buying her sister an expensive stroller. Sending gifts made her feel better about not being there in person.

"Stephanie really hoped to see you."

"I know, I'm sorry." Whitney knew it wasn't an excuse, but every time she went home, things were just awkward. It was like her family didn't know how to talk to her anymore, and she certainly didn't know how to talk to them. Add that to the fact that she still had extreme guilt for leaving her siblings behind after graduating and moving away. Rosie had told her stories about how much worse things got after she left—their dad drank and gambled more, and since she wasn't there to take care of them, their mother would bring the kids to work with her late into the night. Rosie said they would often fall asleep behind the counter at the gas station. It broke Whitney's heart.

She paused, waiting to see if her mother would ask about her grandkids this time—or Rosie, who Whitney had taken in. Sandy usually didn't, too tied up in her own world and with her own problems. Her mother hadn't been interested in Whitney's life since she moved to Austin. Rosie said she barely heard from her either. Out of sight, out of mind, apparently. Whitney assumed that her mother still held a grudge about her leaving town—she was the free childcare, after all. But it made her sad that her mother didn't even attempt to form a bond with Mia, Charlotte, Chloe, and Mason. Sandy seemed to be missing the grandma gene.

The phone crackled and she heard the sound of an audience cheering. "Gotta go, Whitney. *Judge Judy* is back on."

"Oh, okay. Bye, Mom." Whitney looked at her watch. It had been three minutes.

"Great talk, sis!" She rolled her eyes at her brother's mischievous tone. "Looking forward to our chat next Saturday."

"Me too!" She hoped the brightness in her voice didn't

sound forced. Though she'd realized that not only had she given her brother ten thousand dollars but she'd punished herself further by making them do these calls.

Only nine left.

After they hung up, Whitney looked at her phone again. Still no reply from Mia. She sighed as she took another sip of wine, leaning her head back against the chair and closing her eyes.

The strained talk with her mother reinforced why she needed to patch things up with Mia. How had they gotten so distant? If Whitney was being truthful, she didn't really need to ask herself that question. It didn't take a scientist to pinpoint when she and Mia started drifting apart: it was when she began dating Ace six months ago. She'd gone on a few dates over the years, but Ace was the first guy she'd introduced to the kids.

She knew no man would live up to Michael in her daughter's mind—and she wasn't trying to replace him. But Ace was a good man, and they were having fun. Plus, he made her feel young and sexy again. That was such a gift after the years of hell Whitney had lived through in the wake of Michael's death.

Whitney rubbed at the pain in her chest and sat up straighter. She needed to think about something else. Maybe she should call Tawny to come over. Though her best friend's youngest usually had soccer games on the weekend. And her influencer friends were so busy they all required getting plans on their calendars at least two weeks in advance.

Picking up her phone, Whitney took a picture of her tanned legs in front of the pool. Opening Instagram, she pulled up the photo, added a filter to brighten the shot, and then wrote a caption: Sun's out, y'all! Hope you're having a nice day in your neck of the woods. She added three emojis—a blue wave, a sun, and a wineglass—for some extra color.

There. Now her followers thought she was having fun. Whitney watched as the likes and comments started rolling in, relishing the hit of serotonin that surged through her body. As she dropped her phone in her lap, a sense of satisfaction settled over her.

The phone buzzed on her bare leg, startling her again. Finally, Mia had responded to her text. I'll be home soon. We need to talk.

Good. She was ready to put this argument behind them, though something fluttered in Whitney's belly. She'd never felt nervous around her teen until recently. Whitney used to know everything about her daughter, but now she was practically a stranger.

Taking a sip of wine, she realized her head was a little fuzzy. Oh well, she didn't need to worry about the Mia talk right now anyway. She would sit here and relax. What a novel idea. Truthfully, she was exhausted. Whitney had been hustling for four years. Hell, even before that. She'd raised her siblings, then had her own children, before she even started the blog. If anyone deserved this glass of wine and a wide-open weekend, it was her.

Maybe those meditation exercises Tawny kept trying to get her to do would help. Leaning back in the chair, she squirmed around until she was comfortable. Focusing on her breath, she inhaled for three seconds, exhaled for three seconds. *This isn't so bad*, she thought.

Whitney woke up to a cool hand shaking her warm shoulder. "Huh?" She squinted at the afternoon sun.

Mia came into focus. "You okay?"

Whitney sat up, shaking her head to clear away the haze. Luckily, her robe was tied shut, so she wasn't exposing herself, and she'd managed to put her empty wineglass on the table next to her, even though she had no recollection of doing that. "What time is it?"

"A little before three. Where is everybody?" Mia sat in the chaise lounge two over, leaving plenty of space between them.

Whitney smoothed her hair and ran her fingers under her eyes, hoping to rub away any residual mascara lurking there. She hated that Mia had found her like this, tipsy and sunburned. "The girls are at Ava's house. Mason is napping. I need to wake him soon."

Mia nodded as she looked around the backyard, shifting in her seat.

"I'm glad you're finally home." Whitney swore Mia had grown an inch since she last saw her two days ago. Her fifteen-year-old looked more and more like an adult every day. "And I agree we need to talk. Why don't you start?"

"I was looking at your blog last night . . ." Mia said, her voice cracking.

"Oh really?" Whitney said, eyebrows raised. She couldn't contain her grin. She'd assumed Mia never read her work. "What did you think?"

Mia paused, her leg bouncing like a lid on a boiling pot of water. "I didn't, uh, realize how much of me—my life, my stories, my photos—was featured on it." She kept her eyes trained on her hands, where she was picking at her already ragged cuticles.

Whitney frowned. "What do you mean? You know I create content about our family."

"Yes, but I never really considered what that actually meant. Until now."

"Sweetie." Whitney reached out and touched Mia's knee. "I'm simply a proud parent who loves bragging about her kids."

"You're not though, Mom. You have a million followers on Instagram!" Mia took a deep breath. "I don't want to be featured on your social media or the blog anymore. And I especially don't want those pictures of Dad's funeral on the internet. Can you take them down?"

"What? No." Whitney suddenly felt like her skin was roasting. She stood and started pacing the pool deck, waving her hand in front of her face to get some air. "Blogging and social media is my livelihood. *Our* livelihood. It's a business."

Mia rolled her eyes when Whitney said that, exactly like she had every other time her mother called herself an entrepreneur.

"How do you think we are able to have this roof"— Whitney gestured at the gorgeous house behind them— "over our heads, nice clothes, gourmet food, and anything you could ever want? It's because of that silly little business you just rolled your eyes at."

Mia's cheeks flushed pink. "I appreciate that you make a lot of money. But did you ever stop and think about whether I wanted my picture all over the internet? Or a picture of

Dad's funeral?" She swallowed, her nostrils flaring. "You know how private he was!"

Blood rushed to Whitney's head. It was true that Michael had been very private, and he hadn't been particularly interested in her blogging. But he wasn't here anymore. She was the head of this family, and she didn't think there was anything distasteful about those pictures. She knew as well as anyone that death was a part of life.

"And what about in a few years when I apply to colleges?" Mia continued. "Everyone from admissions counselors to professors to other students will be able to find out anything they want about me."

Whitney clenched her hands at her sides. She was so proud of Mia's plan to go to medical school and become a doctor so she could save people with heart conditions like her father. It was an admirable goal, and Whitney respected it. Why couldn't Mia respect her career?

"Everything is on the internet these days," Whitney said, keeping her voice steady. "Lots of kids your age are going to have to deal with stuff like that."

Mia slowly shook her head back and forth. "Wow, okay." Her face was the color of a tomato, and Whitney couldn't miss the tears that now filled her eyes. Mia's voice was quiet when she finally spoke. "Fine. Leave up the stuff about me. But can you at least take down the funeral photos of Dad? You know he wouldn't want them posted for the world to see. Besides, it's old content." Her tone turned bitter. "I doubt anyone cares about your dead husband anymore."

"Don't call him that," Whitney snapped. "And did you know I've raised thousands of dollars for heart research using those photos and telling our family's story? Doesn't that count for something?"

"I didn't know that." Mia drew in a shaky breath. "But I still want those pictures taken down."

Whitney perched on her lounger. She hated seeing her daughter like this, and she wished she could give Mia what she wanted. But for better or worse, their entire lives hinged on this career of hers. She shook her head. "Mia, I can't."

"Why not?"

"Because your father dying . . ." Her throat caught. She looked out over the pool, sparkling in the afternoon sunlight, and thought of her manager, Taylor. What would she say? "It's why so many people follow me. Because I write about being a widow and a mom and my life."

Mia snorted. "That's ridiculous. And you can still sell people things on Instagram without those pictures of dad."

"I don't simply sell people things on Instagram," Whitney replied through gritted teeth. "My followers care about me and this family, believe it or not."

Mia stared off into space, her chest heaving as she wiped tears from her eyes.

Whitney softened. "Look, I know you hate that I posted those pictures of Dad, but a woman recently told me her husband was having chest pains and she brought him in for testing because of your dad." She reached out to touch her daughter's arm, but Mia flinched and moved away. "Those pictures saved a life."

"You're kidding me, right?" The scorn was clear on her daughter's face. "You could do all that without posting those photos. You know Dad would have hated being seen like that."

Sitting up straight, Whitney squared her shoulders. Maybe one day she would tell her daughter about the financial mess they'd been in when her father died. But today was not that day. Whitney was going to protect her daughter's pristine memories of her father for as long as she could. "I think your father would be proud I've managed to take care of all of us so well. And he'd trust my judgment."

Mia stood up. "Well, I don't." Now it was her turn to pace. "It's all about money with you, isn't it?"

"Yes, it is. Because unlike you, I've been without it." Whitney leaned forward and rubbed at her temples. She looked up at Mia, squinting in the sunlight. "I promise you, you never want to be in the place that I was at your age. And frankly, you don't know the kind of pressure I'm under keeping this family afloat. When you've been at the bottom, starving and scared and lonely, you'll do anything to not be there again." Her daughter would never understand how much better her life was because Whitney gave her what her own parents couldn't: money and time.

Mia sat back down in her lounger, exhaustion on her face. "I don't understand how you could post those pictures of the worst day of my life."

"It was the worst day of my life too. And I survived it. And even thrived. I'm not going to hide that part of myself."

"Was it the worst day of your life?" Mia asked, her eyebrows arched in anger. "Or was it the best because it got you hundreds of thousands of new followers?"

Whitney recoiled as if her daughter had slapped her. Did Mia really hate her that much? "It was the worst," she whispered. "I loved your father, and the life we built together.

Very much." She paused, trying to figure out how to rationalize things to Mia. "Even if I deleted the pictures from the blog, they'll still be all over the internet. That's how it works. The internet remembers everything."

"Can't you at least try?" Mia's bottom lip quivered and she suddenly looked exactly as she did as a toddler, frustrated about not being able to do something.

Whitney squeezed her eyes shut. She knew this ask was virtually impossible. The internet was infinite. How could they ever get all those pictures removed? But she hated seeing Mia so upset, their relationship so fractured.

This was her *daughter*. The person she swore she would do anything for. And this was definitely an anything.

"Okay. I will talk to Taylor about it and see if she has any ideas of how to get the photos taken down."

Mia's jaw dropped. "Really?"

"Really." Whitney could tell her compromise was already worth it. "But you have to promise to start sleeping here again, starting tonight. I miss you. We all miss you."

As if on cue, Mason sleepily padded outside, sucking his thumb. His eyes lit up when he saw Mia. "Mimi!" he cried, running to her and wrapping himself around her knees.

"Hey, buddy." Mia lifted her brother into her arms.

"I miss you," Mason said as he snuggled into his big sister's chest.

Mia gave her mom a tentative smile. "I missed you too."

Whitney was so relieved as she watched them. Mia was back home and they'd figured out a compromise. She wouldn't be surprised if getting the pictures taken down would be harder than they thought. But she'd worry about that later.

October 14 – 5:03 p.m.

Ew, Dorothy: Every time Nit-Whit shows off her pool, I get insanely jealous. I would KILL for that backyard!

October 14 – 5:36 p.m.

The Good Karen: I know. If I think too much about how much influencers pull in each month for posting vapid photos and making stupid videos, I get ragey.

October 14 – 6:17 p.m.

Moose Willis: At least she appears to have spent some time with her children this weekend. She'll probably reward herself with eight hours of beauty treatments. #relatable

CHAPTER 6
MIA

Mia couldn't deny she was happy to be home. She loved spending time with Camila and her parents, but she couldn't wait to sleep in her own bed tonight.

Her mother had made good on her promise to talk to her manager about finding a tech guru to scrub those photos from her dad's funeral off the internet. She'd already texted Taylor, who promised she would get on it first thing Monday. It felt good to have won that battle, like she could breathe again. Mia hoped her mother realized how serious she was about her dad's privacy—and not being used as a prop herself. She'd keep reminding her. But getting the funeral photos removed was a good start.

When Charlotte and Chloe got home from their playdate, they were just as thrilled to see her as Mason had been. They'd all snuggled on the couch and watched a movie.

"Mom!" Chloe yelled when the credits rolled. "I'm hungry. What's for dinner?"

Whitney walked over from the kitchen with an uncertain look on her face. "I just ordered pizzas for you guys." Mason and the twins cheered at the good news. "I'm supposed to go on a date with Ace in an hour, but I can totally cancel if you want me to, Mia."

Mia still wasn't used to her mom dating, and she wasn't exactly a member of the Ace fan club, but she didn't have the energy to get irritated about her mom going out tonight.

"It's fine, Mom. Go."

Right as she said it, her phone pinged. It was Rosie texting that she was on the way home from studying. Rom-coms and manis? she messaged.

That sounded like the perfect night in to Mia, who replied with the painted nails emoji.

She was fine with her mom going out for the night, but she could tell her mom was anxious about it. When Rosie got home, Whitney had them all line up on the couch so they could help pick her outfit. Mia rolled her eyes at first, but her mom's fashion show ended up being hilarious.

The first look was a black jumpsuit with silver heels, which Chloe deemed "too boring."

"Rude!" Whitney said, turning from side to side. "What if I added some colorful jewelry?"

"Next!" Chloe boomed as the other kids giggled.

Whitney huffed off, returning a few minutes later in a bright pink minidress with a ruffle along the bottom and cowboy boots.

"Wow," Rosie deadpanned. "I think I saw a little girl in Mason's preschool class wearing that exact same outfit yesterday."

"You look like Hannah!" Mason shrieked, rolling off the couch and onto the floor as he kicked his legs, making his sisters squeal.

When Whitney appeared from her room the next time, she was wearing a red sequined top, gray sweatpants tucked into Doc Martens, and yellow feather earrings.

"I think this is it." She kept a straight face as she did a spin.

"What. Is. That?" Charlotte's face was scrunched up as if in pain.

"No, Mama," Mason said in total seriousness.

That set off Mia and Rosie, who could no longer contain their laughter.

"What? You don't like it?" Whitney came over to tickle Mason. "I think the sweatpants really work with the sequins."

Soon they were all in hysterics. Mia looked around the room, taking in all the smiling faces. It was so fun and silly and carefree.

"Okay, okay. Let me try again." Whitney went back to her bedroom to put on one more option. "I think I found it," she called, before appearing in a flirty floral dress that stopped just above her knees and strappy gold flat sandals. She looked great—beautiful and comfortable and ready for a fun night out with her boyfriend. (Mia still couldn't believe her mom had a boyfriend.)

"That's it," Mia said, just as the doorbell rang.

"Whew." Whitney smiled at her. "Right in the nick of time."

The twins ran to open the front door, with Mason right behind.

"Wow, it's a party in here," Ace said.

Whitney practically glowed as she walked over to give Ace a kiss on the cheek.

"You look gorgeous," he said, resting his hand on her hip.

"We helped!" Chloe yelled.

"Yes, they did. This was the only outfit that got their approval."

"It's perfect." Ace grabbed her hand, spinning her in a twirl. "You kids did an excellent job."

Mia swore her mom blushed.

"All right, well, you guys have a fun night with Aunt Rosie and Mia." Whitney gave each of her children a hug and a kiss. "Don't eat too much sugar, and don't stay up too late."

The kids groaned in response.

Whitney looked at Rosie. "Bedtime is seven thirty for Mason, eight thirty for Chloe and Charlotte."

"Got it." Rosie nodded solemnly at Whitney before making the kids crack up with an exaggerated wink.

Ace offered Whitney his arm and they headed out into the warm night, waving behind them all the way until they got to his blue sports car. Mia was happy to see Ace open her mother's car door for her. At least he was a gentleman.

"She looks happy," Rosie said from beside her.

"She does." Though seeing her mom with another man still made her heart hurt.

After dinner, Rosie gave Mason a bath and got the twins showered. Then the five of them spent the next hour eating ice cream, playing three rounds of Pictionary, and reading a million books. Finally it was bedtime.

Once the house was picked up and quiet, Mia and Rosie settled onto the couch with popcorn and a basket of nail polish. Mia hadn't known her aunt well when she'd moved in four years ago, but they'd developed a deep friendship second only to her relationship with Camila. Rosie was kind of like her big sister these days. Despite their eleven-year age difference, they both loved pop music, romance novels, and baked goods. Rosie told her about college life and what it was like to be a mature student, while Mia talked to Rosie about how she was fifteen and had never been kissed; how she never quite fit in at school; and how she desperately wanted to be a doctor so she could save people before they had heart attacks like her dad.

"So what's up with you not coming home the last few nights?" Rosie asked her as *10 Things I Hate About You* played on the screen. They were going old-school tonight.

Mia sighed. She didn't really feel like getting into it. "I was mad at Mom. I'm tired of her making me do all those stupid photo shoots. And I found some photos on her blog I didn't like."

"Of what?" Rosie carefully applied navy polish to her big toe.

"Just some stuff I didn't like."

Rosie waved her hand. "Go on."

Before Mia could stop herself, the whole story came pouring out: how she was already mad that her mom forgot the anniversary of her dad's death, then a mean girl at school was making fun of her and mentioned her mom being an influencer, and how Mia found the pictures of her dad at his funeral. Plus all the content about her and the other kids.

When she was finally finished talking, Rosie just looked at her. "Whoa. That's a lot."

"Right?"

Rosie capped the nail polish and settled back into the couch to wait for her toes to dry. "I see what you are saying, Mia, I do. And I'm glad you are setting some boundaries on what you want posted and what you don't. But what your mom has built as an influencer is remarkable."

Mia gave her aunt a look. "I mean, sure, she makes a lot of money. But is she, like, contributing to society?"

Rosie grabbed a handful of popcorn. "She's raising four kids *and* she's putting me through college. You don't think that's meaningful? It's more than our parents did."

Mia knew that her grandparents hadn't exactly emphasized school or been around much when her mom and Rosie were kids. But her mom didn't like to talk about it.

"Can't she get another job? A regular job? Why does she have to share every little detail about her life on the internet? About my life?"

"Take it from someone who has been a cashier at a fast-food drive-through, and a waitress, and a house cleaner, and a nanny—it's hard to scrape by. Finding a good job is incredibly difficult, especially when you don't have a college degree. There is no way your mom could afford any of this"—Rosie gestured at the immaculate living room—"with a regular job. You have so many more opportunities than we ever did, all thanks to her."

"So I'm just supposed to let her post whatever she wants about me?"

"No. You have every right to speak up about what you don't like. Maybe you two could meet every month and go over what content she's going to post, and you can have ultimate veto power."

Mia nodded. "That's a good idea."

"But I don't think it's fair for you to tell your mother how she can tell her story. Yes, your dad died, and that is completely devastating." Rosie reached over and squeezed her hand. "But your mom also lost her husband, who she thought she'd be with forever. Is she not allowed to write about that? To share with other women who have experienced the same thing?"

Mia's eyes burned as that sank in. "I mean, I guess. I don't know what it's like to lose your husband. I just know I miss my dad."

Rosie moved the popcorn bowl out of the way and scooted closer to Mia, pulling her in. "I know, hon. It's hard to understand something if you've never experienced it. Your mother and I were raised by the same people in the same place, yet our lives were very different."

"What was it like for you growing up?" Mia knew Rosie and her mom had had tough childhoods with little money, a lot of fighting, and sometimes not enough food.

Rosie shook her head. "It was tough. There were five of us kids, and Whitney carried a lot being the oldest. By the time I was born, our parents were just too tired to care anymore. They didn't really encourage me to do well in school, or help with my homework, or even make me a meal. Your mom took care of all of us for a long time."

"Were you mad when she left?" Mia asked. She did the math in her head: if Whitney was eighteen when she left home, Rosie would have been only seven.

Her aunt looked at her with wide eyes. "Of course. I was a little kid who didn't understand why her big sister left her. I was angry at her for a long time. But now I see that your mom saved herself. And then she came back and saved me. And pretty soon I'm going to have a degree in computer science. There is no way that would have happened without your mom. I will never be able to repay her."

After their nails were dry and the movie was over, Mia hugged Rosie good night and headed upstairs to get ready for bed. She thought about what her aunt had said as she washed her face and brushed her teeth. Even though her mom hadn't gone to college, the talk of college had always been a big part of Mia's life. Her dad had made sure of that with his Northwestern obsession, and her mom had made sure Mia knew she was capable of anything. Mia had never doubted she would go to college or even thought about the finances of it, if she was honest.

But hearing her aunt talk about how that hadn't been a given for her and lots of other people opened Mia's eyes. She *should* give her mom more respect for making such a good living as an influencer. Mia had never wanted for anything material her whole life. She vowed to appreciate that more, starting now.

CHAPTER 7

WHITNEY

Thank you, kind sir," Whitney said as Ace pulled a chair out for her at a trendy Chinese restaurant downtown. She let her hand linger on his firm arm before sliding into her seat. Ace sat down across from her.

After all the arguing—and making up—with Mia, Whitney was thrilled to be out and having fun. They ordered drinks and appetizers in between telling each other about their days.

Dating was so different from marriage. Light and fun and exciting. Even after six months with Ace, Whitney still got flutters in her stomach before he came over. After eleven years of marriage, she'd forgotten what that was like.

The pure delight she felt when she was with Ace was heightened because she'd experienced very little joy since Michael died. Losing her husband changed her in ways she would never be able to fully articulate. She'd figured she was meant to be single and sad forever. But then, after three and a half years, she met Ace. And while she still got overwhelmed with grief sometimes, now the joy finally outweighed the sorrow.

"I can't wait to dance with you tonight." Ace reached across the table to kiss her hand.

Whitney flushed, covering her face with a girlish giggle. She didn't know if Ace meant at the concert—they were seeing a popular eighties cover band at a nearby outdoor bar—or *after* the concert, but she was excited about both. This man set her on fire. And he respected her dating boundaries. No overnights at her house—she didn't want Mia or the other kids to run into him making coffee or sneaking out before breakfast. And she had to be home every morning when the kids woke up. No exceptions.

Their waiter deposited their drinks, egg rolls, and spicy wontons, and they ordered their main dishes: noodles for her, roast duck for him.

"Mia seemed happy tonight," Ace said as they ate. "Did you two work everything out after the photo shoot? She was pretty angry that day."

"Yes, she was," Whitney said with a laugh. She wanted to keep things light; her rocky week with Mia was the last thing she needed to think about right now. "But we compromised on some things, so I think we are on the same page again."

"Parenting seems so hard." Ace leaned back and took a drink of his beer. "I admire you for doing it. I never wanted to."

Whitney almost spit out her wine. "Really? Never?" She had gone into this relationship with her eyes wide open— Ace was a forty-two-year-old bachelor, after all. If he had wanted to get married, he would have. But they hadn't really talked about kids. When they were introduced by a mutual friend, he'd known she had four kids. She just assumed that meant he wouldn't mind having kids in his life. "Why are you with me, then?"

Ace grinned. "'Cause you're hot. And fun." She must not

have looked impressed, because he added, "And you're smart and a kick-ass businesswoman."

Whitney rolled her eyes. "That's better." She liked that he appreciated her brains and entrepreneurial skills. But she couldn't deny it was also nice to be appreciated as a woman outside of motherhood again.

And she wasn't going to worry about his no-kids comment. Not tonight. Whitney didn't know what she wanted out of this relationship anyway. She'd heard stories about young moms who were engaged or even remarried within two years of being widowed. But Whitney had barely dated until she met Ace—between work and the kids, there just wasn't time. And truthfully, she didn't have the interest. Michael had been the only person she wanted to be with.

Whitney took a sip of wine. She needed to stop thinking about this. Who cared if Ace didn't want children? Did she want to be a wife again? To share a house and money? Did the kids want a new dad? Mia certainly didn't. Sure, she would love to have someone in her life to share the highs and lows with, someone who could support *her* while she was carrying the massive weight of her career and family. But all that mattered right now was that Whitney and Ace had a great time together. When she was with Ace, she felt like herself again. Or at least the part of herself that wasn't just a mom.

After Michael died, she'd spent months—*years*—being lonely and sad. It wasn't the big events that were the worst, as you would think—the birthdays, the anniversaries, the holidays. On those days, Whitney was flooded with calls, messages, gifts, and invites—those days passed quickly. It was the days before and after the big events that were miserable. And the nights. The nights were always long and lonely. After the kids were in bed and the house was picked up and quiet, Whitney would crawl under her covers and turn on the TV, just to cut the silence. Sometimes she'd call Tawny, but usually she'd write. She'd pour her heart out to her followers. The community she'd built was better than any grief group. Sometimes it felt like her connection with the other women going through the same heartbreak as her was the only way she survived.

She felt so seen on social media. And she felt that way with Ace too.

Their entrées arrived right as Ace finished telling her about an issue he'd had at work that week. He was VP of marketing at a tech company, so he was good at problem-solving and communication.

"So, about the photo shoot—the photographer said we should get the proofs early next week." Whitney tried to sound nonchalant as she took a bite of noodles. "Should I post them or wait a bit?"

"Oh, excellent." Ace took a big bite of his food. Whitney waited patiently as he chewed. "Can I see them first? Then we can discuss the best time to share."

"Of course." Whitney smiled but couldn't push the thought away that Ace was getting cold feet about being revealed on her social media. Maybe this was all too big and strange for him—and it was strange. Most couples didn't have to declare their relationship to a million people. She took another sip of wine and reminded herself that nothing had to be decided right this very second. "Works for me."

After finishing their meal, they walked hand in hand to the bar that was having the outdoor concert. When Ace went to get them another round, Whitney pulled out her phone and took a few photos, including of his back. She loved when her followers asked about her mysterious new man. Sure enough, seconds after she posted the photos on her Stories, messages started flooding in.

Who is that hunk?

Love your shoes!

When are you going to reveal your new guy's face?

Whitney was giddy when Ace returned. He handed her a vodka tonic before pulling her in for a deep kiss.

How lucky am I? Whitney thought as the band took the stage, her boyfriend's hand wrapped around her own. Soon they were bouncing to the music and singing along. As they danced, Whitney relished the feeling of her heart pounding in her chest, sweat coating her back, and her boyfriend's hands on her hips. Everything else slipped away. She forgot about work, her kids, and all her responsibilities. All that mattered was being present and remembering what she used to be like. Before being a mom. Before grief. Before all the heaviness that life had thrown her way.

October 14 – 11:37 p.m.

Smug Takes: Ugh. She posted more mysterious shots of the guy again. Give it up, Whitney! Nobody cares.

October 14 – 11:39 p.m.

Basic Barbie: So, I live in Austin, and I'm pretty sure I know who the guy is. He's a well-known bachelor about town.

October 14 – 11:41 p.m.

Big Hick Energy: WHAT? Spill the tea!

October 14 – 11:45 p.m.

Moderator: Just a reminder that posting personal information about private citizens is barred on this forum.

October 14 – 11:48 p.m.

Big Hick Energy: @Basic Barbie: DM me.

CHAPTER 8

MIA

Mia was practically skipping when she met Camila at the front of their school a week later. Her mom had made pancakes for breakfast, and while Mia and the kids ate, Whitney told them funny stories about their dad, like the time he grew a mustache for Movember. When the month-long challenge was over, he shaved off only the left side of his new facial hair. He walked around like that for two days until her mom told him she couldn't take it anymore.

"Hello, sunshine." Camila grinned at her. "Having a good morning?"

"Yep. I'm fueled by maple syrup today."

Making pancakes, always with a side of bacon, had been Mia and her father's weekly ritual. They'd started it when she was five years old, not long after the twins were born. Her mom would be up all night nursing the babies, so her dad would sneak in and do the morning feed and plop the twins in their rockers before waking Mia. Then they'd whip together the ingredients while singing silly songs to entertain the babies, and make pancakes dotted with banana slices and chocolate chips in the shape of stars, butterflies, dinosaurs—whatever inspiration struck that week. Those mornings were some of her favorites ever.

"Yum." Camila flung open the door to the school. "Do you have any tests today?"

"Nope. Should be a boring day."

"Lucky. I have a quiz in history. Pretty sure I should have studied more this weekend."

The day before, they'd spent five hours at the skating rink at a party for Camila's dance crew. Mia had actually had fun for once.

She started to say "good luck" but stopped when she noticed that kids were looking at her and whispering.

A chill ran through her bones. *What now?*

As they turned the corner to their lockers, Mia noticed dozens of photocopied pictures plastered around the hallway. Crowds of students were looking at them and giggling. When they saw her, everyone turned away or looked down at their feet.

She pulled a photo off the wall and realized what it was: her twin sisters naked in a bathtub—while she leaned down next to them, grinning, arms covered in bubbles. She was fully clothed, but her sisters were naked, other than bubbles covering them from the waist down. Mia remembered the joy of that day. Chloe and Charlotte were probably about four years old. Seeing her sweet sisters in such a vulnerable state made her tongue turn to cotton. At the bottom of the image, someone had scrawled, "Wow. How embarrassing, Mia," in red pen. That's when she saw Olivia Banks and her cohorts giggling and pointing from down the hall. Three guesses who had done this.

She showed Camila the picture. "It's Chloe and Charlotte." Her voice caught in her throat.

Camila's face scrunched up in fury. She froze for a second before grabbing at every picture within her reach. "What is wrong with you people?" she yelled. "Haven't you heard of child porn? Do I need to turn you all in to the police?"

The hallway went silent at the words "child porn." Mia was sure she was going to faint.

"What's going on here?" It was her biology teacher, Mr. Scott.

When Camila realized Mia couldn't talk, she stepped in, handing the teacher a photo. "Someone printed out pictures of Mia and her sisters and plastered them all over."

He looked down at the picture, and then at Mia. The bell rang out, making them jump. "Get to class, guys," he called with a raised voice. "Don't worry. I'll make sure the principal hears about this."

Mia glanced at Olivia, who wasn't laughing anymore.

As everyone dispersed, Mr. Scott looked at her. "What is all this?"

Leaning against her locker to catch her breath, Mia shook her head. "It's so stupid." She paused. "My mom is an influencer, and that must be a picture she posted a long time ago."

"Got it." He sighed and looked at Camila. "I heard you mention child porn. I don't think these pictures are that, because their . . . uh, genitals . . . are covered." He cleared his throat. "But I will double-check with the principal. He'll be the one to call APD, if necessary." He turned to Mia. "Let's pull down all the pictures, and I'll shred them."

Mia nodded.

The three of them silently started to rip down the photos and put them in a pile. "Do you know who did this?" Mr. Scott asked her quietly when they were finished.

"Probably one of the Filters."

"The Filters?"

"Olivia Banks and her crew."

"Ah. Do you have any proof?"

Mia shook her head. "Just that she seems weirdly obsessed with my mother."

"I'll investigate. Are you okay to go to class?"

She nodded again. She certainly didn't want to go home.

"If you need anything, let me know." Mr. Scott waved them off to class, and Camila gave her a hug before they went their separate ways.

The next few hours passed in a blur of whispering students and a mess of anxiety in her stomach. Mia barely absorbed any of the information the teachers presented in her classes, worrying instead about the moment she would be called to the principal's office. Would the police be there? Would they arrest Olivia?

Her English teacher, Ms. Means, was droning on about literary genres when the classroom door was wrenched open. It was the office manager. Mia braced herself as the woman handed Ms. Means a note.

Her teacher took a second to read it and then looked right at her. "Mia? Principal Nelson would like to see you."

CHAPTER 9

WHITNEY

There were three situations in which Whitney felt most like an influencer. The first was during photo shoots, when she had Tawny, a stylist, and a photographer to make her look like the absolute best version of herself. The second was when someone recognized her on the street and asked for a picture. And the third was when Taylor flew in from L.A. once a month so they could discuss sponsorship deals over lunch.

Whitney was sauntering down South Congress to her monthly lunch with Taylor when a woman pushing a stroller stopped her to ask for a selfie. "I've been following you for years," the woman said as they huddled together for a photo.

It was like Whitney had won Influencer Bingo.

She was feeling a bit like a rock star as she entered her favorite seafood restaurant, a top people-watching spot on South Congress. It was the best place to take in the city and its cast of characters: bearded hipsters on electric scooters, college girls wearing oversized T-shirts and tiny gym shorts, and fashionable young women who were likely also influencers, though with much smaller audiences.

Although Whitney would never say this out loud, it made

her squeal inside to think that she had a manager. When she was growing up, no one knew she existed and her family lived on peanuts. Now she made so much money and was so popular someone needed to manage her career. Life was wild.

She was a few minutes early for their noon reservation. The hostess, who had a thick blond fishtail braid and enviable winged eyeliner, sat Whitney outside on the fabulous patio under the oak trees. She ordered an iced tea, relishing having a business lunch in the sunshine. Leaning back in her chair, feeling the heat on her face, Whitney counted her blessings.

A gentle breeze blew through the trees right as Taylor arrived with a grin on her face and her ever-present phone in her hand.

"How's my favorite influencer?" she asked as Whitney stood to give her a hug.

Eyeing Taylor's adorable printed maxi dress that she'd seen on display at Nordstrom last week, Whitney was grateful she'd worn her new form-fitting dress and Tom Ford heels and burned through two hours to get ready that morning. Taylor's platinum hair had recently been cut into a sleek lob that highlighted her razor-sharp cheekbones, dark eyebrows that she feathered on the edges—a trend Whitney couldn't get behind, personally—and full baby-doll lips that she exclusively painted with red lipstick. Although it hurt Whitney to admit it, her manager was younger than her, thinner than her, and prettier than her. Plus, she had that healthy, well-rested glow of a woman who chose Peloton workouts and green juice over having kids. The thought that it was Taylor, not her, who should have been an influencer often crossed her mind.

"Guess what brand wants to pay you a hundred grand for a campaign?" Taylor asked, raising her eyebrow with a smug look as she picked up the menu. Everything about the woman was sharp and to the point.

Whitney choked on the water she'd just sipped. That was the most money a brand had offered her—ever. "Which one?" she sputtered.

"Target." Taylor leaned back in her seat with a satisfied smile. "All you have to do is three grid posts, three Reels, two blogs, and a few Stories with the family." She raised her glass of water. "We're ordering champagne to celebrate."

"Wow." Whitney was speechless.

As Taylor flagged down the server, Whitney looked out at the bustling city as if in a daze. She knew the campaign wouldn't be a snap like Taylor said—they never were—but a hundred thousand dollars was an obscene amount of money.

Bringing over a bottle of champagne to their table, the server popped it and filled up two champagne flutes.

"I can't believe this." Whitney shook her head and clinked Taylor's glass. Her mind started running through all the things that money could buy, important things. A chunk of the mortgage, several months of her mother's rent, the rest of Rosie's tuition, money for each of her children's college funds. Suddenly, the ten thousand dollars she'd wired to her brother —which had made her stomach turn—seemed like less of a big deal.

"I know! I was so excited to tell you, but I wanted to do it in person to see your face." Taylor did a little shimmy in her seat. "They want to use you for their spring campaign, so we need to shoot quickly. They were very impressed with your audience growth and follower engagement, especially after you posted that tribute to Michael last week."

Whitney's chest tightened when she heard that, Mia's angry face flashing before her. But she pushed away the thought. She was allowed to tell her story any way she wanted. Clearly, it was working.

"And they love that you have children on every level."

"Every level?"

"Toddler, elementary school, and high school."

"Oh, got it." Whitney took a sip of champagne, feeling the alcohol zoom straight to her head. "Though we may have a problem with the high school part."

Taylor looked like she was trying to furrow her brow, but not a single wrinkle appeared. Botox. "What do you mean?"

With a sheepish look on her face, Whitney sat back and sighed. "You know how I asked you to get those photos of Michael taken down?"

Taylor nodded. "Bad move, by the way. Those photos are an essential part of your story."

Whitney grimaced. "I know, but Mia and I had a big fight about them. We made up, but she's saying she doesn't want to be featured on my social media or blog anymore."

"Oh lord." Taylor waved her hand in the air as if trying to swat away an annoying fly. "She's just exploring boundaries and all that. That's totally normal for a high schooler." She sipped her champagne and gave Whitney an encouraging smile.

"I just need to tread carefully." Whitney's entire body suddenly felt heavy. "I don't think there is any way she'd agree to a photo shoot with Target right now."

Taking a deep breath, Taylor looked like she was choosing her words carefully. "That's a problem. Target wants the whole family for the campaign."

"I know," Whitney said. The mood at their table was no longer jubilant. "I don't know what to do."

"You need to talk to Mia." Taylor was in no-nonsense mode now. "Explain the situation. She's a smart girl. She'll understand."

"I'm not so sure."

"This deal has to happen," Taylor said firmly. "This will skyrocket you to the next level. Think of the fees you'll be able to demand for other partnerships going forward."

No doubt Taylor, who got twenty percent of every deal she made for her clients, would enjoy Whitney getting a rate increase as well.

"Mia's really upset."

Taylor gave her a tight smile. Whitney could tell she was tired of talking about this.

"Sweet-talk her. Turn on your charm, Mama." Taylor took another swig of champagne and chuckled. "Or bribe her if you have to. Tell her it's for her college fund. Or a trip to the Bahamas or whatever. Remember: this could set your entire family up for life."

"Okay, okay," Whitney said, though she wasn't convinced. Mia had been angrier than she had ever seen her the other day. She took another sip of champagne, feeling it lighten her limbs. But surely Mia would understand why the Target campaign was so important, especially when Whitney explained all of her financial responsibilities. She'd make her a Power-Point presentation if she had to.

"Good." Taylor nodded, putting down her empty champagne glass and plastering on a smile. "She'll come around. They always do. Every kid needs their mom."

* * *

AN HOUR LATER, Whitney trudged up the walkway to her house. The champagne was starting to wear off, and in its place a headache was forming. Unlocking the front door, she threw her keys on the console table in the foyer and picked up a stack of bills that sat there, unopened. Her stomach churned as she flipped through the credit card bills, the notice that the mortgage payment was due, and a doctor's bill from when Chloe broke her arm falling off the monkey bars and had to go to the orthopedic surgeon three times.

Being the breadwinner created immense pressure sometimes, but it made scoring a hundred-thousand-dollar sponsorship deal that much sweeter. The only person she could count on to take care of herself *was* herself. She'd learned that the hard way.

Looking around her quiet house, Whitney wished someone was here to celebrate with her. Truthfully, she wished Mia was here. All she wanted to do was talk to her daughter, find out how school was going, listen to the *Hamilton* soundtrack, or go to the Alamo Drafthouse for a movie and a milkshake.

Just then her phone rang. "Hello?"

"Ms. Golden," said a deep voice she'd never heard before.

"Yes?"

"This is Principal Nelson from Austin High School. There's been an issue with Mia. Can you come in right away?"

Whitney racked her brain for a reason she'd get called into school about her reserved, sweet daughter. Was she being bullied? Did she cheat on a test? Whitney knew her daughter had been struggling in biology. Oh god—had someone brought a gun to school?

"What happened?" she asked.

"We'll discuss it when you get here." He had the somber tone of someone who made these calls a lot. "See you soon."

October 23 - 2:07 p.m.

Ashley Graham Crackers: Alert! Alert! I saw Whitney out and about in South Austin today! She's actually very cute in person and super friendly. Who would have thought? (Though her dress was pretty fug. The woman definitely needs a stylist!)

October 23 - 2:10 p.m.

Smug Takes: I love influencer-in-the-wild sightings! How'd her hair look? Are those extensions as awful IRL?

October 23 - 2:13 p.m.

Ashley Graham Crackers: I didn't notice, honestly. I said hi and then we snapped a quick selfie together.

October 23 - 2:16 p.m.

Smug Takes: YOU TOOK A PHOTO WITH HER??? Ew.

CHAPTER 10
MIA

Mia slammed the door to her mother's car as she slid into the passenger seat. That had been *the* most embarrassing twenty minutes of her entire life.

She'd had to sit there and listen to her principal—of a school she'd been at for only a few months!—talk to her mother about "the issue of nude photos of minors." After Principal Nelson assured them that the APD said the pictures "didn't constitute child pornography," he'd tried to play off what happened entirely. He said it was just "kids being kids"—guess Olivia Banks wasn't going to see any consequences—and "that's what happens when your family is in the public eye." He also promised them both that nothing like that would happen again. How he could be so sure, Mia had no idea.

Red-hot rage coiled in her stomach as her mom shook hands with Principal Nelson. Her mother had posted those stupid photos, and now Mia was the one who was going to have to deal with it. There was no way that Olivia and the people at school would ever let her live this down.

Mia refused to look at her mother as they drove home, her

eyes focused solely on the landscape speeding by outside the car window.

"Mia," Whitney said gently when they came to a stoplight.

She didn't reply, angry tears burning her eyelids.

"I am so sorry you had to go through that today, sweetie. Whoever put those photos all over school is a jerk."

Mia remained silent.

Whitney hit the gas when the stoplight turned green. "I know it feels like the end of the world right now, but I promise when you look back at your high school career, this will just be a blip."

Mia turned to look at her mother, her eyes bulging with fury. "A blip? A *blip*? Are you serious? You still don't get it. Your children's privacy was invaded. Hundreds of teenagers have now seen Chloe and Charlotte's naked bodies. How do you not get how wrong that is?"

Whitney's jaw tensed as she stared straight ahead at the road. "Chloe and Charlotte were four years old when those photos were taken, and their private parts were completely covered. What happened today was not the end of the world."

Mia scoffed and turned back to the window. It was unbelievable to think that her mother saw nothing wrong with posting those photos and invading her children's privacy. There was just no getting through to her—which meant she was going to keep doing it. "I will never forgive you for this," she hissed. "Drop me at Camila's. I'm staying there tonight."

Mia waited for her mother to argue with her, but all Whitney did was sigh softly and take the turn to Camila's house instead of their own.

The car had barely come to a full stop when Mia launched herself onto the sidewalk, slamming the door behind her. She didn't look back until she was safely inside the Garcias' house. Her mom's SUV idled outside for a solid minute before it slowly pulled away.

"Mia?" Eva came around the corner looking disoriented and disheveled, like she'd just woken from a nap.

"Hey, Eva."

"It's only two thirty." Eva rubbed her eyes. "Shouldn't you be in school?"

"I got called to the principal's office—with my mom."

Eva's eyes went wide. Mia and Camila were not the kind of kids who got called to the principal's office. "What for?"

Mia's shoulders sagged. She was suddenly exhausted. "Can we talk about it later? I'm going to rest in Cam's room."

"Of course, Pepita." Concern was all over Eva's face as she touched Mia's cheek. "Go lie down. We can talk at dinner."

Mia was sound asleep when Camila burst into the room two hours later.

"Where were you?" Camila threw her backpack to the floor and flipped on the light. "I waited thirty minutes."

Mia groaned and pulled the covers over her face. "Principal Nelson called me to his office to discuss the photos. And my mom was there too."

"Yikes." Camila sank onto the bed. "What did your mom say?"

"She said it was a blip."

"A blip?! What does that even mean?"

"That what happened won't matter in a few years. But she wasn't there. It was awful."

"Totally awful." Camila shook her head. "Want to go get ice cream or something?"

"No." Mia's stomach twisted with anxiety. "I need to do homework."

Camila put on a Harry Styles playlist to soothe her. It helped.

Two hours later, there was a knock on the door. Mia looked up to find Omar standing in the doorway. Only slightly taller than his daughter, he had a barrel chest, warm brown eyes, and an easy smile. He was the guy everyone wanted to be friends with.

"Hey, ladies. I think Mom isn't feeling well again. Can you help me set the table for dinner?"

"For sure," they said in unison. They jumped off the bed and followed Omar to the kitchen.

There was a companionable silence as Omar chopped vegetables, Camila heated up leftovers, and Mia set out plates and silverware. Usually Eva was the one who kept the conversation going, asking everyone about their days and telling funny stories about the preschoolers she cared for. But the quiet wasn't bad either.

Right as they sat down to eat, Eva shuffled into the room, causing them all to jump back up. Omar reached her first, gently guiding her to the table. "Let me get you a plate," he said.

"You okay, Mom?" Camila asked, watching as her dad helped her mom into her chair at the dining room table. Eva's skin had a greenish pallor to it that Mia had never noticed before.

"Just a little tired." Eva took a sip of water, a smile touching her lips as her husband set a plate in front of her. She looked around at the serving dishes filled with grilled chicken, rice and beans, and tortillas. Next to them was a plate of fixings: lettuce, tomato, onion, avocado, and cilantro. "This looks delicious."

"It should. You cooked it." Omar winked as he sat down next to her. "All we did was heat it up and chop a few veggies."

"Still. I appreciate it." Eva looked at Mia and smiled as she smoothed a napkin on her lap. "So, how was school today?"

Before Mia could answer, Omar started to fill Eva's plate. "Not too much," she said, touching his wrist. "I'm not that hungry."

"Are you on a diet or something?" Camila talked around the taco she was chewing.

Mia's eyes widened. She'd noticed Eva was looking thinner too.

"No!" Eva scoffed. "You know I don't do diets. I told you, one of the kids probably gave me a virus." She took a big bite of black beans. "Happy?"

"Immensely," Camila said, wrinkling her nose at her mom.

"Anyway, back to school." Eva wiped her mouth, and Mia noticed she set her fork down. "Tell me about it."

Mia saw Eva and Camila exchange a glance as she took a sip of water. Piling toppings onto yet another taco, Omar was oblivious. But she knew what Eva and Camila were thinking: *Poor Mia.*

Everything she wanted to tell them sat in her chest like an inflated balloon. As the silence stretched on, the balloon got bigger and bigger until it was going to explode. Finally, when the silence was too much to bear, Mia cleared her throat and started talking. "Last week, I went on my mom's blog, and I found pictures she'd posted from my dad's funeral. Of me sobbing next to his casket." Her voice broke, and she cleared her throat. "And she showed a picture of my father. Dead." Eva's and Omar's heads snapped up. They made eye contact, mouths agape.

Eva reached for her hand. "I'm so sorry. You shouldn't have seen that."

"No. She shouldn't have posted it." Mia's chest was burning now. Even though the food smelled delicious, anger had overridden her hunger. She scrunched her napkin in her hand. "Shouldn't I get a say in what images and information about me are on the internet?" She looked out the kitchen window, where a neighbor was walking the dog as her young son scootered next to them.

"Have you tried to talk to your mom about all of this?" Eva asked, pushing her plate away.

Mia nodded. "We got in a fight about it, and she finally said she'd take down those photos."

"That's good." Eva looked relieved.

"But it gets worse." She rubbed at the back of her neck, which was tight as a rubber band.

Eva's and Omar's eyes widened. Mia knew what they were thinking: *There's a worse part?*

"Someone at school found photos my mom had posted of my twin sisters in the bathtub and plastered them all over the school today."

Omar put his taco down, shock evident on his face. "Ay dios mío," he muttered.

"She's also posted photos of Mason in his underwear."

"What?" Camila said.

"Yeah. For a story about potty training. I didn't tell you

that." Mia shook her head. "His whole life is going to be on the internet." With his wavy light-brown hair, green eyes, and dimples, Mason was a carbon copy of their father. "Is there anything I can do about that?"

Eva and Camila looked at each other, faces pale.

It was Omar who spoke first, surprising them all. "I could help you explore your legal options."

"Omar!" Eva exclaimed. But he kept going. "My firm doesn't handle cases like this, but I play Ultimate Frisbee with a hotshot lawyer in town who does. He's a really nice guy. Would you want to talk to him?"

Eva pursed her lips. "Do you really think it's our place to help Mia talk to a lawyer?"

Omar locked eyes with his wife. "I don't know, but this seems wrong. Doesn't it?"

"Yes, but this isn't an episode of *Law & Order,*" Eva replied. "This is Mia's family." Although Eva had never been close with Whitney, Mia could tell she felt like she was violating mom code or something.

All eyes were now on Mia.

Crossing her arms over her chest, Mia sat back in her chair. She'd never considered a lawsuit; she didn't know anything about courts or trials, other than what she saw on Eva's favorite shows. This suddenly felt like a very big moment in her life instead of merely a conversation over dinner. She looked at Omar. "Do you think the lawyer could do anything?"

There was a deep sadness on Omar's face that Mia had never seen before. "I have no idea. But it doesn't hurt to ask. Your mom shouldn't be posting these pictures without your or your siblings' consent. It isn't right."

"This is a big problem for everyone our age," Camila chimed in. "All our parents have posted pictures and stories about us on Facebook and Instagram and Twitter since we were born." She looked at her parents and shrugged. "No offense."

Eva waved her off. "None taken," Omar said.

Camila tried again. "What I mean is we're the first generation that has to deal with all of this. Plus, you have the added issue of your mom being an influencer. She's reaching a lot more people than normal."

"A million people on Instagram alone," Mia said. "And those are only the ones who follow her. Anyone can look at her account." She stared down at her plate, sensing they were all waiting to hear if she was going to take Omar up on his offer. Was it worth putting herself out there for this? It couldn't hurt to see what the lawyer thought, right? Though what if he said she had no case? Mia's stomach flipped. What if he said she did?

After a few more moments, she looked up and made eye contact with Omar. "Yeah. Let's do it. I'd like to know what the lawyer thinks about all this."

"I'll reach out to him tomorrow." Omar gave her a small smile before picking his taco back up and taking a big bite. Clearly, he hadn't lost his appetite.

Mia watched as Eva slowly stood and started to clear the table. Reaching out to stop her, Mia put her hand on Eva's arm. "It's okay. I've got it."

Eva nodded before patting her hand and sitting back down. Picking up two dishes, Mia headed for the kitchen, trying to ignore the trouble-filled thoughts she saw reflected in Eva's tired brown eyes.

CHAPTER 11

WHITNEY

Whitney's head had not stopped pounding since her fight with Mia. Or should she say the *latest* fight with Mia? Because the hits just kept on coming. No matter what she said or did, it was completely wrong in the eyes of her daughter. And no matter how many Advil she swallowed, the pain still throbbed behind her eyes, down the back of her neck, and across her shoulders.

As soon as she dropped Mia off at Camila's house, Whitney came home and told Rosie about the incident at the school. Her sister flinched when Whitney mentioned that she'd told Mia it would soon just be a blip in her life.

"Oh boy. That is the wrong thing to say to a high schooler," Rosie said.

"Why? It's true," Whitney pressed.

"I mean, sure," Rosie said. "But you only know that with the benefit of age and maturity. In high school, every friend drama or breakup feels earth-shattering. And the incident today sounds pretty terrible. It's not something Mia will easily forget."

Whitney sank down on a bar stool and hung her head in her hands. "Why can't I ever do anything right with her anymore? When I said that, I was thinking about how I thought

I'd never get over when Jena Graham used to make fun of my secondhand clothes in high school. It was awful. But it is a blip now. That's what I was trying to say to Mia, but it came out all wrong."

What she should do was drive back to Camila's house to talk to her daughter. But she couldn't. Ace was coming over to have dinner with the whole family. That had seemed like a good idea when she'd invited him a few days ago, but now she would have to explain why one of her children was not present. And what in the world would he think when he heard about the bathtub pictures at Mia's school? That story was neither "hot" nor "fun."

But maybe it was time for Ace to see what life with four kids was really like. Because even though he said he did not want kids, she had them, so they needed to figure out how this equation was going to work. What was the point of see- ing each other if he couldn't imagine a life with her *and* her children? Especially when she was having issues with the oldest kid practically on a daily basis.

She was feeling insecure because she'd emailed Ace the big reveal photos days ago, and he'd neither responded nor mentioned them to her. She didn't know what to make of that, but it didn't seem good.

Between worrying about her relationship with Mia and her relationship with Ace, Whitney's brain felt like it was melting. Maybe a drink would take the edge off. She headed to the kitchen. At least the house smelled delicious. Rosie had picked up two rotisserie chickens, mashed potatoes, and a salad from Central Market on the way home from school, bless her. Whitney had planned to make a special meal, but that wasn't in the cards tonight. She poured herself a glass of white wine and took a sip. Within seconds, the vise on her head loosened ever so slightly. She took another sip, massaging the back of her neck as the wine did its magic. What did it mean that wine made her headaches disappear? Did that make them tension headaches or was she just a tired mom with an alcohol problem?

Catching sight of the clock, Whitney jumped. Ace was going to be here any minute.

Passing through the living room on the way to her bedroom, she found Charlotte and Chloe making friendship bracelets while Rosie was curled up with Mason on the couch, reading to him from a stack of books. Her heart swelled at the idyllic scene. Who wouldn't want to be part of this family?

Whitney threw on her favorite black wrap dress and painted on a bright red lip. That's all she could muster at the moment, but it was good enough.

The doorbell rang right at six, making the kids run for the door with Whitney right behind them. Chloe flung the door open to reveal Ace standing there with a bouquet of flowers and a bottle of wine.

"Good evening," he said with a big smile.

"Oooh, flowers." Charlotte took the tulips from him. "Thanks."

"Actually, those are for your mom," he said awkwardly, shifting from one foot to the other.

"Did you bring anything for us?" Chloe replied.

"Chloe!" Whitney said, her face on fire. She heard Rosie snort from the living room.

"Oh, uh, no," Ace stammered, glancing up at Whitney. "Was I supposed to?"

"It would have been nice." Chloe handed him back the flowers, spun on her heel, and went to play with her sister.

"Tough crowd," Ace said with a laugh, though she could tell he was slightly rattled.

"Sorry about that." Whitney gave him a quick peck on the cheek. She hoped the rest of the dinner went better.

It did not. Ace asked Chloe and Charlotte all the standard kid questions—How was school? What were their favorite subjects? Did they play any sports?—but the girls refused to elaborate on their one-word answers. After a while, Ace quit trying, talking instead to Rosie about her classes at UT.

The kicker was when Mason tried to sit in Ace's lap after dinner. Discomfort was all over Ace's face as Mason squirmed on his lap. After a moment, he moved Mason back to his own seat.

Whitney didn't think Ace did it to be mean. He simply wasn't a natural with children. But she was sure that with enough time, he'd get more comfortable.

The night was a bust, but at least Ace helped her clean the kitchen while Rosie bathed the kids.

"I've been thinking," Ace said, wiping his wet hands on a towel. "What if you and I went away together? Just the two of us."

Whitney froze. The thought of leaving with all that was going on with Mia and work was impossible. "That sounds nice, but it's kind of a bad time."

Ace snaked his arms around her waist and gave her a kiss on the neck. "Imagine it: you, me, and a few nights away in Napa. Or somewhere even closer—San Antonio?"

Whitney stepped away from him. "That sounds great. It really does. I just don't think I can get away right now."

"Why not?"

"There's a lot going on with work, and Mia and I are butting heads constantly." Whitney crossed her arms over her chest. "And you haven't replied about the photos of us for social. What's that about? Do you not like them?"

Ace leaned against the counter and pushed his hand through his hair. "No, I do. We look great." He cleared his throat. "But to be honest, this whole launch thing suddenly feels like a lot. Which is why I thought we could get away. Maybe we should figure out what exactly we're doing before we tell all your followers." He paused. "Besides, if tonight is any indication, I'm not ready to be a stepdad."

Whitney's head snapped up. "No one asked you to be."

"I know. And your kids are great. I'm just freaking out a little. It's a lot of pressure."

She looked into his worried eyes and her heart softened. She had to remember this wasn't a normal dating situation. She and the kids were a package deal, and Ace was right: that *was* a lot. She had been trying to force a relationship between Ace and the kids, but why? There was no rush. They'd build a relationship organically if she gave them the time and space to do it.

"I get it." Whitney reached over and grabbed his hand. "Can we rewind a bit? A week ago, we were just having fun. Fun isn't stressful. Fun is easy. And I need easy right now too."

Ace smiled and gave her a kiss. "Deal."

After some more wine and cuddling on the couch, things were back to normal between the two of them. They were on the same page that no big decisions needed to be made right now.

The next morning, Whitney wondered if she could go away with Ace. A romantic getaway sounded amazing. She just needed to fix things with Mia first. As she was lying in bed mulling it over, her phone pinged. It was Brendan.

> Stephanie had the baby last night. She's beautiful!

Whitney's heart surged and tears flooded her eyes. Her little sister was a mother. How wonderful.

> Thank you for letting me know. I'll give her a call.

Brendan replied immediately.

> Forget a call. When are you going to come visit?

She leaned her head back against her pillow and groaned. Even though she would love to meet Stephanie's new baby, she had no desire to go home. Every time she saw her family, someone inevitably drank too much and started a fight. There was usually crying at some point during the visit, and at least one person always asked her for money. Just thinking about it made her feel wiped out. She did not need any more drama in her life right now.

As Whitney struggled to reply to Brendan, the suffocating feeling of so many people pulling at her, wanting to see her and spend time with her, made her lightheaded. Yet the one person she wanted to see—Mia—didn't want anything to do with her.

Hatefollow.com

October 25 - 8:07 p.m.

Taylor Thrift: Man, Whitney has been SO boring lately.

October 25 - 8:15 p.m.

Retail Therapy & Rainbows: I actually liked that Halloween baking project she posted. My three-year-old loved it and it killed an hour before naptime. Win-win.

October 25 - 8:23 p.m.

Smug Takes: I've been obsessively checking Instagram every day because I'm sure she's gonna reveal the new boyfriend any minute. Then things will get real interesting. Let's go!

CHAPTER 12

MIA

Mia was sitting in a quiet office filled with brown leather and bookcases, and she couldn't make her legs stop jiggling. Even with her heavy backpack sitting in her lap, she fought the urge to jump out of the chair. Should she be doing this? Was she really considering suing her mother?

Glancing over at Omar sitting next to her, she saw that his face was calm. He caught her looking at him. "You okay?"

"Yeah." Mia pushed her hair behind her ears before wiping her damp palms on her sweatshirt sleeves.

"Don't be worried." Omar reached over and pulled her backpack off her lap. He placed it on the floor between their chairs. "Caleb is a really nice guy. We're here to talk to him. Nothing more than that."

Mia nodded. She appeared to have lost all ability to speak.

"Hey, guys," a deep voice said from behind them. Mia turned to find a tall, thirty-something Black man wearing a stylish navy suit and with a face that could only be described as sculpted closing the door behind him.

Omar stood up, so Mia did too, but she kept her bulging eyes on the carpet. She couldn't wait to tell Camila that her dad was friends with the world's hottest lawyer.

"Omar!" he said, putting his hand out and pulling Omar in for a clap on the back. "How are you, my man? Still playing Ultimate?"

Omar laughed. "Barely. I try to play pickup games once or twice a month, but my body screams at me every single time."

Caleb let out a deep laugh.

Mia's heart fluttered. *Even his laugh is amazing.*

"I understand that," he said. "I have trouble keeping up with all the young kids myself these days." He turned to Mia and offered his hand. "My apologies. I don't get to talk Ultimate Frisbee much these days. I'm Caleb Bradford. Nice to meet you. Mia, right?"

She nodded, staring at the hand he had stuck out for her to shake. Quickly wiping her palms off on her jeans, Mia placed her hand in his. "Nice to meet you." She hoped she didn't sound as nervous as she felt.

They sat back down as Caleb strode around his desk, taking a seat in front of the many framed degrees on the wall. Vanderbilt University, University of Texas School of Law. Paired with his movie star looks, it was all very impressive.

Sitting back in his chair and crossing his legs, Caleb looked at her thoughtfully. His deep brown eyes were curious. "I have to be honest with you both: I don't get many teens in here." He gave them both a warm smile. "Omar told me a little about your situation, but I'd like to hear why you wanted to chat today, Mia."

She cleared her throat and took a deep breath, straightening her spine. "Okay, so, my mom is an influencer. Do you know what that is?"

Caleb chuckled. "Yes. I'm not *that* old."

"Sorry," she said with a grimace. "So, she started this blog when I was, like, seven. I'm fifteen now. I don't know how many people read it, but I know she has a million followers on Instagram. And she makes a lot of money."

Mia filled him in on the past few weeks, from the photos of her dad to the bathtub photos plastered around school.

"Have you asked your mom to take the photos down?"

"I did. She agreed to take down the photos of my dad, but she doesn't think there is anything wrong with the bathtub photos."

Caleb raised his eyebrows.

"She also makes us do photo shoots a lot. Some of them are ads for companies."

The chair creaked as Caleb leaned forward. "She's never asked your permission for any of this?"

"No." Mia paused, feeling uncertain. She'd never really told her mother no before last week either.

"So why are you here today?" Caleb asked.

Omar cleared his throat. "We wanted to talk to you and explore Mia's options."

"Actually," Mia blurted, "I want to be emancipated, like Drew Barrymore." She glanced nervously at Omar, who was staring at her, slack-faced. Mia realized she had never asked Camila's parents if she could live with them. She hadn't thought that part through. She hadn't really thought any of this through.

"I see." Caleb turned in his chair to look out the window to their right. The seconds ticked by as Mia waited for him to say something.

She gave Omar a worried look. Was the meeting over?

Finally, Caleb spoke. "First of all, I know for a fact that you can't be emancipated."

"But Drew was only fourteen!" Mia dipped her chin down, embarrassed about her outburst.

"You're right." Caleb remained cool and calm as he spoke. "But all the celebrities you've heard about being emancipated were in California, where the minimum age is fourteen. In Texas, it's seventeen—or sixteen if you're living alone and managing your own finances. Which I'm assuming you're not?"

Staring down at the floor, Mia shook her head. She didn't have a job, or even a license to drive yet. Her parents had always taken care of her. She'd certainly never had to worry about money the last few years. Her mom bought her anything she needed or wanted.

This suddenly felt pointless. It took everything she had not to stand up and run out of the office.

"But there are two interesting things about your case."

"There are?" she asked, hope rising in her voice.

"Yes." Caleb leaned forward. "First, there's the issue of privacy. I'd have to do some research, but as far as I know, no child in America has sued their parents for posting something on social media they didn't like. One thing we will have to contend with is the US parent-child immunity doctrine, which says that a child cannot sue their parents and parents cannot sue their children."

Mia's shoulders slumped as she tried not to cry.

"There have been a few exceptions through the years, usually for abuse. But—and this is a big 'but'—your mother is not an average parent. She has a huge audience and is posting deeply personal images and stories about you. That's a big deal."

Nodding slowly, Mia felt a buzzing sensation build in her chest. He didn't think she was being dramatic. He understood why she was so upset about the pictures from her father's funeral and the bathtub photos. He understood.

"Secondly, I want to explore the fact that you've essentially been creating content for your mother for almost as long as she's been doing this. From giving her story ideas to appearing in photos and promotions, you could be classified as an employee."

"I never thought of that," Omar muttered.

Caleb pulled out a calculator. "Let's say you've been a part-time employee for the past eight years." He started tapping in some numbers. "Say you should have been paid ten dollars an hour. That's two hundred dollars a week and ten thousand, four hundred dollars a year. That means your mother owes you as much as eighty thousand dollars."

Mia swallowed. Eighty. Thousand. Dollars. "That's a lot of money," she squeaked out.

"It is," Caleb replied with a nod. "Now, I have a question for you, Mia." He waited to continue until she looked up and met his eyes. "Are you prepared for what this could do to your family?"

Her throat went dry, and her heartbeat kicked into high gear.

Caleb kept their eye contact. "If you file this suit, your mom will probably be really angry."

"I know." Her mom would be livid.

"But have you thought about what that means?" Caleb pressed. "It'll be months before the trial, so you'll have to see your mom, day in and day out, knowing how angry she is at you."

Despair bloomed in Mia's chest as she thought about how tense her home would be. It would be unbearable for all of them.

"Could I live with the Garcias?" She glanced at Omar, hoping he would say yes.

Caleb raised his eyebrows at Omar.

"I'll have to talk it over with my wife and daughter, but I'm sure Mia could live with us until the trial is over," Omar said, shifting in his seat. Mia gave him a grateful smile. If she lived with Camila and her family, she'd miss Mason and his warm snuggles. She'd miss talking to her twin sisters too.

"Okay." Caleb nodded at Omar. "I can propose that to your mom's lawyer." Caleb fixed his gaze back on Mia. "You should also know that this case could get a lot of attention. If your mother really is as popular of an influencer as you say, this could be front-page news. And you would be the poster child for kids who want their privacy back—literally. This could set a legal precedent for what parents can post about their children online."

The room was quiet. No one made a sound as Mia was given time to process everything Caleb had said.

Closing her eyes, she imagined two doors. Behind door number one was uncertainty. The court could make her mother stop posting about her and her siblings altogether. Maybe she could even help other kids who were dealing with their own privacy issues. But Mia could also lose. Either way, she would become the one thing she had never wanted to be: the center of attention.

If she picked door number two, she would move on with life as if nothing had ever happened. She'd go back to the same old thing: photo shoots, being blog content, and having no say in what was posted about her or her family. Her stomach twisted with anxiety just thinking about it.

"Mia?" Caleb's deep voice brought her back to the present. (Seriously, this guy sounded like an insurance commercial.)

Feeling a calm settle over her, Mia opened her eyes and looked at Caleb. "I understand. Now I have a question for you."

A playful smile lit up Caleb's face. "Shoot."

"You're talking like you're taking this case. Are you taking my case?"

Caleb looked her square in the eye. "I think you have a good case. An important case."

Mia nodded, pressing her hands together to hide the shaking. "Okay. How much do you cost?"

The lawyer chuckled. "Like I said, I think this is going to be a big case. And you're fifteen." He cleared his throat, his smile fading. "Have you ever heard the term 'pro bono'?"

That sounded familiar. She'd probably heard it on a TV show once. Her heart felt like it was doing gymnastics in her chest. "You'll do it for free?"

Caleb nodded.

"Why?"

"This case could change internet privacy laws for children forever."

Mia was quiet for a moment. She took slow, even breaths. "I have one more question. Do you promise I'll win?"

Caleb looked at her seriously and shook his head. "I can't promise that. No lawyer can. There are too many variables that are out of our control. But I can promise you that I will build the very best case for you that I can. And I definitely want to win."

For now that was enough.

Mia reached her hand across the desk. "Deal." Caleb smiled as he shook it.

CHAPTER 13

WHITNEY

Wrapped in a towel with a squeaky-clean face and a freshly waxed bikini line, Whitney paged through a magazine while waiting for her massage therapist. She took a deep breath of the herbal scents perfuming the wood-paneled spa waiting room, the tension evaporating from her body. It had been four long days since her latest fight with Mia, and her daughter had barely uttered a word to her since. Mia spent all of her time at Camila's house, coming home only to shower and sleep. Whenever Whitney tried to speak to her daughter, catching her early in the morning before school or right before bed, Mia had an excuse for why she couldn't talk—usually involving having to study or going to bed ASAP because she had an important test the next day.

Whitney sighed. If she was being honest, she had no idea what to do about Mia. Her mom and dad hadn't exactly modeled good parenting for her, and she'd already been gone when her siblings were in high school. At this point, she'd prefer Mia yell at her again instead of freezing her out. At least then they would be talking.

She was at a loss on how to handle the situation or what her next move should be. Shutting down her work was out of the question, but Mia was definitely not in the mood to compromise. The one saving grace was that she knew her daughter was safe because she was at the Garcias' house. While she and Eva had never become close—Whitney had been overwhelmed with the twins when Mia had first met Camila—they always exchanged pleasantries. And then in the years after Michael died, she'd been in survival mode. While Whitney hadn't ever gotten to know Eva and her husband well, she was positive they were good, caring people. Maybe she should invite them over for dinner. Then Mia would have to talk to her.

Leaning back on the cold, smooth leather couch, she let herself relax. It had been a busy day. On top of having Mia constantly on her mind, she'd shot three sponsored-content videos with Gabby in the morning and volunteered at the twins' fall school party instead of eating lunch. After that she ran home for her weekly phone call with Taylor and then had a two-hour Zoom meeting with Amazon about the fashion line.

Now she was ready to relax. Whitney had had a standing Friday-afternoon appointment here for the past few years. Some might call it high-maintenance, but part of her job was to look good, so Whitney considered it a necessity. Designer clothes, beauty treatments, diets, trainers. It was all a requirement of living in the public eye—and keeping up with other influencers. Even though she was supposed to be "your average mom," she couldn't look like one. Which was why she had a rotating schedule of treatments, including manis and pedis, extensions (hair and lash), waxing, highlights, and Botox. Even thinking about the list made her tired.

Right as she started to drift off, Whitney heard a voice call her name.

"That's me," she said, opening her eyes and tipping her head forward to smile at the tall, stout, forty-something woman with rosy cheeks and long blond hair braided into two thick ropes down her back. "You caught me right before I fell asleep."

"My name is Olga. Follow me." The woman looked exactly as her name suggested: like she could throw a sheep over her shoulders and run five miles without breaking a sweat.

Whitney followed Olga down the hall and into one of the massage rooms. Taking off her robe, she flopped down on the table, ready to be even more relaxed.

An hour later, she awoke to Olga gently shaking her shoulder. "Miss? Your massage is finished."

Whitney lifted her head groggily, slobber wet on her cheek. Her entire body felt like jelly. "I slept through all of it?"

Olga nodded. "You must have been very tired." There was an awkward pause. "I'm going to leave you to get dressed. I'll meet you in the hallway when you are ready."

"Thank you." Whitney waited until Olga left the room before hoisting herself up on the massage table. She shook out her neck and stretched her arms up over her head, trying to wake up. While she knew she should have been embarrassed—*lord help me if I talked in my sleep, or worse: farted*—Whitney chalked up her exhaustion to all the stuff she'd been dealing with lately.

Once in her robe, she opened the door and found Olga waiting for her. "Here is some cucumber water. You must hydrate."

Whitney took the water gratefully, chugging it down in one gulp. "The massage was excellent. I feel like a new woman."

"Good." Olga gave her a swift nod. "I hope you get some rest."

"I'm sure I will sleep well tonight. Thank you."

She headed back to the locker room to shower and get dressed. Her entire body felt looser, like her tense muscles had transformed into Silly Putty. She'd have to book Olga again. *That woman is a magic worker*, Whitney thought as she slid on her shoes and grabbed her bag.

Strolling to the lobby area, she found the desk empty. Knowing that the receptionist often gave first-timers a short tour of the spa, Whitney headed over to the wall gallery of beauty products for sale and picked up a face cream she'd heard great things about. She almost choked when she saw the two-hundred-dollar price tag on the bottom. But then she reminded herself that supporting local businesses was important. And besides, she worked hard. She deserved a little treat now and then.

She heard the tap-tap of the receptionist's heels heading her way.

"Sorry to keep you waiting," the pretty redhead said. "How were your treatments today?"

Whitney placed the face cream on the stark white desk. "Wonderful, as usual. Olga is amazing. I fell asleep!"

"That's awesome." The redhead rang up the new cream

and Whitney's treatments. "I've heard Olga gets all the kinks out."

"That she does."

"Excellent. Your total today is six hundred twenty-seven dollars."

Whitney pulled out her credit card with a tight smile. Even now, all these years after growing up without new shoes or even a candy bar from the grocery store checkout line, she had to remind herself that she could afford this.

The receptionist handed her a small bag with her new face cream in it. "See you next week!"

Heading for the door, Whitney wanted to snap a picture of the spa's exterior so she could give the business some love on Instagram.

She was digging through her bag to find her phone when the front door opened. She looked up with a pleasant smile on her face. (You never knew who could be coming through the door. A follower? Another influencer?) She was surprised to find a bearded young man wearing a baggy T-shirt and even baggier jeans. This didn't seem like his kind of place.

"Whitney Golden?" he asked.

"Yes?" she replied, a guarded note in her voice.

He handed her a white envelope. "You've been served." He turned back to the door, pushing it open before she could even comprehend what he had said.

"What?" A wave of nausea surged over her and her knees went weak. Confused, she watched the man's retreating back as the spa door swung shut behind him. That envelope couldn't be for her, could it? Dropping her bags on the floor, she frantically slid her finger under the flap to open the envelope.

Her cheeks heated with rage and her hands started to shake as she skimmed the document:

CIVIL COURT OF THE CITY OF AUSTIN

Plaintiff: Mia Rose Golden
Defendant: Whitney Ellen Golden

You are hereby summoned . . .

"She's suing me?" Whitney whispered. A warm sensation swept up her body from her toes to her head, like a pressure cooker about to burst. "She's *SUING* me!?" Now she was yelling.

"Ms. Golden, is everything okay?"

Whitney turned to look at the receptionist, who she suddenly realized had the same copper-colored hair as her daughter. Her ungrateful, hateful daughter.

"I'm fine," she choked out, struggling to breathe. She grabbed her bags off the floor and pushed out the door and onto the street.

Stumbling down the sidewalk like an injured wild animal, Whitney couldn't see straight. Her life was falling apart, yet everyone in downtown Austin was going about their business. People shopped and sipped cocktails, met up with friends, and clocked out at work, ready for the weekend. Struggling to put one foot in front of the other, Whitney paused to watch a group of people pedal by on one of those bars on wheels. Yet another way the world had gone mad.

When she got to her car in the parking garage, Whitney

wrenched open the door and threw her bags inside. Flinging herself into the driver's seat, she willed her stomach not to heave. Her teen daughter was suing her. Why was Mia doing this? What would her readers think? What would her *advertisers* think? The words "Target" and "a hundred thousand dollars" flashed in her mind. *Oh god, oh god, oh god.* Leaning her head onto the steering wheel, Whitney opened her mouth and screamed.

October 27 – 6:37 p.m.

Ew, Dorothy: Nit-Whit's been awfully quiet today. Think something's going on?

October 27 – 7:05 p.m.

Taylor Thrift: No, it's Friday. She's either at the salon or the wine bar.

October 27 – 7:16 p.m.

The Good Karen: I'm sure she had a very stressful week at "work" and needs to treat herself.

CHAPTER 14
MIA

Sitting on the Garcias' couch, Mia tried to work on her algebra homework. Her mind kept drifting, because she knew from Caleb that her mother was getting served today. She didn't know when, and she didn't know where, but she assumed she'd hear about it as soon as her mother did. It was going to be a shock to her mom, for sure, so Mia was prepared for her phone to blow up with calls and texts.

Eva was cooking dinner in the kitchen. She'd finally gotten over her never-ending cold, it seemed, and was making flour tortillas to use for chicken enchiladas. It already smelled delicious. Mia's stomach grumbled. Even though she knew Eva would have gladly made her a snack, she hated to impose. She'd been hanging out here for four days straight eating their food, using their toilet paper, warming their couch, going home only to shower and sleep. Her dad used to joke that guests were like fish: they began to stink after three days. Turned out he'd stolen that from Benjamin Franklin. But Mia was definitely worried she was becoming a stinky fish.

Scrolling down the page, she clicked on the last part of her homework. A few more problems, and she was done. The sound of a car screeching to a stop made her look up.

Eva poked her head out of the kitchen. "What was *that*? It sounded really close." She headed for the window to peek out.

Hopping off the couch, Mia went to look too. But there wasn't a car wreck in front of the house. It was her mother's very large SUV.

As they watched from the window, Whitney swung out of the driver's side, slamming the door shut behind her. She stomped up the walkway, heading for the front door. The color of her mother's face was as red as the chilies currently sitting on Eva's cutting board. Mia could see the veins popping out of her neck. Was this how an aneurysm started?

"Crap." Mia looked at Eva, her eyes wide. The shock on Eva's face mirrored her own.

Mia opened the front door, bracing for contact with her mom. "What are you doing here?" she asked, stepping outside with Eva right behind her.

The look in her mother's eyes could only be described as crazed. "Suing me?" Her eyebrows were practically up into her hairline. "You're suing ME?" That last part was nearly a shriek.

Mia backed up as she came closer. Guess her mother had been served.

"Calm down."

"Don't you dare tell me to calm down," she hissed, pointing a finger at Mia's face. "I'm your mother. The mother who has done everything for you your whole life. You need to stop this."

The little hairs stood up on the back of Mia's neck, but she held her ground. "Do you think I wanted to do this? You gave me no choice."

Neighbors were starting to come out of their homes, watching Whitney rant and rave. Mia wouldn't be surprised if the scene was on TikTok within the hour.

Whitney noticed the neighbors too. She stopped and took a deep breath, visibly trying to take control of her emotions

"Would you like to come inside and discuss this privately?" Eva asked quietly.

Mia felt dizzy. *My mother in the Garcias' house?*

Whitney glanced at Eva, her face unsure. After a long pause, she finally nodded. "Yes, thank you."

Eva led everyone inside, motioning for them to sit in the living room.

Mia sat down on the couch, hoping her mother would choose the chair across from her. She did.

"Whitney, can I get you something to drink?" Eva didn't appear to know what to do now that everyone was inside.

"No, thank you." Whitney rubbed at her forehead. "But you can tell me how my fifteen-year-old managed to file a lawsuit against me."

Eva's face went pale as she sat down in the other chair. "My husband helped her," she whispered.

"Are you serious?" Anger flashed in Whitney's eyes. "You could have talked to me first."

Before Eva could reply, Mia interrupted. "I talked to you by the pool and after meeting with Principal Nelson. It was clear you don't see anything wrong with exploiting your children for likes, so I had to do something drastic."

Whitney looked to the ceiling in disbelief. "Why didn't you talk to me *again*? I've tried to talk to you every single time you've been home, which isn't much. I've called, I've texted." She paused, tears shimmering on her cheeks. "I was trying to give you space, but clearly that was a bad move."

Mia didn't know how to reply. It was true that her mother had reached out every day, but she had been too stubborn to reply.

Whitney kept talking. "Do you realize what this lawsuit could do? It could tank my business. Who will pay for our house? Our food? All of our bills? And what about Grandma's housing? Or when Uncle Brendan gets in trouble and needs money? Did you think about any of that? This could ruin us."

Mia's stomach quivered and her mouth went dry. She knew they had a lot of money, but her family's financial specifics were a mystery to her. And she definitely hadn't known her mother paid for her grandmother's rent or sent money to her favorite uncle. But that didn't change anything. "I don't know, but what you are doing is wrong."

Whitney's neck and cheeks turned splotchy, and she suddenly looked exhausted. "It's not that black-and-white, Mia." The look in her eyes now turned to pleading. "There aren't a lot of jobs that pay a high school graduate what I make as an influencer."

Seeing her mother like this made Mia's heart sting. But not as much as the image of her father in his casket or her naked sisters in the bathtub, plastered all over the school.

Whitney took a deep breath. "Okay, if I try to take all the pictures you don't like off the internet, then what? Will you drop this charade? Can everything go back to normal?"

Mia stood up and took a step away. Normal? What was normal? Being featured on the blog and social media against her will? And what about her siblings? "No. I don't think things will ever be 'normal'"—she emphasized the word with air quotes—"again. I don't want you to post about me or make me be in photo shoots. And I don't think Chloe, Charlotte, and Mason should be either. At least until they understand what agreeing to it really means."

Whitney slowly shook her head back and forth. "Mia, that's impossible. You want me to shut down everything? How? It's why we can afford to live the life we have."

"Can't we, like, downsize?" Mia asked. "We don't need that huge house or that fancy car or a lot of the things we have."

Whitney sighed. "It's not that simple."

Mia balled her hands into fists. "I can't believe you." She gave her mother a searching look. "If you loved me, you'd take my concerns seriously and figure something out."

Whitney sighed again. "Mia, everything I do, I do for you and your siblings. One day you will understand that."

Mia shook her head. "Whatever. All I know is you can't post about me anymore."

Whitney furrowed her brow. "That's what I don't understand. You're demanding privacy from me, but think of all the attention you're going to get with this lawsuit. This is going to be everywhere."

Mia frowned and crossed her arms over her chest. "That may be true, but that's the risk I'm willing to take for my life to not be plastered all over the internet. I'm not stopping the lawsuit."

"Fine." Hunched and holding back tears, Whitney stood and headed for the door. She looked like she'd aged ten years during their conversation. "You know how to reach me if you change your mind."

A wave of sadness washed over Mia as she watched her mom get into her SUV and drive slowly away.

"You okay?" Eva said behind her.

Mia nodded, sniffling. The tears came fast and furious. She didn't know what to say or do.

"I'm so sorry." Eva pulled Mia into her warm chest for a hug. "You can stay here as long as you need."

"Thank you." Mia sat down on the couch in shock. She couldn't believe that her mother's concerns about finances outweighed Mia's valid points about internet privacy. Her mom had chosen her career over her children, over her. And that meant the lawsuit was happening. For real.

CHAPTER 15
WHITNEY

Whitney's mind was ablaze as she drove home. She'd never been part of a lawsuit before. Did she even know anyone who had been? Surely Brendan did—but that was the crowd he ran with. Whitney had worked for twenty years to be an upstanding citizen and good mother. And now her daughter—a child who arrived after nine months of growing in her body and two hours of pushing—was suing her. And with Camila's parents' help! How dare they?

The whole thing was unfathomable. Half of her wanted to scream and yell and bite somebody's head off. But the other half was so embarrassed. What were her friends and family going to think? What about her followers and sponsors? If they got word of this, they would leave her high and dry in an instant. She didn't claim to be the smartest businessperson in the world, but she knew that.

Taking a right onto their street, she pulled into the driveway. Whitney cut the engine but couldn't will herself to get out of the car. If she stayed there, cocooned inside her quiet SUV, could things stay the same? If she never told anyone else that Mia was suing her, did that mean it wasn't really happening?

As she pondered these questions, the front door of the house opened, and Rosie poked her head out.

When Whitney's gaze met her sister's, Rosie gave her one of her enormous grins and raised her arms in the air. "I got in!"

Whitney squeezed her eyes shut. Her sister had gotten into the study abroad program in Australia. That meant she was leaving her too.

Rosie walked toward the card, her forehead creased in confusion. "Everything okay?" she called.

Whitney leaned forward, pressing her forehead into her steering wheel. If she told her sister about the lawsuit it would make it real, and she didn't want this to be real.

Rosie tapped her knuckles on the window. "Whit?"

She turned to look at her baby sister, her eyes filled with tears. "Congratulations."

Rosie pulled open the car door, a note of panic in her voice. "What's wrong? Did something happen?"

Whitney turned her face away. "Mia's suing me. So there's that."

All the air left the car. "What?" Rosie asked quietly. Whitney felt her warm hand on her arm. "Why? How?"

"For posting pictures she doesn't like of Michael and the kids." She looked at her sister now. "And for all the money I apparently haven't paid her for her work. Camila's parents helped her get a lawyer."

"Jesus." Rosie sounded as stunned as Whitney felt.

"Yeah. And I'm pretty sure she's going to move in with Camila's family permanently." Whitney's lips trembled as she held in a sob.

"Oh, sis." Rosie unclipped Whitney's seat belt and pulled her into her arms. That's all it took for the dam to break open. Sobs racked Whitney's body. "Shh, shh." Rosie ran her hand down Whitney's hair. "It'll be okay. We'll fix this. Let's go inside."

When they opened the front door, the sounds of happy children filled the air.

"The kids are eating dinner," Rosie said as they walked toward the kitchen. "I told them they could eat in the living room and watch a movie for a Friday treat."

"Thank you." Whitney sniffled and sat down on a stool at the kitchen island. "I really am so happy for you, but what am I going to do without you?" She didn't know if she could survive without Rosie. How was she supposed to parent her three younger kids right now? Should she tell them their sister was suing her? Would they even understand what that meant?

Rosie placed a glass of wine in front of her. "Let's worry about Australia later."

Whitney took a grateful sip. "I don't know what to do." Her heart felt like it had been scooped out of her body. "Who do I call? What do I say?" She hung her head in her hands. "I should call Taylor and tell her."

Rosie shook her head. "No. It's Friday night. Let's have a nice dinner with the kids and relax. You can call her tomorrow."

After forcing down a quesadilla, getting the kids to bed, and drinking three glasses of wine, Whitney poured herself into bed. But the wine didn't do its job; she was still wide awake hours later.

Slipping into her robe, she grabbed her phone off the

nightstand before tiptoeing toward the door. Her head was swimming as she headed into the kitchen. She needed a snack.

Inside the fridge, she discovered that a local restaurant had sent over a charcuterie plate, which Rosie must have put in the fridge. She pulled the whole thing out, along with a can of LaCroix, and set everything on the island.

Hunched on a bar stool, nibbling on crackers and cheese, her mind returned to the lawsuit. Growing up with parents who were never around and were certainly never loving, Whitney had promised herself that she wouldn't be like that. And she wasn't. But she had still managed to fail spectacularly nonetheless. From where she sat, she could see a picture of her and a glowing ten-year-old Mia on the fridge. It was from their last trip before Michael died. They'd visited Michael's mother in Chicago and had the best time taking pictures in front of The Bean and shopping along the Magnificent Mile. Whitney's chin trembled. How had things gone so wrong between them?

As her brain swirled with dark thoughts, Whitney wished she had someone to talk to. But it was after two in the morning. Everyone she would normally turn to—Rosie, Tawny, Ace—was sound asleep.

What she wanted was to share with her community. But would they even be on her side? The desire to share the details her own way burned inside of her. Should she try to control the narrative? *Could* she control it?

She cleaned up her mess in the kitchen, and then headed to the living room. She sat down on the couch and looked around the impeccably decorated room. Sometimes, she still couldn't believe she lived here. That she'd *earned* this life. It was then that a light bulb went off: she needed to fight this lawsuit. She loved her daughter, but Whitney didn't think Mia truly understood what she was asking of her. Didn't your brain not fully develop until you were twenty-five? That must have been what was going on here. Whitney still had hope that Mia would come to her senses.

Even though a part of her knew she shouldn't, she picked up her phone and opened the Instagram app. Her community, her people, would understand. And they should hear it from her first.

"Hi guys, sorry I was a bit MIA today." She dabbed at her eyes, which reflected back at her red and swollen. "There has been some turmoil in my family that you may hear about soon, so I wanted to tell you about it first."

She took a deep, shaky breath. "My daughter Mia is suing me." She had to choke those last words out. "I can't get into the details, but I wanted you to hear it from me before you read about it somewhere online. Please know that I'm still going to keep blogging and sharing in this community. I can't answer questions right now, but I'm here. I'm not going anywhere."

Even though it was two in the morning, the comments and DMs started pouring in immediately.

OMG! We are behind you 100 percent, Whitney.

That is crazy! Stay strong.

Why would Mia do such a thing? Is she okay?

Yes! Go Mia! Finally, someone is standing up for the kids of influencers. Y'all deserve this.

Whitney shut down her phone before she saw any other mean comments. She knew they'd keep rolling in, but she was calmer after getting that off her chest. She sighed, hoisting herself to her feet. As she walked toward her bedroom, she trailed her hand along the back of her exquisite six-thousand-dollar couch.

Now that she'd shared her truth, it was like the elephant was no longer in the room. She'd get through this. She was strong. And now she could sleep.

October 28 – 2:24 a.m.

Smug Takes: Whoa. Whitney posted that Mia is suing her!

October 28 – 2:32 a.m.

Waxing and Chillaxing: It must be so hard to have such a vile mother.

October 28 – 2:33 a.m.

Smug Takes: Mark my words: This is going to get messy. (Though Whitney is already messy, so . . .)

October 28 – 2:45 a.m.

Moose Willis: I'm so happy Mia did this! Why don't these influencers see how gross it is to make most of their income off of their non-consenting children? Some of them say their children "give them permission" to post certain things. But those kids have NO concept of what they are agreeing to.

CHAPTER 16

MIA

Mia was eating breakfast with Camila and her parents Sunday morning when there was a knock on the door.

Omar went to answer it and called, "Mia, it's for you!" a moment later.

Mia looked at Camila, eyebrows raised, and shook her head. It was too early in the morning for this.

She assumed it was her mother again, but when she came around the corner, it wasn't her mom waiting for her in the foyer—it was Rosie.

"Aunt Rosie?" Mia couldn't keep her voice from cracking.

"Hi, Mia. I heard about the lawsuit." The usual smile on Rosie's face was gone, and her voice was flat.

Mia didn't know what to do with that. "Yeah."

Rosie took a deep breath, her face a storm cloud. "I'm really disappointed that you didn't try harder to find a solution with your mom before going nuclear."

"Try harder to find a solution?" Mia couldn't believe her ears. Didn't her aunt realize her mom had forced her to take action? "I should have known you would side with her. You always do. And just so you know, I've voiced my concerns to her several times. She doesn't care! Did she tell you about the bathtub photos?"

Rosie flinched. "Yes. I'm sorry you had to deal with that. But I don't think it's worth suing over."

"Oh, so I can plaster some naked pictures of you around the school, then?"

"That's not the same thing," Rosie said with a scowl. "And you know it."

"Because we're kids? We still have rights, you know, and the right to privacy is one of them."

"So you're suing your mom and putting your whole family in the public eye?" Rosie's tone was sharp. "Make it make sense."

"It makes sense to me." Mia opened the door and held it for her aunt. She was so numb that she couldn't even cry anymore. All she knew was that she was done with this conversation.

Rosie glared at her, but Mia could see the pain in her eyes. "Fine. I just wish you could see your mother for who she really is."

"I do." Mia's tone sounded harsh even to her.

Her aunt shook her head as she stepped out the door. "Oh yeah." She turned back. "I also wanted to tell you I got into the study abroad program in Australia. I leave right after the holidays."

Mia swallowed the lump in her throat. Her aunt, who'd never even been on an airplane, had applied for the program on a whim. She was going to be halfway across the world for five months. "Wow, congratulations."

"Thanks. I'm really excited." Rosie cleared her throat.

"You know, I didn't come here to fight with you, Mia. It just makes me really sad to see you and your mom like this. And I wanted to know if there was anything she could do to get you to drop the lawsuit."

"It makes me really sad too. But I already told her: she needs to shut everything down. She's not willing to do that."

"This isn't a switch to flip; this is a career. She needs time. But I hear you." Rosie gave her a sad smile. "I'll keep talking to her."

"Thanks." Though Mia knew there was no hope.

Rosie reached out and touched her hand. "I'll miss you. So much."

"Me too." Mia watched her aunt walk away, not knowing when they would see each other again. Yet another way her life was changing.

* * *

SHE WAS STILL thinking about their conversation Monday afternoon. When the final bell rang, she trudged to her locker. As she pulled out the books she needed for that evening's homework, she racked her brain for somewhere to go other than home. Well, Camila's home. She knew Eva would probably be waiting for her, but she wanted to be alone.

Shutting her locker, she leaned against the wall and watched as the hallway emptied out. All her classmates seemed to have somewhere to go. Out with friends or home, most likely. Camila had dance practice today, so Mia had no one to go to a coffee shop or bookstore with. She could walk to the Froyo place down the street, but she wasn't hungry.

What she wanted was to have some time to think, where no one stared at her or whispered about her family. Or asked her how she was doing.

Mia started walking before she even knew where she was going. Jumping onto the 801 bus that ran through the city by going north and south on Lamar Boulevard, Mia watched the Austin landscape go by. Everything brought back memories of both her father and her mother. The bus zoomed down Lamar, and Mia's mood lifted when she saw Torchy's, where her father always ordered a fried avocado taco. And there was her mother's favorite jewelry store. She had bought Mia a pretty horseshoe necklace from there last Christmas.

Her phone pinged as the bus crossed over the bridge above Lady Bird Lake, though locals called it Town Lake, refusing to acknowledge the name change. Mia wasn't surprised to see a text from Eva.

> Everything okay?

> I'm good. Running an errand. Be back by dinner.

Eva sent her a thumbs-up emoji.

Mia stood up as the bus rolled to a stop at Auditorium Shores. Exiting into the sunshine, she felt a surge of energy run through her body. She loved this part of town. Her dad used to bring her to Zilker Park and the hike-and-bike trail nearly every weekend when she was younger. Feeding the ducks and swans, flying kites, and people-watching were some of her favorite things to do.

Hitching her backpack tighter on her shoulders, she started walking toward Zilker Park. She looked at her watch. Five o'clock. She didn't know if her lawyer would be playing Ultimate Frisbee right now, but it couldn't hurt to head that way and see.

Watching the world zoom by, she remembered all the picnics and adventures she'd had with her father down here. He loved to be outside, soaking in the sun and getting exercise. An editor for the local newspaper, the *Austin American-Statesman*, he could wax poetic about the joys of Austin for hours. The kooky people! The amazing weather! The delicious food! The festivals! The live music! There were so many things that made this city great, and Mia's father had made sure she knew about all of them.

Mia knew her dad would have hated that she was fighting with—and suing—her mother. But she also knew he'd understand her side and be proud that she was standing up for herself. She'd never been very good at that. In kindergarten, she'd been bullied by the biggest kid in her class. He'd stolen her snack every day. Mia had never said a word to anyone. Not her parents or her teacher. She simply took the abuse. Finally, it was Camila who had shoved the boy to the ground and told him to leave Mia alone. He had too. When her dad had heard about it, he'd sat her down and told her she needed to stand up for herself. "You've got to fight for what is right, Mia," he'd said. "Remember that."

It was only about a twenty-minute walk from the bus stop

to the massive green space that was Zilker Park, but Mia was dragging by the time she got there. Maybe she needed to start running, like her dad. Would it be weird to start running, when that's what killed him?

At Zilker, she found a heated soccer game, dozens of dogs playing ball with their owners near Rock Island, and at the far end of the field, a group of people chasing a Frisbee as it flew through the air.

With her head down, Mia headed for the Frisbee players. She knew Omar sometimes played a pickup game after work—he called it "Happy Hour"—so maybe if Caleb wasn't there, she could get a ride home with Omar. It would be better than taking the bus.

Mia surveyed the crowd of guys and girls of all ages, colors, and sizes standing around watching two teams of seven players as they ran, passed, and leaped into the air—all trying to get their hands on the flying disk. It looked like a fun game. Mia could see why Omar liked it.

That's when she saw him. Her hunk of a lawyer, sweaty and chasing a Frisbee in athletic shorts and a T-shirt with the sleeves cut off. Right as he leaped up to grab the disk flying through the air, Mia saw him recognize her. And then he collided with someone from the opposing team.

"Oh no!" Mia gasped as Caleb slammed into the ground. If she had caused her lawyer to break a limb, she would never live it down.

Caleb rolled onto his back and groaned. Someone from his team reached down to help him to his feet. Once he was up and had caught his breath, Caleb motioned at her to come over.

Mia ran up to him. "I'm so sorry. I wanted to talk. I didn't mean to distract you."

"I'm getting too old for this." Caleb wiped his brow and brushed the dirt off his shorts before limping to a nearby camping chair, where he reached for a Nalgene full of water. He pointed to the chair next to his. "Sit."

Mia gingerly slid onto the chair, trying to take up as little room as possible. She saw some of the other players looking at her and whispering. It probably wasn't every day that a teenager showed up to disrupt a game.

Caleb grimaced as he rubbed his shoulder. "To what do I owe this visit?"

"My mom got served on Friday."

"I know." Caleb wiped his face. "I had them do it at the spa you told me she goes to on Fridays, so your siblings wouldn't be around."

"She freaked out."

Caleb raised his eyebrows as he sipped more water. "No one enjoys getting served."

"We had a big fight. On the lawn. Well, Omar's lawn. And then my aunt told me she didn't agree with me at all. And now I'm having second thoughts."

"I see." His tone was calm but his jaw clenched as he turned his gaze to the Ultimate game in front of them.

"If there is this much drama already, it's only gonna get worse."

Stretching his legs in front of him, Caleb winced. "True. But a few days ago, you were in my office telling me why this was a case worthy of me taking. And I still think that Mia was correct."

"You do?"

"Yes. I do." He looked out at the field, watching the game for a few moments before turning back to her. "But you're right. Things are only going to get tougher from here on out."

Mia's ears started to ring as she let that wash over her. She already couldn't stand the attention and upheaval. To think of anything worse made her feel like she was suffocating.

Leaning back in his chair, Caleb looked at her thoughtfully. "Only you can know for sure that you're up for this. That's your decision, and your decision only. But I, for one, would hate to have someone post pictures of my sisters in the bathtub all over school."

She cringed. "Yeah. It was pretty horrible." Looking out at the Frisbee players, Mia noted how happy and carefree they all looked. What she wouldn't give to feel like that. "What would you do?" she asked, turning to make eye contact with the man who was willing to represent her for free.

Caleb rubbed at a patch of dirt on his knee and took another swig of water. "I'm more than double your age, and a Black man, so I've seen some . . . stuff. There's a lot of injustice in this world." He shook his head and cleared his throat. "I don't want to get into all that right now. But I believe you've got to fight for what is right, Mia."

Her heart seized as she heard her father's words from so long ago repeated once again. Caleb gave her a searching look. "Besides, if you don't do it, who will?"

CHAPTER 17

WHITNEY

It was Wednesday, but Whitney was still recovering from the worst weekend of all time. After her late Friday-night confession, she'd woken up to a dozen irate voicemails and texts from Taylor.

The tone of her manager's messages had gotten increasingly unhinged. So much so that Whitney had been scared to call her on Saturday morning, briefly wondering if Taylor would refuse to represent her any longer. There was no way she could find a new manager in the middle of this shitstorm. She saw now in the light of day how stupid she had been to share information about the lawsuit with her followers before she had talked about it with Taylor, before they'd come up with a strategy. Before she'd even *told* Taylor. No wonder her manager was furious.

When she'd finally worked up the courage to make the call, Taylor had answered calmly. Too calmly. "Hello, Whitney."

"Taylor! I'm *so* sorry that I posted about the lawsuit before I told you about it." Her voice shook. Instead of letting Taylor speak, Whitney kept going, trying desperately to defend the indefensible. "Rosie suggested I wait to talk to you until today, but then I had a few drinks. I wasn't thinking straight, on top of being super emotional. I was crying and thought my followers would understand. It was stupid. I was stupid. Again, I am so, so, *so* sorry."

She took a deep breath after her spiel, bracing herself for Taylor's reply. Even though Whitney was the talent, she was enormously loyal to Taylor, who had swooped in and helped her organize her money, her business, and her life after Michael passed away. Taylor had saved her. They were a team; Whitney couldn't imagine doing this job without the other woman. Squeezing her eyes shut, she mentally crossed her fingers that Taylor wasn't going to can her as a client.

"It's okay," Taylor said quietly. Whitney could tell she was struggling to maintain her composure across the phone line.

"It is?" Whitney exhaled. "I thought you were going to break up with me." A nervous giggle escaped before she could stop it.

"I was." Taylor let her statement hang in the air as Whitney's gut dropped to the floor. "But I've been up all night and had a lot of time to think. I've also watched your followers tick up by two thousand in the last hour. You know people love to watch a car crash, so I think we can use the lawsuit to our advantage."

"You do?" Whitney squeaked. She hadn't even logged on to Instagram yet. "How?"

Taylor was back to her all-business self when she replied. "I've developed a three-pronged plan. First, we craft a message and you reach out to all of the companies you work with to let them know about the lawsuit and assure them that nothing is going to change with your content creation going forward."

"Okay." Whitney could do that.

"Then, we have my other clients share their support for you." Taylor represented twenty-five influencers, though Whitney was one of her top-three cash cows.

"That's a great idea," Whitney said.

"Last but not least, we go back through every campaign offer that you've turned down because you felt it wasn't authentic, and you tell them you want to work with them now."

"What?" Whitney sputtered. "I turned down those campaigns for a reason. I don't think it would be smart to take crappy campaigns for crappy money. That doesn't make sense."

The line was silent for a moment. When Taylor started talking, there was venom in her voice. "You know what doesn't make sense, Whitney? What you did last night, telling your followers about the lawsuit before you told me." Even though they were on separate coasts, she could feel Taylor's hostility through the phone. "And frankly, you don't have the luxury of being *authentic* anymore. Until we see how this thing plays out, you need to take every campaign you're offered. Do you understand? Because there is a good chance that your entire career may go up in flames in the next few months. We need to wring out every dollar we can in case that happens."

Whitney took a deep breath and rubbed at the throbbing pain hammering her forehead. While her natural instinct was to dig in her heels and refuse to do what Taylor wanted, she knew this wasn't a time to be stubborn. Although she liked to believe she was a supermom who could do anything, there was no way she could deal with the lawsuit's impact on her career alone. She needed everyone in her corner she could get. And that included Taylor.

"Okay, okay. I'll do it." She didn't have any other choice.

"Good." Taylor's voice was pleasant again. "I've sent you the drafts I wrote for you to send to your clients and my other influencers. I want those all out by the end of the day."

"Today? But it's Saturday. The kids—"

"I don't think this can wait," Taylor said, cutting her off. "Do you?"

"No. I guess not."

"Good. Get those emails out. I'll check in later, after I get some sleep." Fatigue had creeped into Taylor's voice. Whitney realized how exhausted her manager must be.

"We're a team, Whitney. Don't forget that."

"Thanks for sticking by me. Get some rest."

* * *

FIVE DAYS LATER, Whitney was the one who needed to rest. After sending hundreds of emails and sweet-talking the handful of people who would actually get on the phone with her, Whitney had learned she was already tainted. Few of Taylor's other clients seemed to want to touch her with a ten-foot pole, though a handful did do Instagram Stories proclaiming their shock and surprise about the lawsuit and defending the use of their own children on social media. And it appeared her manager had been right. She could no longer be picky. The only company that responded about a partnership was the cheap sparkly phone cases only the newest influencers worked with. Several of her current clients had already dropped her, and she was waiting with a pit in her stomach to see what emails she received today. So far Taylor hadn't heard anything from Target or Amazon. Whitney was trying her best to believe that no news was good news.

The one ray of hope was that her Stories about Mia suing her had gotten more than five million views in the twenty-four hours they were up—the most views she'd ever gotten, by far. It was both thrilling and nauseating. People truly couldn't look away from the wreckage.

On Monday morning, the *Austin American-Statesman* had published a front-page article that blared "Local Mommy Blogger Sued by Daughter." Whitney was even more mortified to recognize the byline as one of Michael's old coworkers.

This morning, Taylor called and let her know that Amazon had backed out of their clothing line deal, citing the morals clause in the contract Whitney had signed. According to the company, Mia's lawsuit against her could be viewed as public condemnation.

After they hung up, Whitney paced her office, wringing her hands as she imagined the money in her checking account ticking down, down, down. How was she going to pay for next month's bills? For this house's ridiculous mortgage? Why hadn't she planned better? Saved more? She'd been so stupid.

All she wanted to do was crawl into her bed and sleep for a year, but she couldn't. She had to get ready for an afternoon meeting with a lawyer Taylor had set her up with. His name was Barton Briggs, and apparently he was a character—and a damn fine lawyer. She hoped so, because right now it felt like only a superhero could fix her mess of a life.

* * *

HER STOMACH WAS a wreck as she pushed open the shiny glass doors to Briggs & Mullins Law, which was located in the center of Austin's bustling downtown. When the elevator pinged open on the eighth floor, Whitney made eye contact with the receptionist, who barely smiled at her. She could only imagine what these people must think of her. What kind of mother gets sued by her own child?

Before she could even tell the receptionist her name, a young woman with blond curls and a pencil skirt appeared and told her she was Mr. Briggs's assistant. The blonde led Whitney down an art-lined hallway to the conference room.

"Here we are," the woman said, gesturing for her to take a seat. In the center of the conference table sat bottles of water, cookies, and a coffeepot. "Mr. Briggs will be right in. Feel free to grab refreshments."

After thanking her, Whitney strolled over to the window to take in the exquisite view of the Texas State Capitol.

"She's a beaut, isn't she?" a deep voice boomed behind her.

Turning with a plastered-on smile, Whitney found a very tall, very solid fifty-something man wearing a dark suit, a Stetson, and cowboy boots. Barton Briggs looked like a guy who'd played football in high school. "Great view." She held out her hand. "I'm Whitney Golden."

Mr. Briggs shook her hand. "Nice to meet you, Whitney. I'm Barton Briggs." He turned to the thirty-something brunette next to him. "And this is my cocounsel, Kelsey. She'll be taking notes as we chat."

"Nice to meet you," Kelsey said without smiling. "I'm a big fan."

Whitney didn't know if she believed her.

Once they were all seated, Barton placed his hat on the table and leaned back in his seat. "So. What can I do for you today, darlin'?"

Whitney prickled. She hoped Taylor hadn't set her up with a misogynistic lawyer. Maybe it was further punishment for not telling her first about the lawsuit.

Clearing her throat, she took out the document she'd been served and pushed it across the table. "You may have seen in the *Statesman* that my teenage daughter, Mia, is suing me. I've been an influencer full-time for four years, since my husband passed away unexpectedly. Mia never had a problem with it, but recently she's been demanding I take down specific photos and content she doesn't like. And now she's gone and done this."

"I'm sorry to hear that." Briggs picked up the letter. "I have two teens myself, and they are quite the challenge. I like to say, 'Teens: you can't live with them, you can't shoot 'em.'"

Whitney chuckled nervously while Kelsey remained stone-faced.

Briggs skimmed the document. "Do you think there is any validity to your daughter's lawsuit?"

Whitney blew out a deep breath. "No. I'm posting about my life."

"Uh-huh, uh-huh. What about paying her for her work?"

Whitney nervously spun her water bottle. "I mean, work? She doesn't work for me."

"I've seen Mia on your Instagram quite a few times," Kelsey piped up.

Whitney bristled. "Because she's a part of my family. Of course my social media features my children—I'm incredibly proud of all four of them. But it's not like they are working forty hours a week for me."

Barton raised his eyebrows at her. "How many hours a week do you think she is working for you?"

Whitney couldn't believe this line of questioning. Sitting up straighter, she looked up at the ceiling. "A few, sometimes. We do photo shoots, but then I use that content for months. And sometimes I write about our relationship. But, again, it's not like she's my employee."

"Okay. I get the picture. This operation seems very loose. But we are going to need you to look back over the last four years and see how often Mia worked for you."

"She didn't work for me!"

"You may think that, but the judge may have a different perception."

Whitney felt like her head was a ball of flames about to launch into the atmosphere. Weren't these people supposed to be *defending* her? Yet she already felt like she was on trial.

Barton leaned back in his chair and rested his hands on his ample belly, which was straining his pressed white button-down. "Have you considered settling? Throw a little money at the problem, and it may go away."

"I don't think this is about money," Whitney said in a strangled voice. "Mia wants me to totally quit posting about her and her siblings. I don't think that's feasible."

"Why not?" Kelsey asked.

"Contracts have already been signed, and I can't break them. I'm the breadwinner for my family. And I have a lot of financial responsibilities for my extended family as well."

Barton and Kelsey exchanged a glance. "We understand," Barton said, kindness in his voice. "The good news is the law really protects parents in this regard. Have you ever heard of the parent-child immunity doctrine?"

When Whitney shook her head, he continued. "It's the

legal notion that a child cannot bring legal action against his or her parents for civil wrongs the parents commit while the child is a minor."

"What does that mean?"

"It means that Mia doesn't have much of a case."

Whitney breathed a sigh of relief.

"But asking for back pay for the work she did for you may be another issue."

"Ahh!" Whitney threw her hands into the air. "But she didn't work for me. I don't know why you keep saying that."

Kelsey looked shocked for a moment, but Briggs didn't flinch. He'd clearly seen worse.

"I'm a mom who posts about her life on social media, and she's my kid."

Kelsey cleared her throat. "I actually crunched some numbers, and Mia has appeared in ten sponsored posts this year alone."

Whitney's face flamed. Ten. *That number can't be correct, can it?* "And I pay for one hundred percent of her food, housing, and clothing. Besides, these photo shoots are fun! I don't see what the big deal is."

Briggs held up his hand, effectively silencing her. "Now, Whitney, you call yourself the CEO of this company, so you can't say that your daughter was simply being a daughter in all those photo shoots."

Whitney felt like her brain was splitting open. If this questioning was only a fraction of what being on trial would be like, she didn't know if she could handle it.

Briggs continued. "The good news is you influencers are essentially operating in the Wild Wild West. There are no laws about posting about your children, but that may soon change. We need all of the information, so we can defend you to the best of our ability."

Whitney took a deep breath. "Apologies for my outburst. This is an emotional time."

Briggs reached out and patted her hand. "It's going to be all right. As I've said, I don't think your daughter has much of a case. And due to the media attention, there's a chance the judge may expedite the trial."

He smiled. "I know it's not fun for you, but it may work in our favor to get this over quickly."

That's what Whitney wanted too.

"There is one more important thing we need to discuss," Barton said as Kelsey slid a paper over to him. "Mia's lawyer has filed an agreement of temporary guardianship for Mia to live with Omar and Eva Garcia. Were you aware of that?"

Whitney swallowed rapidly, trying to stop the contents of her stomach from launching onto the conference table. "No," she said quietly. "What does that mean?"

Barton squinted at the paper. "Looks like counsel is recommending Mia live with the Garcias before and during the trial. You'd pay them a small allowance for Mia's room and board and give your daughter some extra spending money. Once the trial is over, no matter who wins, Mia will return to living with you." Barton looked up at her. "It's probably a way to prevent you from influencing her before and during the trial." He chuckled. "Which is kind of ironic."

Whitney didn't laugh. "I can't allow it. Mia needs to be with me, with our family."

"I knew you were going to say that," Barton started, "but I actually think this might be a good thing. Give Mia some time to cool off. You never know what could happen in the next few months—she could miss y'all so much that she drops the lawsuit."

"Not likely." Her daughter was as stubborn as she was.

Barton leaned back in his chair yet again. "You know the old saying: If you love someone, set them free. If they come back, they're yours."

Whitney noticed that he didn't finish the rest of the saying: "And if they don't, they never were." That was the part she was afraid of.

* * *

LEAVING HER LAWYER'S office, Whitney was all frayed, like a live wire that was suddenly exposed to the elements. She couldn't believe her daughter, her firstborn, wasn't going to be living with her for the next who knew how long. Barton had said it could take up to a year for the trial to make it to court. How was she supposed to survive without seeing her daughter for a year? How was she supposed to explain Mia's absence to her other children?

When she arrived home, Whitney found Rosie feeding the children yet again. When her sister saw her face, she wordlessly poured her a glass of wine. Whitney shouldn't drink—she'd been relying on alcohol way too much lately—but how else was she supposed to survive this?

Accepting the wineglass gratefully, Whitney took a sip. The alcohol was doing its thing, relaxing her as it flowed through her veins, when the doorbell rang.

"Who could that be?" she asked Rosie, who was working on stir-fry for their dinner.

Her sister shrugged, focused on the chicken she was searing. "Probably UPS with a package."

Whitney's heart fluttered. Maybe it was Ace. She'd welcome a little cuddling with a big, strong man right now.

"Coming!" she yelled, stepping out of her heels as she headed toward the front door.

Her drink in one hand, Whitney flung open the door and stumbled, almost dropping her glass of wine.

Standing on her doorstep, luggage in hand, was her mother-in-law. The woman who never thought she was good enough for her son. They hadn't spoken since about a year after Michael died. Judith had come to visit, and the trip had been so awkward and even more painful for them both. The hole Michael had left in their family was never more obvious. After that, Judith stuck to phone calls with the kids and sending cards and presents for their birthdays.

"Judith? What are you doing here?" Her mother-in-law looked exactly the same as the last time she'd seen her. Her gray hair was still bobbed and she still wore her standard uniform of tortoiseshell glasses, cropped pants, and those chunky white sneakers that only grandmas seemed to find fashionable.

"I found out that my granddaughter is suing her mother," Judith said in her no-nonsense manner that only a Chicago teacher of thirty-five years could have. She pushed through the front door with her bags. "Where else would I be?"

November 1 - 7:03 p.m.
Trash Panda: How is this lawsuit going to work, exactly? Is Mia not going to be on the blog going forward? Is she even living with her family?

November 1 - 7:04 p.m.
Retail Therapy & Rainbows: I have no idea, but maybe this will change how much influencers are allowed to share about their kids online. Good.

November 1 - 7:07 p.m.
Ew, Dorothy: I'm an attorney who deals with a lot of family law cases. Mia is likely staying with a guardian for the foreseeable future. Which is so sad, because her siblings are probably incredibly confused and miss her terribly. Whitney needs to do whatever her daughter wants and quit posting about her. Those poor kids.

November 1 - 7:10 p.m.
Thirst Trap: Not to dox myself, but I know Whitney IRL. I can say with confidence that she's a bad mom. Worse than you even know.

November 1 - 7:23 p.m.
Vegan Vampire: You know Whitney in real life? Spill!

November 1 – 7:24 p.m.

Moderator: I will not hesitate to shut this forum down if one of you breaks the rules. Clearly, this is a litigious family, and I do not want to deal with that.

CHAPTER 18

MIA

After third period, Mia headed to the student lounge, where she and Camila met daily to debrief each other on their mornings.

Her phone started to vibrate in her pocket right before she entered the lounge. She unlocked the screen and saw a text from Chloe. Her mom had gotten both of the twins a "dumb phone" at the start of the school year, so they could call and text in emergencies. Chloe and Charlotte loved to send her texts that were simply blocks of emojis. Seeing her sister's name on her phone screen made her heart twinge.

But instead of the emojis she was expecting, her sister had sent her actual words.

> Where are you? Why haven't you been home?

She groaned.

"What's up?" Camila appeared at her side.

"Chloe wants to know why I haven't been home. What am I supposed to say?"

Camila cringed. "Didn't your mom tell her what the deal is?"

"No idea." Mia followed Camila into the lounge and sat down next to her on a couch. Before she could type out a reply, Chloe sent another text.

> Everyone at school is talking about us. I heard Mackenzie's mom say that you're ripping our family apart.

"Oh no," Mia whispered.

Mia turned the phone so Camila could see the text. Cam's eyes almost bugged out of her head. "Good lord."

"Yeah." Mia's fingers flew across her phone's keyboard as she typed out her reply, knowing Mackenzie's mom would probably feel differently if she knew about the bathtub pictures that had been plastered in her high school's hallway.

> I'm sorry you're dealing with that. You can tell Mackenzie's mom that I'm standing up for something I believe in.

Mia sighed as she hit send. How in the world was she supposed to explain all this to her little sisters?

Chloe didn't reply immediately, so Mia sent a second message.

> I love you and miss you. Can we talk later?

This time, Chloe replied swiftly.

> Ok. Love & miss you too.

She ended the message with a string of heart emojis in every color of the rainbow.

Mia had to giggle as she slid the phone back into her pocket. She really did miss her sisters. She'd have to figure out some way to see them soon.

"Everything okay?" Camila asked.

"As okay as it can be right now," Mia replied.

"I have something to cheer you up. Have you seen the school paper?" Camila held up the newest edition so close to Mia's face it practically hit her in the nose.

"No," Mia said, pushing the paper out of her way. "Why?"

"Because they wrote an opinion piece about your case."

"Seriously?" She couldn't believe how fast everything was moving. It had been only a week since her mom was served.

"Seriously." Camila held the paper out to her. "See for yourself."

Hands shaking, Mia grabbed the paper and looked at the front page. There, in black and white, was a huge headline: "Mia Golden Is Fighting for All of Us."

She looked at Camila, eyes wide. "Yeah," her best friend said. "It's pretty good."

As Mia started reading, it was like all the hustle and bustle around her disappeared. No more hollering students, no more shushing teachers. All the noise evaporated as she read the op-ed from the newspaper's editor in chief.

Mia Golden Is Fighting for All of Us
By Alex Liang

I've heard many of my fellow classmates making fun of Mia Golden's privacy case against her momfluencer mother. They say things like, "What's the big deal? It's a few photos of her as a kid." Or "If my mom made as much money as hers, I'd let her post whatever she wanted." Or "Who cares? No one looks at that crap anyway."

But what my fellow students don't seem to understand is that Mia's case is going to set a precedent that will hugely affect all of our lives. We were all born between 2005 and 2009, right when mommy blogs and parenting forums were starting out. Social media was new and it was fun, but there were also no rules put in place—and there still aren't. One British study found parents post about 1,500 images of their kids on social media before those kids turn five. That's almost a picture a day.

You've probably never stopped to think about the seemingly silly things your mom or dad or even grandparents have posted about you. Of course, there have always been those embarrassing photos where you look goofy or still have your braces or baby fat. But unlike when they are in a private photobook, now they can be found in a public Facebook album. And what if you're applying to Harvard? Do you want the admissions officer to find out that your mom asked for math tutor recommendations for you every year of high school via Twitter? Or would you want your future boss to find that adorable video your dad posted of you at two and a half, naked and on a potty?

I, for one, am tired of always being an afterthought in this country. We're the collateral damage of school shootings, when politicians offer thoughts and prayers and say "things could have been worse." We're the collateral damage while baby boomers pretend climate change doesn't exist. Like the world's young people aren't inheriting a planet that is dying. It's the American way to ignore the issues they deem unimportant—or don't want to deal with.

We are the first generation to face the ramifications of growing up with social media, which means we are the first generation to fight for our right to online privacy. Every kid deserves a say in what is posted about them by their parents online or even if they can post anything about us at all. Mia Golden is helping us all to get that. Instead of mocking her, we should be thanking her.

"Wow," Mia said. Her cheeks were pink as she looked up at Camila. For the first time, she felt like one of her classmates understood why she was doing all this.

"I know, right? Do you know who this Alex guy is?"

"No idea."

"I wonder if he's cute?"

Mia rolled her eyes, but her stomach did a flip. "Do I need to thank him?" She paused, considering. "I should thank him."

"Couldn't hurt. You need every person on your side that you can get."

Over the next three class periods, Mia noticed a definite shift in how the other kids treated her. There were still whispers behind her as she walked by or entered a classroom, to be sure, but the way people looked at her was different. No one made comments about her mother or the lawsuit. Even Olivia Banks didn't utter a word of contempt when she took her seat in social studies. "Good article," some guy she didn't know called out as she walked to lunch, as though she were the one who wrote it.

Mia bowed her head and kept walking, but there was a smile on her face.

When her study hall period came around, she headed to the second floor, where the student newspaper offices were located, connected to the journalism teacher's classroom.

The room was empty, so Mia walked through it toward the back, where there was another open door. On the far wall was a huge blue-and-gold sign that said: "All the Austin High School News Fit to Print." Computers lined the long row of desks in the room, but there was only one student sitting at them.

She lifted her hand and knocked on the door frame. "Excuse me. I'm, uh, looking for the school paper's office."

The student looked up. Wait, was he a student? He was tall, trim, and quite handsome, with black rectangular glasses and expertly gelled dark hair. But it was his clothing that confused her. Instead of the usual Texas high school boy look of baggy athletic shorts and a T-shirt, this guy was wearing a slim white button-down, black jeans, and a skinny black tie.

"You found it," he said, scanning her over with limited interest before dropping his gaze back down to the computer.

"Okay, uh, great." She bit her lip and rocked on her feet. "I'm, uh, actually looking for Alex Liang."

"You found him," the man-student said, not bothering to look up at her this time.

"Oh, hey. Hi. I'm Mia Golden."

"I know who you are." This time he looked up, piercing her with his dark eyes.

"You do?" she squeaked. And then thought silently, *You idiot! Of course he knows who you are. He wrote an article about you.*

She held her breath as Alex stood up, strolled around the desk, and stuck out his hand for a shake.

When he released her hand, she wiped hers on her jeans as he leaned against the desk, his legs nonchalantly crossed at the ankles, red Converse on his feet.

"Oh. Okay. Uhh . . . I wanted to thank you for what you wrote." She was finding it very hard to make eye contact with this student. Man. Person.

"No need to thank me," he said with a lazy shrug. "I was only speaking the truth."

"I appreciate it. They haven't made it easy on me." She didn't elaborate on who "they" were.

He smirked. "Yeah, sometimes the students here can be idiots."

She couldn't hold back a giggle. "I've noticed that."

Instead of laughing along with her, he stared at her, as if waiting for her to say something brilliant. That's when she spotted the Northwestern flag on the wall behind his desk.

"Northwestern?" She nodded at the flag. "My dad went there."

"Cool. I'm waiting to hear about early acceptance to the J-school." He snapped his fingers and pointed at her. "Wasn't your dad an editor at the *Statesman*?"

Her skin started to tingle. "Yeah." She wondered what other details about her family he'd picked up while doing research for his op-ed.

"Nice. I want to work in news too."

"Oh, cool." That was the most interesting reply she could think of at the moment. "Okay, well . . . thank you again."

He nodded, standing up straight and walking around the desk to his chair. "No problem." Alex turned his attention back to his computer.

Mia waited a few seconds, her feet feeling locked in place, before turning and walking toward the door.

Just as she crossed the threshold, she heard Alex call to her, "I hope you win your case!"

She looked back, shocked to find him smiling at her. "Me too."

CHAPTER 19
WHITNEY

Knitting. Judith was always knitting. On a stool at the island while eating breakfast. In a chaise lounge by the pool. On the couch while watching *Jeopardy!* every afternoon at four o'clock, while Mason played with his trucks at her feet. It drove Whitney crazy.

Judith had been here for a week already, and Whitney hadn't seen her mother-in-law without needles and yarn in her hands or within reach once. It made her wonder if it was a nervous tic, a way for Judith to keep her hands busy at all times.

Ace had made himself scarce since Judith had arrived. He said he had nothing against her, but Whitney could understand that hanging out with your girlfriend's husband's mother was awkward, to say the least. Judith was great with the kids, though. She got down on the floor to build block structures, race cars, and create Play-Doh sculptures with Mason, and she spent hours talking to the twins, listening to the latest playground gossip and quizzing them for their math and spelling tests.

It was a far cry from Whitney's own mother, who didn't bother to ask about her grandkids half the time.

This morning, Whitney was sitting—okay, hiding—in the

breakfast nook, working on her laptop, when Judith strolled in, a cup of coffee and her knitting in tow. She was working on a sweater for Mason, which didn't seem like the best use of her time since he would maybe wear it for a month before the weather turned balmy again. And by the next Texas "winter," he'd have doubled in size.

Bustling around the kitchen, Judith took a tub of yogurt out of the refrigerator and then grabbed Whitney's favorite gluten-free granola from the pantry. According to the symphony of clanking that commenced, Judith was making a yogurt, fruit, and granola parfait.

Whitney sighed, forcing herself to focus on her computer screen.

"Everything okay?" Judith asked.

"Oh yeah. Work stuff." According to an email she'd received from Taylor, Whitney had lost another sponsor. But she wasn't going to tell Judith that. The one saving grace was that Target hadn't backed out of their deal. They'd postponed her campaign until after the trial, but their marketing VP, who was a young widow with children herself, apparently had a soft spot for Whitney. "Teens are hard," the VP had told Taylor. "I'm sure this will all blow over."

Sitting down with her breakfast, Judith gave her a thoughtful look. "May I ask you a question?"

Whitney nodded warily. The only thing Judith seemed to like more than knitting was digging into her life. Whenever they were alone—which was far more than she would have liked—Judith would ask her an innocent question that clearly wasn't innocent.

"What is it, exactly, an influencer does?"

Whitney closed her eyes, trying to maintain her composure. "I've built up a community of followers who look to me for help on things to buy or do, and sometimes they ask me for advice on parenting or fashion or working out."

"Okay . . ." Judith waited for Whitney to say more. A longtime first-grade teacher, she had a knack for knowing when she should simply listen.

"Think of influencers as modern-day magazines, but all the content is us, instead of models and celebrities and . . . experts." Whitney paused. "That doesn't sound so great, but it's about being real. My followers know I always tell them the truth, about everything."

Taking a bite of her parfait, Judith didn't look impressed . . . or persuaded. "So you put everything on the internet?"

"Not everything. I like to say that my content is heavily curated."

Judith took a sip of coffee. "By content, do you mean your life?"

"What? No. I just mean, I don't post anything that my followers wouldn't aspire to."

"Like a big fight with your daughter. And a lawsuit."

Whitney rubbed the bridge of her nose, trying to fend off the headache that was building. "I had to post about that. I can't conceal it from my followers."

"Or a husband dying suddenly." Judith's voice cracked.

Whitney's throat constricted. "Yes." She shut her laptop, looking Judith in the eye.

"You have to understand. I was devastated when I lost Michael. I didn't know how I was going to survive—as a mom, as a woman—or what I was going to do for money. I posted those photos of his funeral when I had a small audience. They were my friends! That's how it felt anyway. I had no idea it would blow up. I went from twenty thousand followers to two hundred thousand practically overnight. And it grew from there. I would have been insane not to take the opportunities that were handed to me."

Judith blinked back tears. "The pictures were hard to take. To see my son like that again . . . it made me relive one of the worst days of my life. I'm sure Mia feels the same."

"We deleted those photos." Whitney sat up straighter, knowing she would never have an explanation that would satisfy her mother-in-law. Especially one who had made it clear she didn't think Whitney was good enough for her son by suggesting she sign a prenup days before their wedding. (Michael had shut that down real quick.)

"You may have deleted them from your site, but they are still easy to find in other places."

"I'm sorry about that. We are trying to get all of them taken down. It's harder than we thought it would be." She needed to talk to Taylor about this again and figure out what the holdup was. "Honestly, talking about Michael's death has been like therapy for me. I'm not trying to hurt anyone. I'm simply trying to survive, and hopefully help other women along the way. You may not agree with it, but I've been able to create a business that supports my family while also spending a lot of time with my children. If you have another way that I can make six figures at home, please let me know."

Judith's eyes darkened, and she picked up her knitting. "You're right. It's your life."

Whitney wiped her hand down her face. She looked at her watch. "I need to head out soon." She had planned to write a blog post and schedule her social media for the rest of the month, but she no longer wanted to be at home.

"Can you stop the lawsuit?" Judith asked.

Whitney sighed, standing up. "That's up to Mia."

Judith stood as well, heading to the dishwasher with her empty bowl and coffee cup. "I was going to talk to you about that. I'd like to see her. Can you give me her cell phone number?"

Whitney's stomach burned. Judith was going to get to talk to Mia and hug and kiss her. Even though she was jealous, she knew she couldn't keep her mother-in-law from her granddaughter.

"Of course." She pulled out her phone and texted Mia's number to Judith with rigid fingers. "I need to get ready for a lunch meeting." That was a lie. She had no lunch. "Then I'll swing by and pick up the girls after school. I'll see you this afternoon."

Gathering up her things, Whitney breathed easier as soon as she walked out the front door.

The thought of going to a coffee shop to work wasn't appealing. She knew she'd end up going through her DMs. She'd started reading them again since the lawsuit was announced, and what she saw every day was mentally crushing her.

Congratulations! You are officially the worst mother in America.

I truly didn't know someone could exploit their children and their dead husband. And then I heard about you. Whore.

Go kill yourself.

Go kill yourself.

Go kill yourself.

She thought about those messages even when she wasn't on her computer. How could she not? The cruel things strangers said to other people on the internet—especially those who chose to put their whole lives out there for public consumption—would make even the most devoted nun question her faith.

Not to say Whitney didn't get messages of support. She did. But even one malicious message could burrow into her brain and live there forever. The most bizarre part was a majority of these people chose to follow her. If they didn't like her content or thought she was fat and ugly or truly believed she was a bad mother, why didn't they click unfollow? She would never understand the glee these people got out of trying to take her down a peg.

What she needed was to burn off her frustrations. She headed to the hike-and-bike trail around Lady Bird Lake to get some fresh air. After walking the three-mile loop from MoPac to Lamar, admiring the skyline and people-watching, Whitney was much more relaxed—and starving.

She picked up her phone. Eleven a.m. Maybe Tawny was available for lunch.

What are you doing right now?

Tawny replied instantly.

> Vacuuming. Why?

> How would you feel about tacos and some company?

> I would feel great about that.

> Excellent! I'll be by in 30.

Whitney practically skipped to her car, excited to see her friend for the first time in way too long. Tawny lived in a cute house in East Austin, and one of their favorite taco trucks was on the way.

She arrived at Tawny's front door right on time with a bag of barbacoa and al pastor tacos in one hand and a tray with two mango aguas frescas in the other.

Tawny opened the door with a big smile. "Hey, stranger. Come on in."

Entering Tawny's colorful home, Whitney placed the food on the kitchen table and gave her friend a big hug. "I'm so glad this worked out. I've missed you." They still texted on an almost daily basis. It was meeting up that seemed impossible these days.

"The feeling is mutual." Tawny eyed the food. "This looks amazing. I'm famished."

"Me too." Whitney sat down at the table and started pulling tacos out of the bag. "I needed to get away from Judith, so I walked three miles on the hike-and-bike trail."

Tawny chuckled as she took a bite of a taco. She swallowed. "Oh my lord, this is so good." She took a sip of her agua fresca. "Has it been that bad having her here?"

"Not bad, per se. More like awkward." Whitney focused on scarfing down her first taco. She really should have had more than coffee for breakfast. When she'd finished the taco, she picked up her drink. "She asked me for Mia's number today." She raised her eyebrows at Tawny as she took a swig. "That's when I had to get out."

"Oh man. How's everything going with that?" Tawny's head tilted to the side, pity etched across her face.

"Horribly. I miss her so much." Whitney sat back in her chair and crumpled up the taco wrapper. "And I can't help feeling angry. Judith was giving me crap about the photos of Michael today, which, I mean, she has every right. But have you seen the stuff people post on Instagram and TikTok? I've seen parents post photos and videos of their little girls in skimpy outfits and bikinis for likes, babies covered in their own feces, not to mention kids with cancer getting chemo—or even dead, believe it or not. It's insane. And what about those YouTube families who post every move their children make? Yet *I'm* the one getting sued? It doesn't make sense."

"Maybe your case will change what other parents are allowed to post," Tawny said.

"You mean if Mia wins."

"Well, yeah."

Whitney flinched. "So you think Mia will win?"

Tawny blew out a deep breath, clearly choosing her next words as carefully as a tightrope walker about to take their first step. "I think Mia has started an interesting conversation about children and their privacy online." She pursed her lips. "I'm on TikTok a lot—I want to see what my kids are seeing. And it's bad, Whitney. There are parents exploiting their kids all over social media. I'm not saying you're doing that, but . . ."

"But you are saying that, aren't you?" Whitney crossed her arms tightly over her chest, her appetite all but gone now. "You've known me for twenty years. I thought you of all people would know I would never do anything to harm my children."

"I do know that. And I also know the pressure you are under to make money for your family." Tawny stared down at her hands. "Did you read the comments on that video you posted of the twins eating ice cream last week?"

"Yes." Whitney thought back to the short video she had posted of the girls giggling while licking matching mint-chip cones. It had been a sunny day and she was craving ice cream, so she'd taken them out for an after-school treat. She'd captioned it something like "Sugar rush!" "I mean, the first twenty or so. Why?"

Tawny rubbed at her forehead. "You should go back and look at the comments—all of them. There are some gross comments about the girls. Sexual comments."

Whitney threw her hands up. "That's disgusting. It's an innocent video!"

"I agree." Tawny's voice was slow and calm. "But there are plenty of warped people on social media who are looking for pictures and videos of little girls. And you have such a large

following, it's impossible to know where your content is end-
ing up."

Whitney's stomach clenched. She suddenly felt the need
to go back and read every comment that had ever been posted
on her social media accounts.

"Look, I know you're a wonderful mother, but I also know
you're stubborn as all get-out." Tawny raised her eyebrows at
her. "You should take some time and consider Mia's right to
privacy. And the twins' and Mason's too."

Whitney shook her head back and forth, rubbing at the
throbbing in her chest. "I've considered everything."

"Have you?" Tawny asked, her eyes blazing now. "Because
what Mia is asking for seems totally reasonable to me." She
picked up her drink and took a sip. "And if I'm being honest,
I can't believe you were willing to let her move out of the
house."

Whitney pushed her chair back from the table and jumped
to her feet. "But I wasn't willing. The court ordered it."

Tawny placed her drink on the table with a whack. "Listen to yourself, Whitney. How did this get so far? You're her
mother. You need to make this right."

"I don't know how." Whitney practically growled with
frustration. "And I can't believe my best friend in the whole
world doesn't support me."

"I'm sorry. But I can't." Tawny sat back and stared at her, a
closed-off look on her face.

Suddenly lightheaded, Whitney steadied herself on the
table. She'd lost her daughter and now it seemed she had
lost her best friend too. "I guess we're not all perfect mothers
here, huh?" While Tawny's kids had gone through the typi-

cal tantrums and puberty phases, they'd always been good kids. She'd never had to deal with anything like this.

Whitney grabbed her bag. "I should go."

"C'mon, Whit. Don't leave." Tawny's eyes were pleading, and she gestured to the tacos. "You've barely eaten anything."

"It's fine. I have a lot of work to do." She gave her friend a tight-lipped smile. "See you later."

Whitney headed for the door, leaving Tawny at her kitchen table, surrounded by the debris from their taco lunch.

* * *

SHE SPENT THE next few hours mainlining espressos, crafting social media posts, and messaging with Taylor—and she turned off comments on the twins' ice cream video just to spite Tawny. The time went faster than she expected, and before she knew it, it was time to pick up Chloe and Charlotte from school. The bell rang right as she pulled into a parking spot. Whitney headed to the grass area where parents congregated to wait as their kiddos filed out of school.

Noticing a group of stylish moms she recognized off to one side, she raised her arm in the air and called, "Good afternoon!"

But instead of replying, the women turned toward each other, essentially turning their backs on her.

Feeling her cheeks heat, Whitney wrenched her arm back down to her side. She could hear the blood rushing through her ears like a river after a storm. First Tawny accused her of exploiting her children and then these moms were rude to her? She couldn't believe it. Not only had she been a part of this school community for ten years, but those moms were her people. They were exactly the kind of women who would be her followers. Bitches.

A fake smile remained on her face as her brain swirled with embarrassment. The twins ran out the school's double doors, squealing when they saw her. Usually, Rosie picked them up from school. After the encounter with those rude moms, Whitney was going to keep it that way.

"Hi, girls." She bent down to give them hugs. "I missed you." Chloe and Charlotte chattered about their day as she held each by the hand and they headed back to her car. Whitney made sure to keep her eyes down, not making eye contact with any parents.

The girls settled into the back seat, and Whitney wrenched open the driver's door, launching herself into the front seat. Clicking her seat belt into place, she saw her wild and sad eyes in the rearview mirror.

"Mom?" asked Charlotte.

"Yes, sweetie?"

"What's a lawsuit?"

Whitney swallowed, trying to wet her suddenly dry throat. She turned in her seat and looked at the twins. "Why do you ask?"

"Everyone at school is saying Mia is suing you," Chloe said matter-of-factly. "Can kids even sue their parents?"

Whitney's shoulders sagged as she turned and looked out the windshield. How was she supposed to explain this to her ten-year-olds?

"Did you do something bad?" Charlotte asked right as Chloe blurted, "Does Mia not want to be part of our family anymore?"

Whitney's stomach was in knots as she chose her words carefully. "Of course Mia wants to be part of our family. But she is really angry with me and the role she plays in my work. She hired a lawyer to sue me."

"What does that mean?" Chloe asked. "Will her lawyer ask us questions?"

"No, no—I don't think so." Though she didn't know the answer for sure. She needed to ask Barton if he or Mia's lawyer planned to talk to the girls.

"Is someone going to take us away if Mia wins?" Charlotte asked, a hitch in her voice.

Tears welled up at the corners of Whitney's eyes. "Oh gosh, baby—no!" She reached back to put her hand on Charlotte's knee. Forcing a smile, she looked at each girl in turn. "I promise you are safe, and I will try my best to keep you both out of the courtroom. I'm really sorry kids are talking about us at school. This is really none of their business. But if you have questions, you can always come to me, okay?"

"Okay," Chloe and Charlotte replied in unison, their fears calmed for the time being.

Whitney took a deep breath as she started the car.

"I miss Mia and want her to come home," Charlotte said quietly from the back seat.

"Me too," Chloe said.

Whitney looked at her sweet daughters' sad faces in the review mirror. "Me too."

Her limbs and her heart were heavy as she put the car in reverse and slowly backed out of the parking spot.

November 8 – 5:36 p.m.
Ew, Dorothy: Anyone notice that older lady in the
background of some of Whitney's videos? Did she hire a
nanny to raise her kids?

November 8 – 6:12 p.m.
Smug Takes: Could it be someone from CPS, perhaps? You
know the courts have to be looking into Whit's fitness as
a mother.

November 8 – 6:12 p.m.
Retail Therapy & Rainbows: Actually, I think that's
Michael's mother. I remember seeing photos of her at
his funeral. Maybe she's come to talk some sense into
Whitney.

November 8 – 6:15 p.m.
Taylor Thrift: We all know entirely too much about this
woman . . . I mean, stranger.

CHAPTER 20
MIA

Walking down the hallway at her school was suddenly a new experience for Mia. Out of the blue, everyone knew her name and they seemed to want to get to know her.

"Hi, Mia," said the perky blond debate champion from her biology class.

"Hey," Mia replied softly, tucking a lock of hair behind her ear.

"How's it going, Mia?" asked the gorgeous Black artist who was the reigning homecoming queen.

Mia smiled shyly, wondering how in the world Jade Smith knew her name. She was a senior, so they didn't even have a class together.

"Looking good, Mia," chortled the class clown from her English class as his friends chuckled around him. That one made her blush and duck her head.

Even Olivia Banks was being nicer to her. She'd smiled at her the other day and actually complimented her shoes this morning. It was almost too much to take.

Hightailing it to her locker, Mia switched out her morning class books for the afternoon books. She couldn't wait to get to the cafeteria to meet Camila for lunch. It was nacho day, and she was starving.

As she headed toward the cafeteria, her phone vibrated in her pocket. She fished it out and noticed a voicemail from a random number. She clicked the play button and held the phone to her ear while using her finger to block the noise of her fellow classmates in her other ear.

"Hi, Mia, it's Grandma." Mia blinked and stopped walking, nearly getting run over by the football player behind her.

"Sorry," she mumbled, moving out of the line of traffic and leaning against the bank of lockers.

She started the message over, and her breath caught in her throat. Hearing her grandma's voice made her heart swell. "I know this is probably a big surprise, but I'm in town and would love to see you. Let me know when you are free, and I will meet you anywhere. Just name the time. Love you."

She hadn't seen her grandma in years. The last time she'd come to visit, a few months after Mason was born, they'd baked cookies and played games, and her grandma had told her stories about her dad's childhood while combing her hair. Imagining the feel of her grandma's soft hands in her hair made her heart squeeze like a squishy stress ball.

Mia had asked her mom once why they didn't see Grandma anymore. Her mom had said things weren't the same after Dad died, that it was too hard for Grandma to come down and see them without him. But Mia didn't understand that. Didn't losing all of them make her grandma feel even worse?

"Hey."

Shaking her head to clear it, Mia looked up to find Alex

Liang standing in front of her. He looked adorable in a red checked button-down, a black tie, and skinny black jeans, with his black hair spiked so perfectly he could have walked out of the pages of a magazine.

"Oh, hey." Mia still felt dazed as she gazed at him. Going from hearing her grandmother's voice in her ear to seeing a hot guy right in front of her was a weird kind of whiplash.

Alex looked at her expectantly. "Can I help you?"

"What do you mean?" Mia was like a deer in headlights as she looked into his eyes.

Alex gestured behind her. "You're standing in front of my locker."

"Oh!" Mia leaped away from the wall. "Sorry. I got a surprising voicemail, so I was taking a moment to process it. I, uh, didn't know this was your locker."

Alex looked intrigued as he spun his lock to the right, then the left, and back to the right. "Who was the voicemail from?" He snapped his locker door open. "If you don't mind my asking."

"Oh no. It's fine." Mia's palms started to sweat as she held on to her backpack straps for dear life. "It was from my grandma, who I haven't seen in years. She's in town and wants to meet up."

Turning to look at her as he moved books between his locker and bag, Alex raised his eyebrows. "Wow. I bet that was kind of shocking."

"Yeah, it was. But in a good way. I've missed her."

Alex slammed his locker and slung his messenger bag strap over his head. "Then I'm glad she reached out." He jerked his thumb toward the cafeteria. "Heading that way?"

She nodded, falling into step with him, though her appetite had suddenly vanished, replaced by butterflies.

"I heard you're staying with your friend Camila lately."

He's hearing things about me? Mia's cheeks glowed with the thought. "Yeah. It's hard to live at home when you're suing your mom."

Alex chuckled. "I can imagine." As they entered the cafeteria, Mia saw him nod toward a table filled with guys and girls. Several were on their phones, showing their screens to each other, while others turned toward Mia and Alex, gawking at her with curiosity. One girl in particular, dressed in a trendy oversized blazer, looked Mia up and down, no doubt noting her incredibly unstylish outfit.

Mia's eyes flicked to her normal table with Camila, where her best friend sat with a wide smile on her face.

Her cheeks were hot when Alex turned back to her. "I'm gonna go grab lunch, but keep me posted on everything. The trial, your grandma meeting, your mom. You're definitely the most interesting person at this school right now."

Mia couldn't hold back the laugh that echoed out of her. "I doubt that, but will do."

With legs like Jell-O, Mia walked over to where Camila was grinning like a fool.

"What. Was. That?" She was clearly holding in a squeal.

Mia shrugged. "Nothing. I happened to be leaning against his locker, that's all."

Camila choked on the bite of the sandwich she was chewing. "That's all? That's all?" she sputtered. "You were chatting! With a boy. I need details."

Mia sighed. Truthfully, she was tired of all the turmoil in

her life. "Let me get some food, and then I'll tell you about my grandma's call."

"Grandma?"

"Yep. It's been a big ten minutes."

* * *

As soon as the final bell rang for the day, Mia met up with Camila once again and started walking to her house.

"Are you going to call your grandma back now?"

"I don't know. Do you think I should wait a few days?"

"I don't think you need to play hard to get with your grandma."

"True." Mia pulled her cell phone out of her pocket and, taking a deep breath, hit the call-back button on the message her grandma had left.

Ignoring Camila's stare, she gnawed at the cuticle on her thumbnail while listening to the phone ring.

"Hello?"

Closing her eyes, she let the sound of her grandma's smooth voice envelop her.

"Hi, Grandma."

"Mia?" She heard her name catch on her grandma's tongue. "It is so good to hear from you. I've missed you so much."

She couldn't stop the grin that formed. "I've missed you too."

There was an awkward pause as they both tried to figure out what to say next.

"Why are you in town?"

Her grandmother cleared her throat. "I heard about the lawsuit."

Mia's breath caught in her throat. Sometimes she still for-got her issues with her mother were out in the world for all to see. "Oh."

"I thought maybe you and your mother could use my help . . . somehow. I don't know." As she paused, Mia could hear the high-pitched voice of a small child in the back-ground. "I had to see you."

"Where are you?" Though Mia suspected she knew where her grandmother was.

"At your house."

Mia stopped walking. Why did she feel betrayed to know her grandmother was with her mother and siblings? She shouldn't, but she did. "It's not really my house anymore."

"Oh, honey. Yes, it is."

Mia sighed. She had been stupid to assume her grandma was going to come to town without seeing the twins, Mason, and her mom. Her grandmother hadn't seen Mason since he was a few months old. Her heart ached a bit when she real-ized that. Mia would have loved to see that reintroduction. Her little brother was affectionate with everyone, and surely threw his pudgy arms around their grandma in a big hug, even though there was no way he remembered her.

"Can I see you? I'd love to take you out for ice cream, like we used to do."

Grandma was talking about all those times they'd gone to Amy's Ice Creams when she was little. It had been her dad's favorite place, and he'd made sure it was hers too. She couldn't remember the last time she'd had a Mexican vanilla cone with whatever "crush'n" sounded good that day.

Pushing away the feeling that her grandma was staying

in enemy territory, she tried to infuse excitement into her voice. "Sure. Amy's on West Sixth Street after school tomorrow? I can get there around four forty-five."

"Great. I'll be there. Can't wait!" Her grandma really did sound thrilled to see her.

Hanging up her phone, Mia slid it into her pocket.

Camila gave her an encouraging smile. "That sounded like a good call. And getting ice cream will be fun."

"She's staying at my mom's house."

Camila's eyes widened. "Oh. Awk-ward."

"Yep."

Camila looped her arm through Mia's. "Doesn't matter. I'm sure it'll be great."

Mia forced a smile. She wished she could be as positive.

* * *

THE NEXT DAY, after her last class, she hustled out of school, jumping on the crosstown bus that stopped the closest to Amy's. Mia's leg bounced as she watched downtown Austin fly by the window. She hoped she'd recognize her grandmother. Closing her eyes, she could picture her grandma's gray bob and glasses. But more important, would her grandmother recognize her? Hopefully she didn't look the same as when she was twelve. Talk about embarrassing.

After getting off the bus, Mia walked the last few blocks to the ice cream shop, nibbling at her fingernails until she tasted blood.

"Oh, great." She'd ripped the cuticle of her thumbnail off, and now it was bleeding . . . again. Stopping on the sidewalk, she rummaged through her backpack for a tissue.

"Jackpot." She pulled one out of a little travel bag, wrapped it around her finger, and started walking again. Her fingernail biting had gotten out of control lately. Holding her hands out in front of her, she spied nails bitten down to the quick and ragged cuticles, several tinged with dried blood. Thankfully, her Northwestern sweatshirt was a little big. She pulled at the sleeves, hoping they covered up enough of her hands that her grandma wouldn't notice the carnage that was her fingertips.

The bell above the door jingled as she opened it, searching for a woman who looked like her grandma. It didn't take long to spot her: she knew it was her grandma as soon as she saw her striped T-shirt, cropped pants, and white sneakers. Her signature outfit was still exactly the same.

"Mia." Her grandmother held out her arms as she walked toward her, pulling her into a warm hug.

Mia blinked back tears. She'd missed being hugged by a family member more than she realized. "Hi, Grandma." She pulled back and looked at her grandma with an embarrassed smile. She hated crying.

"I can't believe how grown up you are!" Grandma reached up and wiped away a tear that had escaped.

Smiling tightly, Mia took a step back. She suddenly needed some space. "Yeah. A lot happens in three years when you're my age."

Grandma gave a sheepish nod before arranging her face into a careful smile. "You're right. I'm sorry I missed it." Looking around the colorful, crowded ice cream shop, she gestured to the counter. "Should we order?"

Mia nodded, pretending to peruse the menu, even though

she always got Mexican vanilla. She could feel her grand-mother staring at her.

After they got their treats—her grandma picked a mint-chip milkshake—they headed to a table to sit down.

"What?" Mia hated the feeling of being watched.

"Nothing." Her grandma smiled, taking a sip of her milk-shake. "I can't get over how gorgeous you are."

Her cheeks flamed, and Mia knew that her face was the color of a beet. "Thanks, I guess." She looked into her grand-ma's green eyes, which were exactly like her dad's. "I'm pretty nerdy, though."

Throwing her head back, her grandma laughed out loud. The sound was so delightful Mia giggled too, even though she also sneaked a look around to make sure no one had turned to stare at them. Luckily, everyone seemed engrossed in their own ice cream concoctions and conversations.

"Nerds are my favorite," her grandma said, a twinkle in her eye. "You know, your father was a big nerd in high school."

"He was?" She remembered her dad's messy dark hair and big eyes that crinkled when he smiled. She'd never thought of him as a dork, though he did wear tall white socks with sneakers.

"Oh yeah. He had big, thick glasses. And he loved comic books and sci-fi movies . . ." She started giggling. "And he was in the marching band." She paused, dabbing at the edges of her eyes with a napkin. "I loved those years, the ones that straddled him being a kid and a full-fledged adult. We had the best conversations, when he would talk to me, of course. He was so curious and intelligent and saw the world in such an interesting way."

Mia nodded, taking a bite of her ice cream. "I remember. He was my favorite person in the world."

"Me too." Her grandma smiled sadly, leaning back in her chair. "I'm so sorry I disappeared from your life. I simply couldn't handle Michael not being here anymore."

"It's okay," Mia said quickly, even though she didn't mean it. She would have given anything to have had her grandma's support the past three years.

Reaching out, her grandma covered Mia's hand with her own. "No, it's not. There is no excuse for my behavior. I should have been there for you, and I'm so sorry." There were tears in her grandmother's eyes now. "I'd like to be there for you now, if you'd let me. This situation with your mother is not going to be pleasant."

Mia kept her eyes on the graffiti covering the small table where they were sitting. There were so many questions she wanted to ask her grandmother: Why hadn't she wanted to see her grandkids anymore? Had Mia done something to upset her? Grandma had always sent presents and cards, but it wasn't the same.

Before her dad died, there had been nothing she liked more than hanging out with her grandma when she came for a visit. Everyone was so enamored with the twins, but her grandma had always showered her with attention, buying her stacks of books from the discount bookstore and taking her out for ice cream, exactly like this. They'd go on hikes with her dad and swim for hours in the neighborhood pool.

When her grandma quit visiting, it hurt. She'd lost a parent and a grandparent in one fell swoop. Could she open her heart to that kind of pain again?

"I'd like that," she whispered. "But it's really weird that you're staying with her."

Her grandmother sighed. "I know. But your sisters and brother are my grandchildren too." She chuckled. "Mason is really something else."

Mia giggled. "He is, if by 'something else' you mean a mini tornado."

"I do. I'm exhausted after ten minutes with him."

Mia's smile faded and she bit her lip. She'd do anything for a squishy toddler hug right about now.

Slouching in her seat, she looked into her grandma's eyes. "Do you think I'm doing the right thing?"

Her grandmother squirmed in her seat. "Oh, Mia. That's a complicated question."

Mia furrowed her brow. "Is it?"

Sighing, her grandmother looked down at her hands. "I'm not a fan of a lot of the stuff your mother has posted through the years." She paused, seeming to consider her words. "But I also wish you two could have worked this out on your own."

"I tried." Mia dabbed at the corners of her eyes, wishing her grandma would side with her. "She wouldn't listen to me."

Her grandma reached over and patted her hand. "What you are doing is very brave. I wish you didn't have to do it, is all. And even though I'm staying with your mom, I want to see you as much as I can. As much as you'll allow. Okay? We can go to the bookstore and go on hikes." She smiled softly. "Whatever you like."

Mia nodded. "That sounds good." Glancing up at the big clock on the shop's wall, she realized it was already six o'clock. "Oh, wow. It's getting kind of late. I should head home to Camila's house. Dinner is at six thirty."

"Of course." Her grandmother stood up and gave her a hopeful smile. "Can I drive you home? I rented a car so I could have some independence. I'm not a fan of this city's traffic, though."

"Yeah, it's pretty bad. And sure, I'd like that."

As they left the ice cream store, Mia was hopeful they were on the way to rebuilding their relationship, together.

CHAPTER 21

WHITNEY

Whitney and Ace were dressed to the nines and heading out on the town. They'd barely seen each other recently, though they'd had a long conversation about the lawsuit. Ace agreed with her that Mia had gone too far. Between the lawsuit, work, and Judith, things had been too unstable, so she'd tried to keep him distanced from the mess that was her life. But tonight they got to celebrate Whitney being named the City's Best Influencer by *Austin A-List* magazine. (Before the lawsuit, obviously.)

Even though she had no idea what was in store—Would people be nice to her? What would they say?—her spirits lifted as they headed down MoPac. She'd had her doubts about attending tonight's event for the city's society magazine when she was persona non grata, but now that she was dressed and her hair and makeup were on point, with Ace beside her, Whitney was happy to be out of the house. Lately, she felt trapped in that place. Especially since she knew Judith had met up with Mia. She was dying to know how Mia was, what she'd said, but she didn't feel comfortable asking her mother-in-law.

Whitney's eyes were wide as they pulled into the driveway

of a house in Austin's ritzy Westlake alcove. The house for tonight's event was simply stunning. Three stories tall with a pristine white exterior that had a mix of rounded and straight edges, the house sat atop a cliff overlooking Lake Austin. And the view was as breathtaking as the house.

Austin's desire to "Keep It Weird" was legendary. And while there were plenty of hippies, musicians, and artists in the city, there was also plenty of money—with more arriving from California, New York, and Dallas every day. Tech money. Oil money. Real estate money. Influencer money.

Whitney knew her hard-won assets were nothing compared to those of some of the city's socialites and CEOs, but it was far more than she'd ever thought she would be worth.

A valet in a black vest strolled up to the driver's side door to take Ace's keys, while another opened Whitney's door, reaching for her hand to help her out. She gave the tall, lanky twenty-something with floppy hair a smile, watching as his cheeks instantly went red.

That gave her a confidence boost as she linked her hand into the crook of Ace's arm. She was grateful to have him by her side tonight, as she walked into the unknown that was this party.

"You look great." She gave him a kiss on the cheek. He was doing the monochromatic look right in a steel-gray slim-cut suit with a light gray shirt and silver skinny tie.

"I had to up my game to match yours." She was wearing a little black dress and electric-pink heels. They were a good-looking couple.

He smiled at her as they walked through the house's entryway and into the all-white foyer with bleached oak floors, a white limestone fireplace, and cream-colored marble counters. The only color in the whole house was from the bold modern painting hung on one wall. Whitney had done her research and knew that if she started to snoop, she'd find a five-hundred-bottle wine cellar with custom steel doors, a media room with red theater chairs and an old-fashioned popcorn machine, and a tiny elevator for the owner's dogs. Her parents would have gotten a kick out of that. "An elevator! For dogs!" her dad would have said while slapping his knee. A wave of sadness washed over her. Their relationship hadn't always been steady, but she sure did miss him since he'd passed away two years ago.

Entering the backyard, where oak trees outlined a sprawling, lush green lawn, they found the party in full swing. At least two hundred people dressed in cocktail outfits and holding drinks gathered in groups, chatting about their holiday plans as waiters handed out hors d'oeuvres. Around the outside of the backyard, bars served drinks and interactive vendor booths displayed beauty products and gave away gift certificates. This wasn't simply a party; it was an experience.

"Whitney!" she heard a voice call out behind them.

They turned to find a short brunette woman in sky-high metallic heels and a bright orange one-shoulder bodycon dress coming their way.

"Ellie! So good to see you!" Whitney bent down to give the magazine's diminutive PR manager an air-kiss on each cheek.

"You too! Thank you so much for coming." Ellie talked in a way that could have easily made her the sixth Kardashian sister. "I know that you have"—she lowered her voice and leaned in—"a *lot* going on right now."

Whitney's face froze, but she tried to hide it. "We're happy to be here," she said with a tight smile. "Thank you for featuring me in the magazine."

"Oh, for sure. Our readers love you." The woman flipped her hair. "Grab a drink and something to eat. We'll announce the awards in about thirty minutes. And don't forget to grab a gift bag when you leave. Enjoy!" Ellie turned on her heel and headed back to the magazine's table, likely to gossip with her cohorts.

Ace squeezed her arm. "C'mon. Let's get a drink." He maneuvered them through the crowd toward the bar closest to them, passing a pyramid of champagne glasses waiting for someone to pour bubbly down from the top.

As they beelined for the bar, Whitney swore she heard her name whispered in multiple snippets of conversation.

"That's Whitney Golden . . ."

"The one getting sued . . ."

"Her daughter Mia . . ."

When Ace placed their order, the conversations around them stopped entirely as people turned to stare at her. Whitney's face and neck were hot as she looked around, hoping to see a friendly face. While she knew of many of the people at the party, she didn't actually *know* them. But the way they were staring at her confirmed that she was the talk of the town—and not in a good way.

They got their drinks and headed back out into the crowd, where there was more whispering.

"I hate influencers . . ."

"I knew a kid would sue eventually . . ."

Holding tight to Ace's hand, Whitney kept her head down and positioned her body behind her boyfriend, trying to hide. Ridiculous, she knew, but suddenly the spotlight was too hot.

They set their drinks down on a cocktail table. That's when she saw a group of women staring at her from a few lengths away. A tall woman with long black hair, clad in a skintight turquoise dress and strappy silver heels that highlighted her toned physique, held court. It was her least favorite local blogger, Jessica Morris.

Also an influencer, Jessica stayed within the health-and-fitness space and had about five hundred thousand followers. When she'd first started out, Jessica had asked Whitney to meet for coffee. They'd had a nice chat and had even discussed meeting up again. While that had never happened, they'd seen each other at events and been cordial. But then one day, Whitney had been shopping in a local clothing store, and the owner had made a comment that Jessica was bad-mouthing her, saying Whitney had stolen one of her content ideas and that most of her followers were bots. Livid, Whitney had avoided Jessica ever since.

When she caught Whitney's eye, Jessica headed their way.

"Whitney!" She held out a hand to her. "So nice to see you."

Whitney stiffened but she accepted Jessica's outstretched hand. "Hi, Jessica. This is Ace." Whitney widened her eyes at her affable boyfriend. She hoped he knew what that meant. "Jessica is a health-and-fitness influencer in town."

"Nice to meet you, Ace." Jessica was all smiles. "I'm so

sorry about the *lawsuit*." She leaned in and whispered the last word like it was a bad one. "Congrats on the award tonight. I'm sure that feels good, when there is *clearly* so much turmoil at home."

Whitney's eyes narrowed. She hoped Jessica felt the daggers she was shooting at her.

"Are you receiving an award tonight too?" Ace asked with feigned innocence.

Jessica bristled as she took a sip of her bloodred wine. "No. Just here to enjoy the party with my friends, who I should get back to. Congrats again, Whitney." She sauntered over to her groupies, who'd been watching their exchange with interest and were now gossiping, eyes sparkling.

"What a bitch," Ace muttered, still smiling.

"Right?" Whitney raised her eyebrows.

Ace winked at her as he took a sip of his drink.

The music lowered and Robert Forbes, the editor of *Austin A-List*, appeared on a makeshift stage set up in the middle of the lawn. After talking a bit about the Best of the City awards and how the winners were chosen, he started to announce them. Each winner—from Best Chef to Best Salon to Best TV Personality—went up on the stage to accept their award and say a few words of thanks.

When the award for Best Influencer was announced, Whitney smiled at Ace and squeezed his hand before strolling to the stage, where Rob held out the glass plaque to her.

Right as she took the trophy, a voice called out, "Does her daughter get one too?"

The crowd laughed.

Whitney stopped, her stomach dropping to the ground.

But before she could react, another voice called out, "Is there an award for best exploiter of their children?"

That made Whitney whirl around. "Are you kidding me?" She directed her question toward where the voice had come from. "Like all of you don't do it too."

She pointed at Jessica, who was giggling with her group. "I know that your kid ate sushi for dinner tonight, because you bragged about it on Instagram an hour ago." Jessica glared at her in response.

"Your eight-year-old is scared of water." She gestured to a popular real estate agent to her left. "How do I know that? Because you posted a huge novel on Facebook about how we all need to face our fears. It was masked as you being a good dad, but in reality you were hoping it went viral so more people would call you about selling their house." The Realtor stared down at his toes, looking ashamed.

"And you . . ." She pointed to a short blonde in a canary-yellow minidress with sparkles at the bodice. "Your daughter shills acne cream for you on TikTok. How much money did she bring in for your brand this month?"

The woman's cheeks turned crimson, and she took a step behind the person next to her.

Whitney laughed bitterly. "Do you all not realize that anything that happens in my case will apply to you too? If I lose, no more sharing about your kids, no advertising campaigns with your children. No more being 'authentic'"—she used air quotes, thinking of Mia—"for your audience.

"You're all just as guilty as I am."

She turned back to Rob Forbes and handed him the plaque. "Here. You can have this. I don't want it anymore."

With her head held high, Whitney walked off the stage and through the crowd, grabbing Ace by the hand as she headed out into the sparkling Austin night to retrieve his car and leave.

* * *

WHITNEY WAS SICK to her stomach by the time Ace pulled up in front of her house. Neither one of them had said a word since they left the party.

He turned off the car, and they sat in silence.

She took a deep breath. "I'm so sorry you had to see that. I didn't mean to pull you into all this."

"Yeah." Ace raked his hand through his hair. "That was a lot."

Whitney turned to stare at her boyfriend, mouth agape. She'd expected him to tell her he was proud of her for defending herself. Or at the very least reassure her the scene at the party wasn't that big of a deal.

"Look, Whitney." Ace stared down at his hands. "You're great, and I have so much fun with you. But this lawsuit thing is . . . too much. I'm swamped at work, and I just don't know if I can support you properly through all this."

Whitney stared at his profile in the dark, her heart in her throat. "Right. It is a lot. I get it." But she didn't get it. Michael would have known exactly how to support her. He would have told everyone else to go to hell.

Ace finally turned to look at her. "How about we take a break? Once things settle down, let's see how we feel."

A break. Because everyone knows how well those work.

Whitney's vision blurred as she gazed out the windshield.

Her heart felt like it had been stomped on. She really cared for Ace and had envisioned a future with him. But she needed a strong man who could support her emotionally, and clearly he couldn't. Or wouldn't.

She turned to look at him. She would not make another scene tonight. Maintaining her dignity right now was more important.

"You know what? Let's just call it now. You need someone with less baggage, and I need someone who can hold mine." She opened the car door and hopped out. "Goodbye, Ace."

At least he had the decency to look sad. "Goodbye, Whitney. And good luck."

She walked inside her house, stepped out of her shoes, and sank onto the couch. Whitney was completely numb. She was alone again, but now she didn't have Mia or Tawny either. Her chest was tight as she lay down and pulled a blanket over her body. She curled into a ball but couldn't even cry. This time, she'd brought the loneliness on herself.

November 16 – 9:03 p.m.
ATX Fashionista: Did you see Jessica Morris's Stories?
She gleefully reported that people were rude to Whitney
about Mia's lawsuit at some magazine party. Apparently,
Whitney lashed out.

November 16 – 9:15 p.m.
Yes Way, Rosé: Not gonna lie. I would have paid big bucks
to see that whole thing go down.

November 16 – 9:17 p.m.
Smug Takes: I mean, we all know Whitney had it coming,
right?

November 16 – 9:23 p.m.
Vegan Vampire: I don't know. It doesn't seem very kind to
kick someone when they're down.

November 16 – 9:25 p.m.
Smug Takes: Oh, please! We feel sorry for Whitney now?
The woman who makes millions off her children and
dead husband? Give me a break.

CHAPTER 22
MIA

Mia and Camila were walking home from school after the first day back from Thanksgiving break when Mia's phone buzzed in her pocket.

> How's the most interesting student at Austin High doing?

Mia stopped in her tracks. "Oh my god, he texted me." She held her phone out for her friend to see.

"Who?" Camila barely looked up from her own phone.

Mia swatted her on the shoulder. "Who do you think? Alex Liang!"

"First of all, ow." Camila rubbed at her shoulder. "Second: amazing! How did he get your number?"

"I have no idea. What do I reply?"

"Something funny. And flirty."

Mia gave her a look. "I'm not good at being either of those things."

Camila furrowed her brow. "You're funny. And I can help you be flirty."

After much debate, Mia finally replied.

> Still not that interesting. But interested in how you got my number.

She held her breath until he sent a laughing emoji back.

> I have my sources.

They were still deciding how to reply to that when Alex texted again.

> I'm actually the one with interesting news today. I just got my acceptance letter to Northwestern.

Mia let out a whoop and jumped into the air right there on the sidewalk. "He got into Northwestern!"

"Nice," Camila said.

Mia didn't need Camila's help with this reply.

> CONGRATULATIONS! I AM SO HAPPY FOR YOU!!!!!

He texted back instantly.

> Thank you. I knew you would be. That's why you were the first person I told after my parents.

"Wow." A warm, fuzzy feeling swept through her body.

"What?" Camila was trying to read over her shoulder.

Mia covered her phone with her hand. She wanted to keep this to herself for a second. "I'll tell you later."

She tapped out a reply to Alex.

Seriously? I'm honored.

"Is this how my whole life is going to be now?" Camila moaned as they started walking again. "You texting Alex and ignoring me?"

Mia grinned and rolled her eyes. "Doubt it."

You should be. How was your break?

Mia didn't know what to say to that. She'd had a nice time spending a week at home with Camila, Eva, and Omar, but there had been some weird and lonely moments. The worst was when Camila had told her they needed to talk, and then asked her to move into the guest room.

Mia was shocked. "I thought you liked having me stay in your room?"

"I do," Camila said, fiddling with a loose thread on her comforter. "But I'm an only child. I'm used to having my own space."

"I used to sleep over all the time."

"This is different. You're going to be here for a while." Camila looked up at her with concern. "Is that okay? I'm not trying to be mean."

Mia forced a smile onto her lips to keep her chin from trembling. "Of course. I'll get all my stuff."

The whole family had helped Mia move her clothes and books into the guest room, and Eva had added a bouquet of fresh flowers to the nightstand. But Mia's stomach hurt the whole time. She understood that her best friend needed space—but it felt like an exile all the same.

Since then Mia had been tiptoeing around Camila, going into her room only when invited. It made her miss her family even more.

Things had gotten better on Thanksgiving, when Eva had given the whole family, and Mia, matching green-and-red-striped pj's. Mia and Camila had spent the day watching movies, helping Eva with dinner, and dozing on the couch. It had been a different Thanksgiving than Mia was used to—quieter, no kids moaning they were bored while their mom made them watch the Macy's Thanksgiving Day Parade or fighting over which board game to play. It had been nice.

How did she explain that all over text to a guy she was trying to impress?

As they turned the corner to Camila's house, they saw both her parents' cars in the driveway.

"Sweet, Dad's home," Camila said, walking faster. "Maybe he can convince Mom to let us order in. I'm craving sushi."

"I'm sure Eva has something delicious cooking already. She always does." Mia would rather eat Eva's food than take-out any day.

They were giggling about Alex's texts as they walked up the driveway, but they went silent when Omar opened the front door. The pained look on his face was enough to stop anybody in their tracks.

"What? What's wrong?" Camila asked, rushing into the house. "You look like you've seen a ghost."

Omar's characteristic grin had been replaced with a frown and his dark brown eyes were heavy with sadness. He pushed his thick black hair off his face as he ushered them inside. "You guys may want to sit down."

A shot of ice surged down Mia's spine. *Oh god, this is about me.* "Is this about me?" she whispered.

"Oh no, Mia." Omar patted her back. He waved at the seat on the couch next to Camila. "This isn't about you." He sat across from them in one of the fluffy blue armchairs.

"Where's Mom?" Camila asked, looking around. Eva was always home by now. "Did something happen at work?"

"No. No." Omar looked uncomfortable. "But that's what I want to talk to you about."

Camila covered her mouth with both hands. "Are you getting divorced?"

Mia's stomach had a brick in it. She could see tears pooling in her friend's eyes. *This is all my fault.*

"No. Of course not. Jesus, Camila, let me talk." Omar rubbed at his forehead.

"Sorry." Camila slumped back into the couch cushions, looking relieved.

"It's okay." Omar heaved a deep breath, as if arming himself for battle. "We're not getting divorced. And this isn't about you, Mia." He locked eyes with Camila. "Mom has cancer."

Camila shot forward in her seat. "What? How? Where is she?"

Mia could barely breathe as she watched the panic bloom on her best friend's face. She was instantly brought back to the day she was told about her father's death. The feeling of hopelessness that had consumed her. Like you were drowning and didn't have the strength to swim to the light. Mia would have done anything in her power to protect Camila from those feelings.

Omar put his arm out, like when parents hit the brakes in the car, trying to keep their children from ramming into the dashboard. "Wait, Cam. She's resting right now, but we will answer all your questions. I promise."

Camila scampered around the coffee table and into her father's lap, burying her face into his chest. Mia's heart clenched; she was missing her own dad so much it took her breath away.

Omar started to speak quietly, rocking his teen daughter as if she were still a toddler. "You know how Mom has been really tired lately?"

Camila nodded. "And losing weight."

"Right." He cleared his throat. "She had some, uh, bathroom issues, so she got a colonoscopy last week. They found a tumor in her colon."

Sorrow coursed through Mia. Peeking at Camila's crumpled, gray face, she knew exactly what her best friend was feeling. Disbelief. Denial. Like her heart was being ripped out.

Hugging her arms around her chest, Mia shrank into herself as Omar started talking again, working hard to sound upbeat.

"The good news is it has only spread a little bit, to lymph nodes nearby, so they think with chemo and surgery, she'll be fine." Omar rubbed his daughter's back and looked at Mia. "Okay? She's going to be fine."

He sighed. "But the court case does complicate things."

Camila leaned back and looked up at her father. "Why?"

Mia's stomach heaved.

"It's stressful, for one. But also, Caleb asked Mom to be a witness for Mia's case. We don't know how she will be feeling when the trial finally rolls around, and she doesn't want the world knowing about her health problems. Your mother is a very private person."

Mia shuddered. She couldn't imagine having to discuss her colon with doctors, let alone the judge or the media.

"Plus, we don't know if this will affect our guardianship of Mia." He looked at Mia again. "We need to talk to Caleb about that, okay?"

Nodding, Mia looked down at her shoes. If she couldn't stay with the Garcias, where would she stay? Darkness closed in on her as she watched Omar stroke his daughter's hair. She ached for her own father.

The room's uncomfortable silence was broken by the soft sound of a door opening.

"Mom!" Camila jumped up and ran behind the couch, where Eva had appeared, wrapped in a blanket and looking frail.

"Hi, mija." Eva smiled and held out a thin arm to her daughter.

Mia saw Camila pause, not knowing how to hug her mother. She looked like she could break any second.

Finally, Camila gently took hold of Eva's arm and steered her to the couch.

Sitting down next to her, Eva patted Mia's leg. "Hi, Pepita."

Mia placed her hand on top of Eva's. "I'm so sorry," she said softly.

"Me too." Eva smiled sadly. "But it's going to be okay." She grabbed Camila's hand with her other one. "I'm going to be okay."

Squeezing both girls' hands, she started to tell them about her treatment. "I'm going to have chemo for two days every two weeks. Once it's done, and hopefully the tumor has shrunk, I'll have surgery to remove it and be good as new."

"How long do you have to do chemo?" Camila asked, her voice cracking on the last word.

"Six months."

Both girls flinched. Six months was forever. What about spring break? What about Camila's quinceañera? Eva wouldn't be finished with her treatment until June, at least.

"I know, it's a long time. But the good news is that the kind of chemo they use for colon cancer doesn't cause you to lose your hair." She gave her dark locks an exaggerated flick off her shoulder. "I'd hate to lose my best feature."

Omar winked at her. "You'd be beautiful with a bald head and no eyebrows."

Mia swore she saw Eva's cheeks pinken. It made her feel a tad less afraid that they were being so optimistic.

Camila sat up straighter, a tear slipping down her cheek. "Why didn't you tell us you were having issues? Why didn't you tell *me*?"

Eva reached out and cupped her daughter's chin, wiping away the tear. "Don't cry. I didn't say anything for several reasons. I was embarrassed, for one. I'm not super comfortable talking about my, well, behind. And I didn't want to upset you. You have enough going on in your life right now, and this is a lot to handle." She turned to Mia with a sheepish smile. "I value my privacy and hold things close to my chest. Mia and I are alike in that way. This is deeply personal, and I would like to keep it as private as possible."

Mia nodded that she understood.

Touching her knee, Eva asked, "Do you have any questions, Mia?"

"Will you get the chemo in the hospital or at home?" Mia asked.

"The first few treatments will be at the hospital. But if I do well, they may let me do most of them at home."

"Speaking of home, things are going to be a bit different around here," Omar said. "I'm going to work less and cook more."

Camila groaned, making everyone laugh.

"And we'll probably order in more takeout too." He raised his eyebrows at his daughter. "Can I count on you to help out with the dishes and other cleaning?"

Camila gave her dad the patented teenage look that said, *Obviously*. "Besides, I'm a better cook than you."

"I want to help out too." Mia cleared her throat. "I'm not much of a cook, as we all know, but I can grocery shop and vacuum."

Omar's eyes were kind as he gave her a gentle smile. "Thank you, Mia." He already looked exhausted, and they hadn't even started the journey yet.

Eva pulled them in close. "My girls. I love you both so much."

Mia plastered a smile on her face, but when she locked eyes with Camila, she saw the terror she was feeling inside reflected back at her.

After their talk, Eva went back to her room to rest, while Omar and Camila ran to the store for a few groceries. Mia had lied and said she had a paper to write, because she could tell Camila needed some alone time with her dad.

Upstairs in the guest room, Mia didn't know what to do. She couldn't concentrate on her homework, and she didn't have anyone to talk to. She'd lost her father and sued her mother. Now her second mother was sick? It was all too much.

Picking up her cell phone, she called the one person she could share this information with: her grandma. She felt like a gossip, but she had no one else to talk to. How much could one kid take?

Her grandma picked up on the first ring. "Mia. So good to hear from you, darling."

"Hi, Grandma." Mia could hear the tension in her own voice.

"Everything all right?"

"I have something I need to tell you, but you can't tell my mom. Promise?"

Her grandmother sighed. "I can't promise that without more information. What is this about? Did something happen? Are you safe?"

"I'm totally fine. Something happened with the Garcias." Mia stood up and started pacing her room. "Eva, Camila's mom, has cancer."

Mia heard her grandmother suck in her breath. "Oh no. That's terrible."

"The doctors said she'll be fine after chemo and surgery, but it's still scary."

"That's good." Mia could hear relief in her grandmother's voice. "But it's going to be tough on her. On all of you."

"Yeah. I can't help but think I need to leave. This is a private family matter."

"Oh, honey." She paused. "Maybe I could rent an apartment or a little house for the two of us. Would that help?"

"No." Mia sighed. She'd heard how crazy-high rents were in Austin these days, and she couldn't bear her retired grandmother spending that kind of money on her. And they couldn't ask her mother for the money either. "I'm going to be as helpful for Omar and Eva as I can."

"You're such a sweet girl. I know they love you. I'm sure it will give them comfort having you there."

"Yeah." Mia was suddenly very tired.

"You call me if there is any way I can help or if you need anything, okay?"

"Okay. And you won't tell my mom, right?"

"I promise."

"Thanks, Grandma. I'll talk to you soon."

After hanging up the phone, she sat down on the bed. Sorrow settled into her bones. Mia had never felt more alone than right that second.

She looked at her phone and realized she'd never replied to Alex's last message.

My Thanksgiving was OK. How about you?

Three dots immediately started dancing in the text box, and Mia's stomach fluttered along with them.

> She's alive! I was worried.

Mia laughed. The loneliness she had been feeling a second ago was replaced with the intense desire to make Alex laugh too. She stretched out on the bed and got to work formulating just the right response.

CHAPTER 23

WHITNEY

The only reason Whitney got out of bed these days was because of her mother-in-law. All she wanted to do was wallow in the fact that she was the city's biggest pariah—and she'd been dumped. She would have gotten the kids off to school each morning and then headed back to bed to sleep away her nausea and neck and shoulder pain. But since Judith was watching, Whitney put on a show every day.

Showering, getting dressed, and doing her makeup almost made her feel human again, though the headache and pain remained. Whitney popped four Advil in her mouth and washed them down with a gulp of water before shuffling into her office to sit down at her computer. Two hundred and forty-seven emails awaited her. Her biggest sponsors had dropped her—though most had privately said they'd be back after the trial—and some random woman was waging a vendetta against her, messaging sponsors Whitney had worked with in the past to ask if they were still partnered with her. This lady Instagrammed about it under the handle @HoldWhitneyGoldenAccountable but had blocked Whitney, of course.

Shockingly, her follower number had actually increased

to 1.2 million. She knew that a substantial amount of those were likely hate follows or people who simply enjoyed watching the drama unfold. But followers didn't translate into money.

They were barely scraping by. She'd had to let Gabby go because she couldn't pay her anymore. Whitney had recommended her for a social media job at a local lifestyle website and was crossing her fingers Gabby got it. At least that would alleviate some of her guilt.

At the moment, Whitney was holding on financially through her affiliate-link earnings. Thankfully, many of her followers still bought the clothing, beauty products, and accessories she posted about. But it wasn't enough to pay all the bills. And that was crushing her—and her meager savings.

She'd made a good dent in the emails when her inbox dinged, signaling a new arrival. It was from her lawyer, and "Mia Living Situation Update" was the subject line.

What? That had all been figured out weeks ago. She clicked on the message.

> Howdy, Whitney. I wanted to alert you that Caleb
> Bradford let me know this morning that Eva Garcia has
> cancer.

At first she couldn't make sense of the words. After a moment, they unscrambled. *Cancer. Poor Eva!* Closing her eyes, Whitney flashed back to the emergency room and losing Michael. *Poor all of them.* She didn't wish health issues on anyone or any family.

Mr. Bradford gave me few details, but he did say Eva is starting chemo treatments soon. Eva and her husband said they are fine continuing on as Mia's guardians, but this is a good opening to try to get her back under your roof. Let me know if you want me to file a petition for termination of guardianship.

—Barton Briggs

The hair at the back of her neck stood up. Whitney couldn't believe what she'd read. She had so many questions—What kind of cancer? What stage? How long had they known?—but her primary feeling was one of deep empathy. Juggling work, family, and life was hard enough. Add cancer and the court case into the mix, and you had a recipe for a breakdown.

And it couldn't be healthy for Mia to see yet another of her favorite adults going through chemo after all the trauma she'd already endured in her short life.

"Good morning."

Whitney jumped in her seat. She turned to see Judith hovering outside her office door. "Oh! You scared me. Good morning."

"Everything okay?" Judith asked, frowning.

Whitney gestured to her computer. "My lawyer emailed to let me know that Eva has cancer, which is devastating. But that means Mia may come home." *Assuming she'll want to,* though she didn't say that part out loud.

"I see. That is very sad." Judith turned to head to the kitchen.

Whitney's muscles tensed. That was an odd reaction. She followed Judith into the kitchen and leaned against the island. "Do you think Mia will want to come home?" Her mother-in-law would know best, as she'd been meeting Mia for weekly coffee or ice cream dates.

Judith's cheeks pinkened as she picked up a sponge and started scrubbing at a spot on the counter. "Is that even allowed?"

"I don't know." Whitney swallowed the last of her coffee before setting her mug down. "But I really don't want my daughter exposed to more trauma. Do you?"

Judith stopped cleaning to look Whitney in the eye. "Of course not." She washed and dried her hands before putting a piece of bread in the toaster. "But I know how much Mia loves Camila and her family. I wouldn't be surprised if she wanted to stay and help them."

Whitney could tell by her answer that this was not the first Judith was hearing of Eva's cancer. She narrowed her eyes at her mother-in-law. "You knew, didn't you? Why didn't you tell me?"

Judith sighed, turning to take butter and half-and-half out of the refrigerator. "Mia only told me yesterday. It wasn't my secret to tell."

Whitney slammed her hands down on the countertop. "She can't live like that, among sickness and sadness. We need to get her home."

"You can try." Judith was completely calm in the face of Whitney's anger. "But she told me she wants to stay and support them."

"The hell with that. She's my daughter, and I don't want

her to have to live through yet another traumatizing event."
She took a deep breath, counting to ten as she slowly blew it
out. She was so irritated that Judith had kept a secret from
her, even for only a day. Whitney wanted her daughter home
and under her roof.

She pushed off the kitchen island and headed to her office.
Sitting down at her computer, Whitney typed one line back
to her lawyer: Yes, please file the petition immediately.

* * *

WHITNEY BARELY MADE it to the courthouse by nine the next
morning. Mason had knocked over his bowl of cereal, dows-
ing the TV remote in milk. Judith had decided there was no
better time to put together a grocery list, asking her twenty
questions as she tried to get ready. And she'd misplaced her
phone. After a half hour of searching, she'd finally run out
the door without it. If someone told her she had lipstick on
her teeth and a milk stain on her wrap dress, she would not
be surprised.

Rushing through the double doors, she found Barton waiting for her in the lobby.

"Howdy, pretty lady. Ready to do this?"

Whitney nodded, wishing she had a moment to take a
breath, but Barton grabbed her elbow and ushered her to a
quiet office down the hall from the courtrooms. Her heart
leaped into her throat when she saw Mia, Omar Garcia, and
a handsome man who must have been Mia's lawyer already
waiting.

"Good morning. I'm Caleb Bradford, Mia's lawyer." He
reached out to shake her hand. Omar nodded at her, while

Mia kept her gaze fixed on the carpet. Whitney reached out to hug Mia before stopping herself. Was that against protocol? Were you allowed to hug the teenager who was suing you in the courthouse? There was no manual for this situation.

"Good morning," Barton boomed. Reading the room wasn't one of his strong suits.

"I'm so sorry to hear about your wife," Whitney quietly said to Omar, which got Mia to look up at her. "Please let me know if there is any way I can help."

"Thank you, that's very kind," Omar replied, his eyes tired and filled with sadness.

She gave him a small smile. If Whitney would have run into Omar on the street a few days ago, she wouldn't have been able to stop herself from giving him a piece of her mind. Who helped a teenager file a lawsuit against her loving mother? But today, she left it alone. She knew he was going through hell right now.

The door opened and Judge Sonia Martinez swooped in, saving them from further awkwardness. Instead of a black robe, the judge was wearing a navy sheath dress, black heels, and pearls around her neck. She looked like she'd just left an important meeting.

"Thank you all for coming on such short notice." As they muttered their greetings, Judge Martinez pulled out her desk chair and sat down, pressing her chin against steepled fingers. "I was so sorry to hear about Mrs. Garcia's diagnosis." She looked at Omar. "Especially as I know how hard a cancer diagnosis can be on a family."

Whitney raised her eyebrows at that. If the judge knew

how hard this situation truly was, then she'd have to let Mia come home.

"Mr. Garcia. I know that this is a new development in your family. How are things going?"

Omar let out a deep breath. "We're all sad and scared, obviously, but I have faith that we will get through this. The diagnosis is good—stage two—so the doctors are confident Eva will make it through fine. And she is being a rock star, like always." He smiled.

"Moms always are." Judge Martinez smiled back at him. Clearing her throat, she turned to Barton. "And Mr. Briggs, why did you feel the need to file a termination of guardianship?"

Barton straightened to his full height. "Your Honor, while Mrs. Golden feels for the Garcia family, her daughter has already experienced extensive trauma in her life from her father's death. Mrs. Golden knows that Mrs. Garcia's chemo journey will be challenging, and she believes that Mia should not be subjected to that."

"I see." The judge turned back to Omar. "Mr. Garcia, are you concerned about having Mia under your roof during your wife's chemo treatments?"

Omar chuckled. "Absolutely not. We all love Mia. And to be honest, I could use all the help I can get. Mia is a wonderful girl, and I know she will only help us. That said, we don't want to harm her in any way, so if she is worried about seeing my wife go through chemo, we completely understand."

"All right." The judge shuffled some papers on her desk. "My next question is for you, Mia: Where would you like to live? With the Garcias, at home, or with someone else? Your lawyer alerted me that your grandmother is in town from Chicago. Perhaps you could move into temporary housing with her."

Whitney's stomach flipped. Judith wouldn't dare, would she?

"I would like to stay with the Garcias." Mia's voice was barely above a whisper. "I want to help them while Eva is going through chemo. And I've been happier with them for the past six weeks than I've been in a long time."

Whitney couldn't contain her audible inhale as her lip started to tremble. It was one thing to know your daughter was happier without you; it was entirely another for her to say it out loud in a chamber of law.

The judge made eye contact with her briefly, but Whitney looked down at her feet to keep her tears at bay.

"First off, let me say that I understand your concerns, Mrs. Golden. I know from personal experience that this will be a stressful season for Mrs. Garcia and her family. Cancer is an unpredictable beast, but Mia is a smart, capable young woman. If she is mature enough to bring a case of law against her mother and everything that entails, then I believe that shows she is mature enough to know what she can and cannot handle within her living situation." The judge looked around the room. "She should stay in her current living situation. But Mia: cancer is serious business. If things ever get too overwhelming, I want you to tell your lawyer, so we can figure something else out. That won't make you weak or ungrateful. It will make you human. Do you understand?"

"Yes, Your Honor." Mia shifted from one foot to the other.

Whitney stared at her daughter as darkness closed in around her.

"Good." Judge Martinez nodded. "Due to the circumstances, I've asked the courts to fast-track this case. We will get this taken care of as quickly as possible, and then you can all move on with your lives." She gave them one last nod. "Thank you for coming in today."

Everyone turned and headed to the door, except for Whitney, who stayed rooted to the spot, shaking her head, breathing like she'd run a marathon. Her daughter would rather live with someone in the throes of chemo than her own family. She'd rather deal with the sadness and the vomit and the hospital visits. Her entire body shook as she processed that. Her daughter, who she could still vividly see walking into kindergarten for the first time, didn't want to live with her.

"Mrs. Golden?" Judge Martinez was now standing behind her desk, eyebrows raised in concern. "Are you okay?"

Whitney looked at her, anguish in her eyes. "No. I am not."

Stumbling slightly as she left the office, Whitney blinked rapidly to hold back the tears that threatened to pour down her face. Her lawyer was waiting for her in the busy courthouse corridor.

"I'm sorry that didn't go the way you had hoped," Barton said.

Whitney held up her hand, stopping him. "You need to win this case. You understand me? I want her back."

Barton took a step back, away from the emotional woman. Then he nodded. "Understood."

She marched stiffly out the door and headed home.

The rest of the day unfolded like any other. Whitney ate dinner with her family, bathed the kids, read them stories, and put them to bed. More proof she was a good mother.

Rosie went out for a drink with friends, so Whitney sat down with Judith and told her about the judge's decision. About Mia's decision. Judith had looked as deflated as Whitney felt. She was still stunned hours later, after Judith had gone to bed and she'd made her way through a bottle of wine.

She couldn't stop thinking about the terrible DMs people kept sending her.

You're the world's worst mother.

Mia deserves better. All your kids do.

Kill yourself.

Kill yourself.

Kill yourself.

She squeezed her eyes shut, trying to erase them from her memory. Questions swirled in her head. How did things turn out this way? How did they get so bad so quickly? She'd lost control of her entire life. Whitney poured herself another glass of wine and took a big gulp.

December 1 – 10:47 p.m.
Taylor Thrift: Is it just me or does Little Miss Whit look drunk or hungover ALL the time these days?

December 1 – 10:53 p.m.
Moose Willis: It's not only you.

December 1 – 11:06 p.m.
Olivia Mild: Yep. I would love to know how much she's spending at the liquor store each month. Must be in the thousands.

December 1 – 11:08 p.m.
Vegan Vampire: Also, the hard launch of her new beau we predicted never panned out. He must have dumped her.

December 1 – 11:10 p.m.
Moose Willis: Ouch. Way to kick a woman when she's down.

CHAPTER 24

MIA

After months of Camila dealing with Mia's problems, now it was Mia's turn to take on the role of support system and cheerleader. Usually, Camila never quit moving, but since Eva's cancer diagnosis she'd been either at school or sitting by her mother's bedside. Her energy was low and her smiles were fewer and farther between. She'd lost her glow.

Mia could tell Omar and Eva were worried about Camila too, so she'd asked Omar if he could drop them off on North Loop, home to Austin's best thrift shopping. It took some convincing, but Camila let Mia drag her there after she promised her there would be pizza. Their first stop was Home Slice, where the girls shared a basket of garlic knots and ate giant slices of Margherita pizza. The combination of cheese and carbs seemed to bring Camila back to life. By the time Mia paid the check, Camila was pulling at her arm, excited to check out all the nearby stores.

"I need some new earrings and maybe a cool vintage T-shirt," Camila said as she skipped down the sidewalk. "Ooohh! And I should look at the dresses. Maybe I can find something super unique for my quinceañera."

Mia would have rather been curled up on the couch with

a good book, but she was relieved to see her friend happy again.

They turned into a small vintage shop known for its wide array of cool finds. Despite it being prime Saturday-afternoon shopping time, there were only a handful of customers in the store and one worker behind the counter. Camila glowed as she thumbed through the racks of clothing, separated by era, style, and size. Within minutes, a pink silk bomber jacket with iron-on rainbow patches, a gold sequined top, and an Alanis Morissette *Jagged Little Pill* Tour T-shirt were piled in her arms.

Mia was half-heartedly checking out the accessories, sifting through hats, headbands, sunglasses, and jewelry, when she heard Camila squeal.

"Oh. My. God. Look at this seventies prom dress." Camila held up a lavender floor-length gown with delicate ruffles around the neckline and a thin tie at the waist.

"Wow. That is gorgeous. Are you going to try it on?" Mia asked.

"Obviously." Camila turned on her heel, loot in hand, and headed to the fitting rooms.

Shaking her head with a smile, Mia wandered over to the men's section. Combing through the shirts, she pushed aside a navy-and-orange Western shirt with pearl snaps and couldn't believe her eyes. Hanging on the rack was a black T-shirt screen-printed with the iconic image of Dustin Hoffman and Robert Redford in *All the President's Men*. Her dad had insisted on showing her the movie after they heard a report on the forty-fifth anniversary of Watergate on NPR.

The shirt was exactly something Alex Liang would wear.

Mia's heart fluttered as she examined the shirt. It was thirty dollars. A little pricey for her, but she couldn't deny it was a cool shirt. Would it be weird to buy it for Alex? They'd been texting every day for hours at a time, and she couldn't stop thinking about him. Maybe it would be a nice thank-you for writing that op-ed.

She suddenly felt flushed. While Camila had had a week-long crush on almost every boy in their grade, Mia hadn't really been into a guy in years. Not since Asher Stevens had turned her down at the seventh-grade dance. She'd been so embarrassed, she'd sworn off boys right then and there. But this thing with Alex seemed different. All this texting had to mean something, right?

She'd almost talked herself into buying the shirt when Camila came out of the fitting room wearing the prom dress. "What do you think?" She did a twirl.

Mia shoved the shirt back on the rack and slid another shirt in front of it, her cheeks burning. "You look amazing."

"Yeah, I do." Camila turned back and forth in front of a mirror, checking herself out. "It's beautiful, but I don't think it's right for my quinceañera. I should probably wear a dress from this decade."

Mia laughed. "Probably." She scurried over to a nearby rack of dresses.

"What was that shirt you were holding?" Camila's eyes were questioning.

Mia bit her lip as she looked at her shoes. "Oh. Uh . . . just a vintage T-shirt. I thought it looked cool."

Camila raised her eyebrows. "For who?"

"I don't know, me?"

"A men's shirt?" Camila had a smirk on her face.

Turning her back on her friend, Mia pretended to look at the dresses, quickly flipping through the hangers. Camila already teased her about having a crush on Alex, and she didn't want to give her more ammunition. "Yeah. What's the big deal?"

"Nothing. I've just never seen you shop in the men's department before." Camila did one more turn in the mirror. "I'm going to try on a few more things, and then do you want to grab a coffee?"

There was a cute coffee shop right across the street.

"Sure."

Camila headed back to the dressing room, and Mia walked to the front of the store, where there were picture frames and records displayed near the checkout counter. She smiled at the thirty-something guy behind the counter before bending down to pick up an ornate bronze leaf frame. It immediately reminded her of her mother. A lump formed in her throat. She knew her mom would love it. Mia checked the price tag. She could just swing it, but would she actually ever give it to her mom? Christmas was just around the corner, but what would that look like this year? Only then did she realize this was the first year she wouldn't be spending the holidays with her family. She blinked over and over, willing the tears not to start.

Her legs were wobbly as she stood back up and placed the frame on the counter. "I'm going to get this."

"Cool," said the guy behind the counter. He had a mop of

brown curls and a bit of a paunch. His name tag said Geoff. After scanning the frame, he wrapped it in paper and placed it in a bag. "Is it for someone special?"

"Oh, uh, yeah." Mia handed him a twenty-dollar bill. "For my mom."

"Right on," said Geoff, giving her the change. He snapped his fingers. "Hey. I think I know your mom. Isn't she big on Instagram?"

Mia's stomach plunged to the ground. "Yeah. She's, like, an influencer," she replied, her voice cracking.

"Oh yeah." Geoff handed her the bag. "I'm a foodie and she posted a good recipe, so I started following her."

You follow a momfluencer? That's weird, Mia thought, reaching for the bag. But she wasn't brave enough to say it out loud. "Uh, cool."

"I think I've seen her post your pictures. She's really pretty." Geoff's smile had turned into a leer. "You are too."

It was warm in the store, but a shiver zoomed down her back when he leaned toward her. Her eyes refused to blink as her brain tried to figure out what to say. She had no idea how to respond to the advances of someone more than twice her age. Her feet were welded to the spot.

The tension left her body when she heard the door to the dressing room squeak open. Geoff broke her gaze and they both turned to look at Camila as she threw the pink jacket onto the counter. "I'd never forgive myself if I didn't buy this."

Mia gave a shaky laugh and took the chance to head toward the door. She wanted out of the store and away from this guy.

After Camila paid for her jacket, she skipped toward Mia. "Time for coffee," she sang.

Mia had just opened the door when a meaty hand grabbed her arm.

"Hey. Would you want to get dinner sometime?" Geoff was standing there, a hopeful look in his eyes.

Mia turned to look at Camila, her eyes wide. Her mouth felt like it was full of rocks. *Help me*, she said to her best friend with her eyes.

"Dude." Camila whirled on Geoff, blocking Mia at the same time. "She's fifteen. And you definitely aren't."

Grabbing Mia's arm, Camila pushed her out the door. "Perv!" she yelled as they ran across the street.

It took Mia the rest of the day to calm down. She'd never been hit on other than as a joke by boys at school, so to have an older man ask her out was new territory. And to have it connected to her mother was just disgusting.

The next day, while she was watching a movie with Camila, Mia's phone pinged. It was an Instagram message notification from someone named @VintageGeoff.

"You have *got* to be kidding me," Mia said. She threw her phone down on the couch next to her.

"What?" Camila picked Mia's phone up and looked at the screen. "Whoa. This is officially creepy now."

"*Now*? It was officially creepy yesterday."

"True. Are you going to read his message?"

"I guess." Mia's mouth was bone-dry as she entered her pin into her phone. Clicking on the barely used Instagram app, she opened the message requests.

> Hey, sorry about yesterday. I didn't mean to freak you guys out.
> I thought you were a lot older than 15.

Mia's stomach flipped. "Gross," she whispered.

Camila grabbed her hand, turning the phone to see his message. "Ew. Two words: block him."

Mia hit a button. "Already done."

They continued watching the movie, but Mia couldn't shake the feeling of violation that surged through her body. She felt so exposed, like creepy Geoff was going to knock on the door at any moment.

"Do you think he knows where I live?" Mia asked when the movie's credits rolled.

"How could he?" Camila frowned. "You're here with us."

Mia hugged her knees to her chest. "But what about my family? Can he find where my mom lives?"

"I'm sure your mom has protections in place," Camila said, but there was a hint of doubt in her voice.

Following Camila into the kitchen for a snack, Mia's mind spiraled with ugly possibilities she'd never even considered before. *Did* her mother have protections in place? Their house had an alarm system, but was that enough? There were a lot of creeps on the internet. She hoped her mom had done something to prevent them from finding her—and their family.

* * *

MIA WAS STILL jittery on Monday. But the weekend's incident was forgotten when Mr. Scott placed her biology quiz face up on her desk. "Great job." He gave her a quick smile before moving on to the next desk.

Mia looked down and saw the "99" glowing back at her.

Yes!

She wanted to raise her fist triumphantly in the air, but she controlled herself. All that studying was finally paying off. That's all she ever did anymore, besides helping around the Garcias' house. If she kept her mind busy with school and her body active with laundry, vacuuming, and scrubbing bathrooms, she didn't have to think about the fact that Eva looked more frail every day or that she was about to spend her first Christmas ever without her family. Without her mother.

The last bell of the day rang. Mia automatically checked her phone as she walked out of the school's doors and into the sunshine. There was a voicemail. Weird. No one left her messages besides her mother and her grandma, but this one was from an 847 area code. Clicking the app, she held her ear to the phone, blocking out the noise of the students around her by putting her finger in the other ear.

"Hello, Mia. This is Mavis Fisher. I'm on the admissions team at Northwestern University. We've heard about your case, and I actually was in the same class as your father. We didn't know each other, but I was sorry to hear about his passing. I wanted to call because I'm really impressed with your gumption in filing this privacy case. I think it will be very interesting to see how this pans out. If you're ever in the area, please reach out. I'd love to take you on a tour of the campus."

Mia's insides started to vibrate as her feet quit walking. They were anchored to the grass. Someone from Northwestern knew about her case? And wanted to give her a tour of the school? Throwing her hands into the air, she jumped up and down right there on the lawn, not caring who saw her, for once. But a few seconds later, she realized she had no one to tell the exciting news. It felt weird to tell Camila something good when she was dealing with so much bad. Her mother was out, obviously. And she could tell her grandma, but would it make her sad to hear about Northwestern, since that's where her son went to college? Things were so complicated right now, every decision Mia made felt like it involved breakdancing through a laser grid.

There was one person who would understand her excitement about Northwestern. Alex.

Turning back toward the school doors, Mia went against the tide of kids leaving for the day. Climbing the stairs to the second floor, she felt her heart start to race. Maybe this was a stupid idea. Why would a super-hot senior care about someone from Northwestern calling a silly freshman like her?

The hallways were quiet as she headed to the newspaper office. She found Alex there, along with two other students, a guy and a girl, their heads bent over the same computer.

Mia stood at the door awkwardly, not knowing what to do. For some reason, she had assumed Alex would be alone. He *was* the newspaper to her.

Right before Mia turned to leave, the girl, a serious-looking blonde with chin-length waves, tortoiseshell glasses propped on the top of her head, and an oversized blazer fit for a sixty-year-old professor, looked up. "Can we help you?"

Mia's mouth had cotton in it as Alex glanced up from the pages the trio was reading together. "Oh, hey. How are you, Mia?"

"Uh. Good." She looked down at her feet. *What the heck do I do now?* She probably should have texted him. "How are you?"

"Doing well," Alex said. The pretty girl and the other guy exchanged a glance.

"I got some, um, interesting news. But I can come back, if you're busy."

Alex raised his eyebrows. "Cool. We're on deadline, but I could use some caffeine." He turned to the others. "We're gonna get a Coke. Do you guys need anything from the vending machines?"

The two students shook their heads. It was all very awkward, but Mia was too busy fixating on the fact that Alex had said "we."

He grabbed his phone off the table. "Be back soon."

Mia turned and followed him out of the classroom, trying to mirror his self-assuredness.

"So what's up?" Alex gave her a big smile as they walked.

Mia didn't know what to do with her hands as they headed to the vending machines down the hallway. Finally, she put them in her pockets. "I got the craziest call today."

"Oh yeah? From who?"

"Someone in admissions at Northwestern. She said she's following my case and offered to give me a tour."

Alex stopped walking. "Wow. That's amazing."

Mia's cheeks heated under his gaze. "Not that I have anyone to take me to Chicago." As they stood in front of the machine full of options, she was suddenly parched. "Maybe I could visit my grandma after the case."

"Oh, right." Alex swiped a credit card and hit the button for a Coke. "Does she live there?"

"Yeah."

"What do you want?" He looked at her, his hand still poised over the buttons.

She waved her hand. "Oh. I can get it, it's fine."

"I got it." Alex tilted his head and pointed to the machine, as if waiting for her to decide.

"I'll take a Coke too. Thanks." She smiled as he reached down to grab her soda out of the machine. Their fingers touched as he handed her the drink, making her breath catch in the back of her throat.

Popping open his drink, he leaned back against the machine and took a long swig. As she watched him, Mia couldn't help thinking that it should be illegal for a teenager to be that relaxed and beautiful. Weren't all teens awkward and weird and figuring things out? Or was that only her?

"So are you feeling pretty good about the trial?"

I guess the Northwestern conversation is over. "Oh, uh, yeah. The judge said she's going to make it happen faster because of Eva. My lawyer was happy."

Alex snorted. "Your lawyer. What a weird thing."

"I know, right?"

"Who's Eva?"

Mia turned away from Alex and cringed. *Stupid!* She wasn't supposed to talk about Eva's diagnosis. She turned back to Alex and gave him a tight smile. "Um. Camila's mom is sick. But I'm not supposed to talk about it."

"That sucks."

"Yeah." Mia shifted back and forth on her feet, hoping Alex didn't ask any other questions about Eva.

"Does that make you miss your mom?"

Mia looked up at him with surprise. "Yeah. It does. I love Camila and her family, but I miss seeing my brother and sisters. And my mom." She cleared her throat. "And I worry about overstaying my welcome."

"What do you mean?"

Mia thought about how Camila had asked her to move to the guest room. "You're not really meant to live with your best friend, ya know? I worry about getting in the way or annoying them."

Alex reached out and touched her shoulder. "I seriously doubt you're annoying."

Warmth radiated through Mia as she giggled. Her heart was pounding in her chest; she was sure he could hear it. "You'd be surprised."

Alex threw his head back and laughed, shaking his head as he leaned against the soda machine like she was a comedian. Her eyes widened. *Does he really like me? What is going on?*

She had almost worked up the courage to tell Alex about the Geoff incident when he looked at his watch and pushed himself off the machine. "Chris and Sloane are gonna be pissed. I have to get back to finish the prepress pages. Text later?"

"Okay, yeah." She gave him a shy smile and lifted her hand in a wave. "Thanks for the Coke."

He grinned, making her knees weak. "Anytime."

Mia felt weirdly let down as she walked out of the school

doors. Alex barely cared about the Northwestern representative calling her. Though, realistically, why would he? It wasn't like they were dating or anything. Were they even friends? She had no idea. Maybe he felt like Northwestern was his thing.

Exiting the campus, she turned onto the street to start the walk to Camila's house. Mia looked up as a dirty blue pickup truck sped by. She locked eyes with the driver and froze on the sidewalk. It looked just like Geoff, the creepy guy from the vintage store. And she swore he smirked at her.

Mia's stomach clenched as the truck paused at the stop sign. *If he comes back, run to the school.* But instead of turning around, the driver hit the gas, a cloud of dark smoke swirling out from the truck's exhaust pipe.

Relief flooded her body, followed by doubt. *That couldn't have been him. How would he know where I go to school?* She watched the truck until she couldn't see its red taillights any longer.

The street was quiet now, other than a few birds chirping. Her pounding heartbeat slowly returned to normal. She'd been on edge since she filed the lawsuit, but this was taking things to a whole new level. Mia shook her head. *I'm losing it.*

Ignoring her wobbly legs, she started to walk as quickly as she could. She just needed to get to Camila's house. Then she'd feel safe.

Twenty minutes later, she turned the corner to the Garcias' street. The sight of their bungalow had never made her so happy. As she headed toward the house, she spotted a deer munching grass in a neighbor's lawn. She loved deer. They reminded her of her dad. Baby deer were ubiquitous in their neighborhood each spring, and Mia and her dad always named them. There had been Dot, Unicorn, Vanilla Ice Cream, even Stet—the one her dad had named after some weird editing term.

Mia shook her head, grinning as she thought about her sweet, silly dad. She missed him so much. He was the one she really wanted to tell about the Northwestern call and being freaked out by creepy Geoff. If he'd been alive, he would have protected her, no questions asked. But then again, if he'd been alive, there would have been no court case and no call from Northwestern. She would have been one of thousands of teens trying to get flawless grades in order to score a spot at their dream school. Mia would have preferred that. She knew she should be grateful she had so many wonderful memories of her father. But all she could think about were the memories she'd missed out on since he'd been gone.

The deer startled, noticing her watching it. It took off at a sprint, leaped into a clump of bushes, and disappeared without a trace.

CHAPTER 25
WHITNEY

It was the second week of December, and Whitney was already sick of the holidays. The three trees they'd put up for the October photo shoot still glistened, but she would have ripped them down if not for her children, who loved them. The trees seemed to taunt her, as if they were saying, "Your perfect family act is as fake as we are."

Whitney usually loved the holidays. From the hot chocolate and gingerbread houses to the light shows and holiday events to the presents and elaborate decorations, she did it all big. Even when she and Michael were merely scraping by, she'd scrimped and saved to be able to buy their girls small presents—a book here, a doll there—and to decorate the house and tree. A little went a long way back then. For the past few years, she'd had enough money (and sponsors) to do everything in excess. But this year, she didn't have Mia, and that made everything else pointless.

Every day felt like she was trudging through mud. She wished she could fast-forward through the holidays and get to the trial already. Once that was over, things could get back to normal.

And while she knew her children missed Mia too, they

seemed bound and determined to have the extravagant holiday season they were accustomed to. The twins made sure she bought tickets for the Trail of Lights and the Teddy Bear Tea at the Four Seasons. Even Judith got into the spirit of things, suggesting they go cut down a real Christmas tree to all decorate together. It had been seventy-five degrees and sunny, but they'd made eggnog and pulled out all their family decorations. It had been perfect, other than the part of her heart that was missing. Mia would have loved it, and Whitney hadn't been able to shake that thought the entire day.

While all of this would have been amazing social media content, Whitney posted as little as possible these days. She was paralyzed every time she logged on to Instagram and saw all the other happy families with smiling children. It made her question everything. When she did post, she used photos of only herself or the backs of the kids. Most of the comments she received these days were from her followers saying they missed seeing her children. But Whitney needed to protect them, and herself, right now.

Christmas morning dawned with the kids climbing into Whitney's bed as they yelled, "Santa came! Santa came!" Despite her laughter at their excitement, she had a pit of despair deep in her gut. Mia wasn't there to celebrate with them. Instead, Whitney had dropped presents off for Mia, Camila, Eva, and Omar. She'd left the gifts with Eva during the day while the girls were at school. It was important to her that Mia knew they were thinking about her, but she didn't want to pressure her to see them if she didn't want to.

They joined Judith in the living room to survey the presents under the tree. Rosie helped the kids get down their stuffed stockings, and Whitney hit brew on the coffeepot. Later she would make their traditional Christmas breakfast of cinnamon rolls, bacon, and fruit salad. But now, as she waited for the coffee to brew and her mind to settle, she watched Rosie help Mason open the Play-Doh kit he'd pulled out of his stocking. It amazed her that her baby was already crafting, coloring, and painting and could even spell his name.

She remembered the day he was born. It had been a quick, uncomplicated labor compared to that of the twins, who had arrived through an emergency C-section. But the emotions on that day, without Michael by her side, holding her hand, ready to meet his fourth child—and only baby boy—had been dark. She'd been determined to have a VBAC, focusing on that when Michael's absence overwhelmed her.

Tawny was her birth partner and had taken on the role with aplomb, even when Whitney swore she couldn't push anymore. "You can. You are," Tawny said, her voice as sure as any Olympic coach's.

Once Mason was out and in Whitney's arms, Tawny had called her husband, Jackson, who brought Mia to the hospital to meet the baby while the twins stayed at home with Rosie. Whitney wanted Mia to meet her new brother first. Her sweet eleven-year-old had been standoffish about the baby since Michael died, not wanting to touch Whitney's belly or even acknowledge that their life was about to change again. But in the last few weeks, as Whitney's belly went from big to enormous and the birth got closer, Mia had started snuggling with Whitney while watching movies, placing her ear against her mommy's tummy. She'd whisper to the baby, telling him about their family and the three sisters waiting to play with him.

When Mia walked into the hospital room that day, she'd been hesitant, pausing at the door until Whitney beckoned her over to the bed.

"Hi, sweetheart." She reached out an arm to hug her daughter. Pushing back the blanket that shielded the baby's face, she tilted him toward Mia. "Meet your baby brother, Mason."

Tears glistened on Mia's cheeks as she gently touched his tiny hand, her eyes tracing his face. "He has so much hair," she whispered.

"No wonder I had such horrible heartburn."

Mia's pinkie stroked Mason's nose, running up the bridge and over to his dark eyebrow. "He looks like dad."

Whitney's eyes filled with tears, and her voice caught in her throat. "He sure does."

Whitney swore she watched her daughter fall in love with Mason right before her eyes. And the duo had a special relationship from that day forward. Mia was often the first one to him when he cried, armed with a bottle or a clean diaper. And when Mason threw an epic tantrum, it was usually Mia who got him to calm down.

She should be here now, Whitney thought as she watched her three-year-old play in front of the fireplace. The sadness that strangled her soul was unrelenting.

Rosie came over and put a hand on Whitney's shoulder. "It's not the same without her."

"No, it's not." Whitney smiled sadly. And soon Rosie would be gone too. She was leaving for Australia in just a few days.

Her phone rang, and she went searching for it, hoping it was Mia calling. But it wasn't. It was her mom. It was a holiday surprise—usually she was the one who did the calling.

"Merry Christmas, Mom," Whitney said when she picked up.

"Merry Christmas, Whitney." Her mom's voice sounded small and sad.

Whitney's heart dropped as she walked back toward the kitchen. "Everything okay? You're going over to Stephanie's to celebrate this morning, right?"

"Yes. They should be here soon to pick me up." Her mom paused. "I was feeling a little lonely. I miss Dad."

"Oh, Mom. I'm sorry. I miss him too." Her father had had his faults, like gambling and often lying about it. But he worked hard and always had a joke or a kind word to share. "Did you get the presents I sent?" She'd mailed her mom a package of her favorite treats, including chocolate, new fuzzy socks, and a luxurious lotion, the week before.

"I did, thank you. I'm sorry I haven't sent the kids their gifts yet. Time got away from me."

"It's okay, Mom." Her mother had the same excuse every year. While it bothered her that her children were an afterthought, Whitney knew her kids didn't even notice. They were practically buried in their new toys and the wrapping paper that was strewn all over the living room. "They got more than enough presents."

"Can I talk to them?"

"Of course." She put the phone on speaker. "Kids, Grandma Sandy is on the phone. Can you say Merry Christmas?"

"Merry Christmas, Grandma Sandy!" the kids yelled, barely looking up from their dolls and dinosaurs.

"Anyone want to talk a little bit more?" Silence. Whitney grimaced. "Sorry, Mom. The twins and Mason are distracted by their new toys."

"What about Mia?"

Whitney gritted her teeth. "Oh, ah . . . she just jumped in the shower."

"That's too bad. Tell her Merry Christmas for me."

"I will." Whitney rubbed her forehead. She couldn't believe she had lied to her own mother—and on Christmas.

She handed the phone to Rosie, so she could talk to their mom a bit. After a minute of discussing the weather and her sister trying to tell Sandy about the study abroad program, Rosie handed the phone back with an eye roll.

"I should finish getting ready before Stephanie arrives," her mom said. "Y'all have a nice day. I miss those Christmases when you kids were young. They were . . . magical."

Whitney's heart softened. When she thought back to their Christmases when she was a child, she mostly remembered being worried that there would be nothing under the tree for her brothers and sisters—if there was a tree. But she had to admit, her parents always delivered, even if it was oranges wrapped in festive paper and new toothbrushes. They had always managed to make the day special.

"Merry Christmas, Mom."

After breakfast was eaten and cleaned up, the kids went back to their toys. Whitney, Rosie, and Judith sat bleary-eyed on the couch, discussing what to do for the rest of the morning as they sipped their second cups of coffee. There was a knock on the door.

Whitney looked up at Rosie with surprise. "Who could that be?"

"Maybe it's a package," Charlotte said, not bothering to look up from her new L.O.L. doll.

Rosie, still clad in her robe and slippers, headed to the door.

"Who is it?" Whitney called when she didn't immediately return.

Her sister reappeared in the living room with Mia, who was holding gift bags. Whitney jumped up from the couch, eyes wide, and clapped her hands. Her daughter was here!

"Mimi!" Mason shrieked, running to her for a hug. With a big smile, Mia dropped the bags and bundled him into her arms.

"Me miss you." Mason planted the softest of kisses on his sister's cheek.

"I miss you too." Mia smooched him back. "You're so big! I feel like you've doubled in size since I last saw you." Whitney swore her daughter had tears in her eyes. She knew she did.

"Mia." Whitney's heart swelled as Chloe and Charlotte swarmed their big sister, hugging her around the waist. "Merry Christmas, sweetie."

"Merry Christmas, Mom." With Mason still on her hip, Mia didn't quite look Whitney in the eye but she gave Judith a warm smile. "Thank you for the gifts you sent over. I wanted to bring over a few things for you all. I hope that's okay."

"Of course it's okay." Whitney swallowed around the lump in her throat as she led everyone to the couch.

While Rosie and Judith made small talk to glaze over the awkwardness, the kids mashed themselves against Mia, looking at her like she was a god. Whitney's heart ached to think about how much they missed their big sister.

"Can I get you something to drink, Mia?" Whitney asked. "Orange juice? Sparkling water?"

"I'm fine." Mia gave her a stiff smile before turning to Mason and handing him a gift. "This one has your name on it, buddy."

Mason squealed as he ripped open the wrapping to find the personalized *PAW Patrol* book his sister had made him. "It's me!" he yelled when he saw a cartoon character who looked like him solving cases with the dog superteam. "Thank you, Mimi." He was obsessed with the show, so it was the perfect present.

Mia was known for giving the best gifts, especially to Whitney. When you got boxes of free gifts every week, it was the thoughtful stuff that counted the most. In the past, Mia had made her a framed photo collage that she loved so much she hung it on the living room wall, and she'd gotten her a coffee mug with "HOT STUFF" printed on the side that still made her chuckle every time she used it. After Mason was born, Mia had ordered her a necklace with each of the kids' birthstones in it. Whitney knew Eva or Rosie had probably helped her with that, but she didn't care. It was her most prized possession.

Mia gifted the twins sparkly mermaid-tail blankets and gave Judith a personalized illustration of her four grandkids. "Oh, Mia," Judith breathed. "I love it." And she got Rosie a stylish set of Australian travel guides.

Rosie jumped up to hug her niece and immediately started poring over the books.

"This is for you." Mia shyly handed Whitney a slim box wrapped in festive red paper.

"You didn't have to get me anything." Whitney gave her daughter a sad smile, but what she wanted to say was, *I don't deserve it.*

Everyone stopped and watched as Whitney unwrapped the gift. She peeled back the paper, revealing a photo of her holding Mia when she was only a few months old. Chubby Mia was fresh out of the bathtub in a tiny bathrobe, with tufts of red hair sprouting all over her head and a gigantic gummy smile on her face. Whitney was gazing down at her baby, the immense love on her face evident. Michael sat behind Whitney with his arms around them both, smiling proudly at his girls. Seeing the image took Whitney's breath away. The room shifted as she was transported back to that blissful moment.

"I'd never seen this photo, but Grandma gave it to me." Mia smiled at Judith, sitting across from her on the couch. "I got the frame at that thrift store I love on North Loop."

Whitney dabbed at her eyes, trying to keep her emotions in check. "Thank you. I love it." She ran her finger along the intricate bronze frame. "This is gorgeous. I'll put it in my office."

"You're welcome." Mia had a careful smile on her face, like she was also trying to maintain her composure.

For the next hour, Mia played with Mason, Chloe, and Charlotte, oohing and aahing over their new toys and telling them about the interesting things she'd been learning at school. It made Whitney warm inside to see them all happy like that, together for the first time in a long time.

Finally, Mia said she had to get home for the Garcias' Christmas meal. She hugged the kids, Rosie, and Judith goodbye before Whitney walked her to the front door.

"Thanks for coming over today, Mia," she said, fighting off another wave of tears. "You don't know how much it means to the kids. To all of us, really. We've missed you. *I've* missed you."

"I've missed you all too, Mom." Her daughter's shaky smile betrayed her composure. As she turned to leave, Whitney reached out a hand to stop her.

"Mia . . ." she said. Right then she was ready to agree to all of her daughter's demands. She'd completely quit posting and blogging about Mia and the kids if it meant having them all back together and happy again.

But before she could tell her daughter that, Mia's phone started to ring.

"It's Camila. They're waiting for me." Mia gave her an apologetic smile as she put the phone to her ear.

"I'm on my way," she said, turning back to give Whitney one last wave before she walked out the door.

December 25 – 6:06 p.m.
Olivia Mild: Wow. No mention of Mia on Christmas. Oof. I can't imagine what that family is going through.

December 25 – 7:13 p.m.
Trash Panda: I, for one, feel no sympathy for Whitney. She made her bed, and now she has to sleep in it. Boo-hoo.

December 25 – 7:48 p.m.
Basic Barbie: It's Christmas, so I feel bad for them both. How sad to not spend it together. No mother should be without her children during the holidays.

December 25 – 7:50 p.m.
Smug Takes: Barbie, I think you're in the wrong place. This is a snark site. Take your white-knighting somewhere else. Whitney is destroying her family, all because of social media and the fortune she has made from it. Full stop.

CHAPTER 26

MIA

Mia sighed with relief as she slid into her seat in English class right before the tardy bell rang. It was the first morning back at school after the holiday break. She'd had a nice two weeks with Camila, Eva, and Omar, but Mia was ready to get back to her normal routine—even though that was probably the most un-teenagery thing ever.

During the break, Eva had been recovering from her second round of chemo, so they'd watched dozens of movies. Camila had convinced them to watch the entire J.Lo canon, though they put their foot down at *Gigli*. Their afternoons were quiet, and Mia had had too much time to think. About her family (though her Christmas visit had gone better than expected); about the upcoming trial; about missing her dad; about Eva's cancer. And even though Camila and her parents put on happy faces, it was clear the strain each was feeling.

Between waiting to see if Eva's chemo worked and waiting for word on when the trial would start, Mia felt like her life was in a holding pattern. At least quizzes, tests, and papers gave her some sort of structure and other things to worry about. And worry she did. Her fingernails were bitten so far down to the quick that she'd been having a recurring dream that her fingers got infected and fell off. (Talk about a night-mare. If that really happened, how would she text?)

The dream was especially scary because texting with Alex was currently the only excitement in her life. They bantered back and forth each night before bed. They talked about everything from current events to the trial and their families. Turned out, Alex, the only son of a Chinese dad and a white mom, was under intense pressure to succeed. His parents were worried about paying for Northwestern, and his dad, especially, did not understand why he wanted to be a journalist instead of a doctor. His mom was depressed he was going so far away for college. So, his house was tense too, even though he wasn't dealing with the same things as Mia.

Mia had to admit that her crush on Alex had exploded into a full-blown obsession. She checked her phone constantly, her mood swinging back and forth based on her text notifications. She no longer minded that Camila teased her relentlessly about being infatuated with Alex. Because it was true. Each night, she hoped he would finally ask her out. But she was still waiting.

When her phone vibrated that morning as Ms. Means talked about *The Odyssey*, Mia's heart jumped into her throat. Maybe it was a message from Alex. Stealthily fishing the phone out of her pocket, she clicked it open and glanced down. But the message wasn't from Alex; it was from Caleb.

We have a trial date! March 14. A little over two months away. Time to kick things into high gear.

A shot of ice ran through Mia's body, and her stomach rolled over. It was really happening. What did "kick things into high gear" mean? She'd ask Caleb later. Her hand shook as she slipped her phone back into her pocket.

Part of her was glad to know that all this waiting would be over soon. In two months, she'd find out what her future held: Would she win or would she lose? Would her mom finally quit using her kids as content? Would she move home or stay with the Garcias forever? (Could she stay with the Garcias forever?) But she was also terrified. So many people would be looking at her, judging her and her family. Mia had discussed all these things with Caleb, but now it was really happening. It was real.

Mia nibbled on her thumb, tugging on her cuticle until she tasted blood. Embarrassed, she pressed her sweatshirt on the wound to stop the bleeding. By the time she'd stemmed the blood, the bell rang, and Mia was still lost in thought as she headed out into the sea of students in the hallway. A buzzing sound rang in her head as she walked to her next class.

The rest of the morning felt like she was trudging up a hill in wet clothes. Or maybe that was simply her armpits being damp with anxiety sweat. By the time she met Camila in the cafeteria for lunch, Mia needed a shower and a nap.

"This is good," Camila said when she heard about the trial date. "Not only is that spring break, so everyone will be gone, but you finally get to find out what the judge says and move on." She thoughtfully chewed on her pizza crust. "Besides, you're totally going to win."

After thirty more minutes of Camila's positive talk, hope had broken through for Mia. She *did* have a solid case. Maybe she *would* win. And at least she had an end date to focus on now.

When she didn't see Alex at school that day, Mia texted him about the court date after she'd finished her homework and was lounging in bed.

He immediately responded.

> Nice. Here we go!

We? What kind of a reply was that? As far as Mia could tell, she was the only one braving the stand.

Alex texted again.

> Great that it's on spring break, so we don't have to miss any school.

There was that "we" again.

> Why would you miss school for the trial?

> Because I'm covering it.

> You are?

Mia's stomach churned. She'd assumed Alex would be gone on a senior trip like everyone else.

> This is the biggest case in ages. Of course I'm covering it. I even reached out to the Statesman to see if they want a student perspective.

She hung her head in her hands and moaned. Her crush was going to hear about all of her dirty laundry . . . and her family's too? This was a nightmare.

> Oh.

Mia tried to see the positive side of this new development. Maybe it would be nice to have one more friendly face in the courtroom. Someone else in her corner.

Before she could think of something else to say, Alex texted her again.

> By the way, did you see this?

There was a link.

When she clicked on it, she found a story on a gossip news site called the *Daily Buzz* that said her mother was being investigated by CPS.

Her fingers trembled as she typed.

> That's totally not true. My grandma would have told me.

> Yeah, I figured. That site isn't exactly credible.

Mia didn't know anything about the website, but she did know this conversation was making her uncomfortable.

> I have to go to bed. See you tmrw.

> Night!

As Mia closed her eyes and willed her brain to turn off, she didn't know what made her feel more violated: the story about her mother being investigated by CPS, or the fact that her crush was more interested in the trial than in her.

CHAPTER 27

WHITNEY

Whitney couldn't believe she was standing backstage at the American Heart Month gala, dressed in a fabulous red gown, about to walk the runway in the Wear Red celebrity fashion show. This was the third year in a row she'd had the honor of participating in the February event, yet she was still surprised they hadn't told her not to come after they heard about Mia's lawsuit. Her hands shook as she smoothed the dress along her hips, thinking of the last disaster of a party she went to. If she could make it down the runway and back without having insults hurled at her from the audience, she would consider the night a success.

The announcer called her name. Taking a deep breath, Whitney plastered on a smile and stepped into the spotlight.

"Whitney Golden, who you all know is a great supporter of the American Heart Association, is wearing a strapless Oscar de la Renta gown with a feathered skirt and a beautiful train," the announcer read from his cards. "Let's give her a hand!"

As she walked down the runway, Whitney braced herself for boos, but all she heard from the audience was cheers. Among this crowd, at least, using Michael's tragic story to raise money for heart health and heart disease research appeared to be justified—or at least understood. She paused at the end of the runway, smiling and posing as people in the audience clapped and snapped her picture.

After the fashion show, Whitney headed out into the crowd to have a drink. She wished Rosie were there as her date. She'd missed her sister terribly since she had left for Australia. But she knew from their daily texts and weekly Zooms that Rosie was having the time of her life.

Right as she got to the bar, she heard someone call her name.

"Yes?" She turned to find a petite brunette dressed in a sparkly red cocktail dress who was dragging her embarrassed-looking husband behind her.

"I'm Jane Mumford. I'm the one who told you about my husband you saved. This is him!"

Whitney's eyes widened as she remembered Jane's comment on her Instagram post about Michael nearly four months before. "Oh my goodness!" She pulled Jane into a hug. "I'm so happy to meet you!"

"Me too!" There were tears in Jane's eyes as she introduced her husband. "This is Paul. When I saw you were going to be at this event, we had to drive the three hours from Dallas to be here."

Whitney turned to Paul, a tall, lanky man who looked like he'd rather be wearing Wranglers and cowboy boots than a suit. He reached out a hand to solemnly shake hers. "Nice to meet you, ma'am. My wife tells me I wouldn't be here if she hadn't read about your husband. I'm really sorry you lost him, but I thank you for saving me."

"It was all your wife—she's the hero here. But thank you for coming all this way to meet me. You've made my entire year."

After chatting a bit more, Jane and Paul headed to the dance floor. Whitney was getting her glass of wine from the bartender when there was a tap on her shoulder. She turned to find Tawny standing there with a sheepish smile and her sweet husband, Jackson.

"I hope it's okay that we're here," Tawny said. She looked like a queen in a gown with a sleek black top that flowed into a full skirt adorned with thick rainbow stripes.

"I'm so glad you are." Whitney gave Tawny a big hug. The relief at seeing her best friend was palpable. They hadn't seen or talked to each other since their failed taco lunch months before. "I've missed you so much."

"I'm so sorry about our fight." Tawny's voice was emotional against her ear. "I do see your side. How could I not? Just look at all these people you've helped. And I know everything you do is for your kids."

Whitney pulled back to look at her best friend, tears in both of their eyes. "Thank you, but trust me, I've had my doubts. I'm just glad everything will be over next month."

Tawny took a sip of the cocktail Jackson handed her. "About that: Mia's lawyer subpoenaed me. I have to testify."

Whitney's stomach clenched. "Are you kidding me?" She hadn't even thought about who would be testifying against her.

"Don't worry." Tawny grabbed her hand. "I'll only tell the truth, that you're a wonderful mother who loves her children very much."

Whitney swallowed hard, feeling the room start to close in around her.

Right as she started to spiral, Tawny grabbed her wrist. "There's nothing we can do about the trial now," she said, looking into her eyes. "It's not worth thinking about."

"You're right." She gave her best friend a shaky smile and squeezed her hand. "Can we just drink and dance and have fun?"

"Absolutely." Tawny's eyes were bright as she nodded. "We all need some fun."

For the next hour, the trio danced and drank and laughed. It was exactly what Whitney's soul needed.

In the car service home, Whitney replayed the night. The cheers from the audience. Meeting Jane and Paul. Making up with Tawny. It was the first time in a long time she didn't feel like a horrible person. Whitney shook her head as she looked out at the night sky. She didn't know what to think anymore. Sharing her life online had saved someone else's husband but caused her to lose her daughter.

Hours later, the house was dark and quiet. The kids were tucked safely into their beds. Whitney should have been too, but she couldn't sleep. She'd tossed and turned every night in the weeks since her lawyer had called and told her they had a court date. When she found out that Mia's lawyer got around the parental immunity doctrine by arguing she wasn't simply a mother, she was a brand, she figured they had already lost the case. No judge would side with a brand over a child.

But now, after tonight, when people gushed about the good she'd done with her work, she wondered if there was a chance she *could* win this trial. She'd saved Paul's life, for goodness' sake! The judge had to see that she was more than just an influencer.

It was time for Whitney to prove herself. To show everyone that she was a good mother and a loving wife. She hadn't posted those pictures of Michael to invade his or Mia's privacy—she'd done it because she knew drawing attention to their tragedy could help another family someday.

Although she'd had plenty to drink at the gala, Whitney poured herself a large glass of red wine and took a sip. The alcohol soared down her throat, unraveling her mangled nerves one by one as it headed for her stomach. She let out a soft sigh, calmer already.

Turning on her office light, she took another swig of wine. Her brain was fuzzy around the edges in that glorious way that made you relaxed, without a care in the world.

She sat down at her desk, not knowing what to do with herself. Another sip, more buzzing.

Opening her laptop, she typed "hatefollow.com" into the search bar before she could stop herself. Whitney knew this was a bad idea for her mental health, but tonight she didn't have the willpower to resist. Or maybe she was just itching for a fight.

She braced herself for the hostile words she would likely find. Hell, she wouldn't be surprised if actual sewage poured out of her keyboard.

She'd known about HateFollow for a long time. When her blog had first gotten big, Whitney had spent way too much time perusing the comment boards, reading the mean, dark, and sometimes foul things people—mostly women—said about her. It made her feel awful about herself. But one day, after she'd been up too late reading about how these random people viewed her and then had to deal with her children at six in the morning, she made a vow to never look at those snark forums again. What was the point? Those people only knew the parts of her she was willing to reveal, to sell to them, really. And if they didn't like it, that was fine. Not every book or TV show or movie was everyone's cup of tea. The same could be said for people. She'd decided then and there that she was okay with random strangers on the internet not liking her—and had never gone back on that website again.

But now here she was, tipsy and weak. Clicking on the "Momfluencer" link, she quickly spotted the link to her forum. She was shocked to see that there were 2,400 pages of snark. *Who are these people? Don't they have jobs?*

Clicking back a few pages, she started to read. First they were posting that she was drinking too much. Ouch. Whitney looked at her half-empty glass of wine. Whatever. Every mom drinks sometimes.

Others speculated that Judith was from CPS. Whitney chuckled. Oh, please. If she needed to mention that her mother-in-law was visiting, she would.

Scroll, scroll, scroll. Sipping wine as she read, she found people disparaging her looks, Mia's looks, and her parenting. There was lots of talk about her mystery man—even commenters who correctly guessed that he'd dumped her. And, of course, there was plenty of discussion about the lawsuit. Her skin suddenly felt raw, like she was on fire from the inside out. Gulping the last of the wine, she pushed her glass out of reach.

Even though she wanted a refill, she wouldn't allow herself to have one.

Whitney caught sight of her reflection in the beveled mirror her designer had hung in her office. Her hair was still in the messy updo from earlier in the night, though now it was squashed and lopsided. Mascara ringed her eyes, and her pupils were wide and wild. She looked crazed, but she wasn't crazy. She was angry. How dare these people comment on every inch of her life? They didn't know her.

Putting her hands on the keyboard, she did the one thing she probably shouldn't have: she created a HateFollow account. It took only a second, and within a minute, she'd typed her very first post on the forum.

February 5 - 2:37 a.m.
The Real Whitney: Don't y'all have anything better to do? I'm fine. My kids are fine. And for the record, the older woman in my stories is my mother-in-law.

The replies came fast and furious.

February 5 - 2:38 a.m.
Moose Willis: Is this really Whitney?

February 5 - 2:38 a.m.
The Real Whitney: Yep.

February 5 - 2:39 a.m.
Retail Therapy & Rainbows: Wow. Most influencers don't admit that they snoop on here. Kudos to you.

February 5 – 2:39 a.m.
The Real Whitney: I like to keep it real. Feel free to
speculate about me, but can you please keep my children
out of it?

February 5 – 2:40 a.m.
Smug Takes: You're asking for *privacy*? For your
children? Do you not see the irony here? You're the one
who puts everything out there for public consumption.
Just ask Mia.

Whitney sat back, blinking in shock like she'd been
smacked. It didn't take long for her embarrassment to fade
and anger to take its place.

February 5 – 2:44 a.m.
The Real Whitney: If you actually knew me, the real me,
you would know that everything I do is for my children.

Before she could write another comment—to tell these people how devastated she'd been when Michael died while she
was newly pregnant; to detail how she'd had to handle three
young kids and figure out their finances; to ask these people who
they were to judge her; and to tell them about all the people
who thanked her for raising mountains of money for the American Heart Association tonight—a new post appeared.

February 5 – 2:46 a.m.
Moose Willis: No matter how you spin it, I'm pretty sure
Mia will hate you forever. And your other kids will too,

once they realize their mother was too selfish to get off
the internet when all Mia asked for was privacy.

Whitney stewed inside. How dare they? These people
didn't know the reality of the situation. She started typing,
but the forum quickly became a pile on.

February 5 - 2:47 a.m.
Retail Therapy & Rainbows: Don't worry, though. I'm sure
you can replace your kids with some new ones from
Amazon.

February 5 - 2:48 a.m.
Smug Takes: Here's a suggestion: Get off the internet,
quit drinking, and fix your life.

Whitney shut her computer like it had bit her. If these
people, these strangers, thought she was a terrible mother,
how would a judge ever side with her? She was going to lose
the court case and her career. She was going to lose her family's livelihood.

With the weight of that realization sitting on her shoulders, she picked up her empty wineglass, placed it in the
kitchen sink, and went to bed.

February 5 – 3:05 a.m.
Retail Therapy & Rainbows: Whitney?? Hello?? Where did she go?

February 5 – 3:07 a.m.
Smug Takes: I think we scared her away. Too bad. That was kind of fun.

February 5 – 8:13 a.m.
Trash Panda: Wow. Just read through that exchange. Whitney is unhinged. Somebody really needs to do something to protect those kids.

CHAPTER 28

MIA

Mia was texting with Alex before bed, as had become their routine over the past few months. They told each other about their days, they bantered, and then they wished each other good night.

But this time, just before signing off, he sent a text that made her heart stop.

> What are you doing tomorrow?

Her fingers shook as she typed out a reply.

> Just school. Nothing after that. Why?

She held her breath as dots danced in the text box, waiting for Alex's reply to come through.

> Wanna come over after school? We could watch a movie or something.

Staring at her phone in disbelief, Mia exhaled in a rush and stood up so she could dance like a maniac next to the bed. After a minute, she realized she needed to actually re-ply to Alex. It was best to keep things light and casual, she figured.

> Sure. Want to meet at your locker after seventh period?

His response was swift.

> Cool. See you then.

She'd barely slept, getting out of bed at six so she could shower and do her hair. She even put on lip gloss and a tiny bit of mascara, though she didn't know how successful she'd been. Her best jeans and a fitted T-shirt rounded out her look.

When Mia arrived in the kitchen for breakfast, Camila's eyes lit up. "Who's this supermodel standing before me?"

Eva and Omar watched in amusement as Camila ran over to examine Mia's face. "You're wearing mascara! I knew it. What's the occasion?"

Mia could feel the heat in her cheeks. "Alex invited me over after school."

Camila squealed. "Finally!" She started dancing in the kitchen.

Ducking her head to conceal her smile, Mia slid into a chair. "It's not that big of a deal. No dancing required."

"Oh please." Camila was glowing as she sat back down next to Mia. "You never like anyone, so this is a big deal. I wish I could come record the whole thing."

Mia gave her a horrified look. The last thing she wanted was for someone to document her date with Alex.

"Oh, right. Bad choice of words." Camila speared a bite of the scrambled eggs topped with salsa on her plate. "I'm just excited."

Mia was excited too, but she had to push through and ignore the flutters in her belly all day long.

When the last bell sounded, she couldn't keep cool any longer. She beelined for Alex's locker and was shocked to find him already waiting for her. Guess he was excited too.

"Hey," she said, giving Alex a nervous smile.

"Hey." He smiled back. His intense eyes made her heart do flips. "Ready?"

"Let's go."

She may have been imagining it, but Mia swore people turned and stared as she and Alex walked out to the parking lot. Even though she knew Alex drove a Jeep Wrangler—red, just like his Converse—she made sure to stay a step behind him so he didn't know she knew that.

He opened the passenger door for her, making her swoon, before going around to the driver's side and throwing his bag into the back seat.

When he turned the car on, rap music blasted from the speakers.

"Sorry," he said with a sheepish grin as he turned the music down. "I'm a zombie in the mornings and use music to wake up."

It was thrilling to drive through the streets of Austin with Alex, the wind whipping through her hair, sunshine on her face. If this was what it was like to have a boyfriend, Mia liked it.

When they got to his house, the first thing she noticed was how quiet it was. Alex was an only child like Camila, so there were no siblings to greet him, and she guessed his parents were at work.

"Let's grab something to eat." Alex dropped his bag and removed his shoes in the small foyer, so Mia did too.

She followed him to the kitchen and watched him rummage around in the fridge.

Alex pulled out deli meat, cheese, and mustard and threw it on the counter next to a loaf of bread. "Sandwich?" he asked as he grabbed a plate from a cabinet.

"I'm good, thanks." The knots in her stomach were not conducive to eating anything at the moment.

After assembling his sandwich, Alex grabbed a bag of chips and headed out of the kitchen. "Follow me."

He walked down a hallway and into a den-like room with two couches positioned in an L. Alex threw himself onto the one facing the TV and started scarfing down his sandwich.

"Have a seat," he said between bites.

Mia rushed over to the other couch and sat down, pressing her hands together to hide their shaking. She glanced at Alex, who was way more focused on eating than her. She didn't know what to do or say. What was this? A date? A hang with a friend? Was he interested in her romantically or did he just like texting with her? She was so confused.

Alex finished his sandwich in record time. He jumped up and grabbed a Coke out of the mini-fridge in the corner. "Soda?" he asked.

"Sure." Maybe the bubbles would help her stomach.

Alex brought her a drink and sat back down—this time right next to her. "So, tell me about your court case. Do you know what your lawyer's argument is going to be?"

Just a friendly hang, then, Mia thought as she popped open the can and took a sip. She closed her eyes as the sugar and caffeine flowed through her. "Um, yeah. He's going to talk about how the U.S. has no regulations or laws in place in regards to social media and children, but other countries like France do. Did you know that under French privacy law, anyone convicted of publishing and distributing images of another person without their consent can face up to one year in prison and a fine of forty-five thousand euros?"

"Really, that's incredible," Alex said, watching her intently.

His intense stare made her want to keep going. "And he's going to bring a psychologist and other expert witnesses to the stand to talk about the Coogan Law and stuff like that."

Alex scooted closer to her, reaching up to gently wrap a strand of her hair around his finger. "You have the most amazing hair. It's the color of fire."

Her breath caught in her throat as he played with her hair. "What's the Coogan Law?"

"Oh, uh, it's a law named after this super-famous child actor in the 1920s named Jackie Coogan. When he turned twenty-one, he found out all the money he had earned was gone. So he sued his mom, who happened to also be his manager."

"Sounds familiar." Alex smiled, removing his hand from her hair and running his finger along the top of her hand.

Mia giggled at his touch, which sent lightning bolts

shooting up her arm. "Yeah. The Coogan Law is what still protects young actors in California today."

"Wow. You and Jackie Coogan, saving kids everywhere."

"I guess."

"Seriously, Mia. I'm really proud of you." Alex placed his arm around her shoulders and pulled her close, making her suck in her breath. He stared into her eyes, their mouths inches away from each other. "What you are doing is so brave."

Mia's heart was beating so fast she thought it was going to explode. Alex Liang was about to kiss her.

"Alex, I'm home!" a female voice called out, followed by the slam of a door.

They jumped to their feet right as a woman poked her head in the door. "Oh, hello."

"Hi, Mom," Alex said, running his hand through his hair. "This is Mia."

"Hello, Mia. When I saw a backpack and shoes out front, I assumed it was Sloane."

Sloane? Mia's eyes bulged. The face of the girl from the newspaper room flashed in her mind. *Was Alex dating her?*

Alex's mom swooped into the room, picking up the bag of chips and empty plate Alex had left on the coffee table. "I'm going to start dinner. We're having spaghetti tonight—your favorite." She smiled at her son before turning to Mia. "Nice to meet you."

When they were alone again, all she could think about was Sloane. And that only added to her confusion about this whole situation. Mia stood up. "I should go."

"No, come on. Do you want to stay for dinner?" Alex had a hopeful look in his eyes.

"Uh, thanks. But I should go." She started out of the room.

"Wait." Alex jumped up. "Before you go, I wanted to show you something. Hold on."

He jogged out of the room and was back in thirty seconds with his laptop. Alex sat on the couch and patted the spot next to him. She reluctantly sat back down next to him, watching as he typed something into the search bar: thedailybuzz.com.

"I found some more stories about your case and thought you should see them."

There was a story detailing how much money influencers make and an interview with a psychologist about how putting kids on the internet can mess with their mental health. (*No kidding*, Mia thought.) Along with the made-up story about her mom being investigated by CPS, there was another salacious one: "Whitney Golden on the Verge of Bankruptcy."

"That can't be true," Mia breathed. Though what did she know?

But it was the most recent headline that really upset her: "Whitney Golden Case Shocker: Mia's Guardian Has Cancer."

She sucked in a gasp of air. "What in the F? Why would they care about Eva?"

Alex clicked on the link, and Mia skimmed the story. The unnamed writer found it "shocking" that Mia would choose to live with her friend's sick mother over her own dysfunctional family. Mia was horrified that the exact thing Eva had not wanted to happen had: her privacy had been violated.

The writer knew that Eva had colon cancer and was getting chemo, but he or she didn't seem to know much beyond that. But the thing that took her breath away was the mention of Eva's nickname for her: Pepita. Besides Eva and herself, the only two people who knew about that were Omar and Camila.

Mia stood up again. "I really have to go."

"Are you sure? My mom would love to have you stay for dinner."

"I'm sure—I need to go."

Mia was in a trance as she grabbed her backpack and slipped her feet into her shoes. She got into Alex's car and stared out the window as she tried to piece the puzzle together in her head. It couldn't be Omar who sold the story—why would he reveal his wife's illness against her wishes? So that left Camila. But why would she do such a thing? They couldn't have paid her much for those stories. Would a couple hundred bucks be worth betraying your best friend and your mother? Or maybe Camila was jealous of Mia's relationship with Eva? Maybe she simply wanted to get back at Mia for taking all of her attention away.

When they got to Camila's house, Mia jumped out of the car and ran up the walkway before Alex even said goodbye. "Thanks for the ride," she called.

Once she was inside the Garcias' house, Mia leaned against the wall, completely out of breath.

Camila came around the corner. "What's going on?"

"This." Mia pulled up the story on her phone and showed it to her best friend.

Camila's face fell as she scanned the story. "Mom's going to be devastated."

"You're pretty much the only person who knows all these things about my life," Mia said quietly, still trying to catch her breath. "Including that Eva calls me Pepita."

Her best friend's lip curled as Camila realized what she was saying. "What?"

"Did you sell these stories about us?"

Narrowing her eyes, Camila shoved the phone back at Mia. "Are you kidding me? I can't believe you would even ask me that."

That wasn't a no, Mia thought. "If it wasn't you, who was it? No one knows about Pepita, not even my mom."

Camila laughed in disbelief. "I can't believe you. Of course I didn't do this." She started out of the room before turning back to look at Mia. "Besides, this isn't about you. This is about my mom and her privacy and how upset she's going to be. And if you don't know that I would never do this to her—or to you—then you don't know me at all."

Camila paused, as if biting her tongue. "You know, I think you like all this attention more than you'll ever admit."

With a sinking heart, Mia watched her best friend stomp away. Camila was right. She should have known better than to accuse her loyal best friend of something so stupid. She was just so confused; who else could be selling those stories about her? Heading to her bedroom, Mia wished she could take it all back. But it was too late.

CHAPTER 29
WHITNEY

With three kids and Judith in tow, Whitney pulled open the door of a colorful high-end kids boutique in South Austin. They were shooting an Instagram campaign for the store today. She still couldn't believe they wanted her family to do it—maybe they didn't know about the lawsuit? Or they truly believed any publicity was good publicity? Either way, Whitney wasn't going to question it. She needed the money.

"You're here!" A tall, slender thirty-something woman wearing navy overalls and a red polka-dot T-shirt walked toward them with a grin on her face. "Welcome. I'm the owner, Leslie Cunningham. Huge fan."

Whitney shook hands with her. "Thank you so much. We are happy to be here." She smiled as she looked at her children, who were gazing around the store in awe. The entire back corner contained shelves stuffed with toys. "Your store is adorable."

Leslie nodded. "Isn't it? Thank you for coming in to do the shoot. I know it's a bit unorthodox, but I wanted to get the store in the background." She turned and waved over a hair-and-makeup artist. "Let's get you guys dressed and styled, and then we will get started."

Whitney's heart beat in overtime as she plopped down in the makeup chair. She'd never been asked to do a photo shoot at a store—normally, brands sent packages of clothing for her to try on and post at home—but this had been an offer she couldn't refuse. Now the kids just needed to behave for the next four hours.

When she glanced over to the other side of the makeup area, her spirits lifted to see the twins getting their hair brushed and light makeup applied, while Mason giggled with Judith and Leslie, who had given him a new Hulk action figure. They could do this. It was all going to be okay.

After they slipped on the first outfits of the day—sunny yellow ensembles—Whitney turned and looked at her gorgeous kids. "You guys look fantastic." She pulled the twins and Mason into a hug. She was so proud of them.

They scurried over to the photographer, a tall Black man named James King, a consummate professional in black jeans and a black T-shirt with wire-rim glasses perched on his bald head. "Ready to do this?" he asked with a smile.

James gave each kid a bundle of faux flowers and handed Whitney an empty watering can.

James hit a button on his phone and Kidz Bop started playing. He stepped back behind his camera. "All right, guys. Let's have some fun."

Mason let out a delighted squeal as he hugged the flowers to his chest. Then he started to dance. His moves were so hilarious, everyone started laughing, from the photographer and Leslie to the makeup artist and stylist. Even Judith let out a giggle. Whitney turned to her and smiled as they locked eyes. *Yes, more of this*, she thought.

"That's perfect, Mason!" Click, click, click went James's camera.

Fifteen minutes later, they were done with the first setup. "That went well," Whitney said to Judith as they headed back to the styling area to change their outfits.

"You all looked great," Judith agreed. "Mason was hilarious." She looked at her watch. "It's almost eleven, though. I'll get him a snack before he gets hangry."

"Good idea," Whitney said, taking the white outfit the stylist handed to her.

Leslie swooped in before they could put their plan in action. "Actually, could we do this one setup and then eat? We can't risk staining the clothes."

Whitney exchanged a glance with Judith, and then looked over at Mason. He was happily playing with the Hulk doll and giggling as the stylist threaded his legs into white shorts. Whitney nodded. "He seems okay. Let's do these shots and then eat."

Turned out, it wasn't Mason she should have been worrying about. After they were dressed and James told them where to stand, Whitney realized Chloe had a sour look on her face .

"What's wrong?" she asked.

"I don't want to wear this dress." Chloe stamped her foot. "I want to wear *that* dress." She pointed at her sister's dress, covered entirely in white sequins. Charlotte twirled around in glee, taunting her sister just a little bit. Whitney shot her a look.

"I love your dress." She touched the skirt of Chloe's cream eyelet dress. "It's so pretty."

"I hate it. It's boring." Chloe's eyes filled with tears and her bottom lip quivered. "I want sparkles."

"Okay, okay." Whitney was frozen in place, painfully aware that everyone was watching as she navigated this parenting situation. She glanced up at James, noting his amused expression. It made her die a little bit inside. "You wouldn't happen to have two of the sequined dresses, would you, Leslie?"

The store owner shook her head. "No. I'm so sorry. I only got one of each piece for the shoot. The rest of the spring stock doesn't come in for another month."

Whitney nodded. It was up to her to solve this problem. "Charlotte?" She looked at her daughter hopefully. "Would you switch dresses with your sister? That would be so nice."

"Nope." Charlotte ran her hands down the sequins, making them dance. "I *love* this dress."

She was definitely taunting her sister.

Chloe covered her face with her hands and ran sobbing into the bathroom.

Whitney glanced up at the ceiling and clenched her teeth. *Why must everything be so difficult?* She grabbed Charlotte's hand and pulled her in close. "I'll give you five dollars to switch dresses with your sister," she whispered into her ear.

"Ten," Charlotte replied with a gleam in her eye.

Whitney rubbed her forehead. She knew this was a bad parenting move. But she was desperate. "Deal. But don't tell your sister."

It took twenty more minutes to get Chloe out of the bathroom, switch the girls' dresses, and touch up Chloe's makeup.

Whitney's head was pounding by the time James started shooting again.

"You guys look great," he said, clicking his camera. "Just a few more shots and we can have some lunch."

Mason, who was starting to wilt, widened his eyes at the word "lunch." "But I hungry now."

"I know, buddy." Whitney rubbed his arm. "Just a few more minutes and we will have a yummy lunch."

Mason's face turned purple. "I hungry NOW!"

"Okay, okay." Judith snuck over from the side of the set and held out a string cheese for Mason. "How about this?" Whitney shot her mother-in-law a look filled with gratitude.

"No! Me want cookie!" Mason sobbed, snot pooling under his nose.

Stepping out of the frame, Whitney picked up Mason and placed him on her hip. "It's okay, bub." She rubbed her hand over his tiny, tomato-red face, drying his tears and removing the snot as best she could. "I'm sorry, but I think we need to break for lunch." She looked at Leslie, who clearly wasn't pleased. "James, did you get anything usable?"

"I'm not sure." James walked over to the laptop his camera was connected to and flipped through the photos he'd taken. "I think I can make something work."

"Great." Smoothing Mason's hair as he hiccupped, Whitney turned to the twins. "You girls ready to eat? Then we can finish the shoot and head home for movie night." *Assuming the rest goes perfectly*, she thought, knowing deep in her bones it probably wouldn't.

After a quick lunch, Whitney and her kids put on the last outfits of the day: swimwear. Whitney didn't have time to

worry about how her thighs looked in the tankini they'd selected for her. It was getting close to Mason's naptime, and
she knew they had less than an hour before he had another
meltdown.

James had the girls sit on the floor with sand pails while
Whitney had a beach towel over her shoulder and Mason was
supposed to hold a beach ball.

As James started shooting, Mason threw the ball at Whitney.

She gave him a look but laughed it off as she went to retrieve it. "Don't throw it, Mason. Just hold it."

But she knew the mischievous glint in her son's eyes.
Winding up his arm, he threw the ball at her head as hard
as he could. Whitney dodged to the left, and the ball soared
past her face.

"Mason!" Her cheeks heated as she saw the shocked faces
around her.

Judith stepped out of the shadows. "I got him."

Whitney held her hand up. "No. I have this."

As she walked toward her son, he became his own version
of a toddler Hulk, balling his fists, locking his knees, and
releasing a chilling scream. She grabbed at his arms to pick
him up, but Mason dropped to the ground and rolled onto
his stomach, flailing his arms and kicking his legs.

"I don't want you! I want Mia!"

"Mia isn't here," Whitney said through clenched teeth.

Crouching down, she flipped Mason over and tried to
pull him to his feet. Fighting her with all his might, Mason
pushed off her and then jerked his head forward—smacking
her right in the cheekbone. Hard.

Their audience shuddered.

Whitney grabbed her face, squeezing her eyes shut as she tipped over and hit the ground. Tears flooded her vision as her son continued his tantrum right next to her.

"Oh my goodness, Mason," she blubbered. "That hurt Mama." Her voice was controlled, but she was seconds away from screaming right along with him.

Judith swooped in, picking up Mason and handing Whitney an ice pack.

Once Mason finally stopped shrieking and started sniffling, Whitney pulled him out of Judith's arms and into her own. "Can you apologize for hitting Mama, please?"

Mason raked his arm across his snotty nose. "So-sorry."

"Thank you." She rubbed her tender cheekbone. "That really hurt."

Whitney gave Mason a kiss on the cheek, feeling victorious that she'd gotten through yet another crisis.

That's when she felt something warm and wet.

Pee was running down Mason's leg, soaking his swim trunks and her heels.

Spots dotted Whitney's vision as she wished she could disappear. But she couldn't. She was the only one who could clean up this mess.

An hour later, after they'd changed clothes—she offered to pay for the wet swimsuits but Leslie assured her they could be washed—and the makeup artist covered the round bruise forming on her cheekbone, James finally got the photos he needed.

After saying their goodbyes, Whitney and her family piled into her SUV. The twins zoned out to music, while Mason immediately passed out.

Whitney was beyond exhausted. The kind of exhausted that seeps into your bones and hibernates there until you can escape for two weeks to a spa and they can massage and meditate you back to life. She was also embarrassed. That she couldn't control her children. That everyone watched her get hit by a ball in the face. That her favorite heels were ruined.

"Why do you do this to yourself?" Judith asked quietly from the passenger seat.

Whitney's head thudded. She did not have the strength to dissect the day from hell with her mother-in-law.

"That was so stressful, both for you and the kids," Judith continued. "Most people's careers don't hinge on their children, you know."

Whitney wanted to sob. Instead, she focused on driving.

Judith didn't let Whitney's silence stop her. "Honestly, how long can this last? How long will people want to watch you try on clothes? And what about the kids? Are you going to have another baby after Mason starts refusing to do photo shoots? Because I'm pretty sure that's going to happen any day now." Judith took a deep breath, staring straight ahead. "You're so smart and capable, you could do anything."

Whitney bit the inside of her cheek, wanting to scream. In a perfect world, being smart and capable would be enough. "I don't have a college degree, remember?" *That's part of why you thought I was a gold digger, Judith.*

"Still." Judith dug through her handbag until she found a piece of gum. "There's got to be something better than this."

They were quiet for the rest of the drive. Whitney counted

the minutes until she could climb into bed and sleep for as long as she was allowed.

Once she'd parked and everyone had piled inside the house, there was dinner to figure out. Whitney pulled leftovers out of the fridge and Judith started making a salad. Chloe and Charlotte made friendship bracelets while Mason played with *PAW Patrol* figurines in the living room. He'd woken up from his car nap in a much better mood.

When Whitney's phone rang and she saw Brendan's name on the caller ID, she groaned. The last thing she could handle right now was talking to her brother. She let the call go to voicemail.

Her phone buzzed a moment later. She picked it up and listened to the message.

"Everything okay?" Judith asked, slicing tomatoes.

Whitney put her phone down and sagged against the island. "My mother broke her hip. I have to go home."

February 23 – 7:06 p.m.
Ashley Graham Crackers: Anyone else feel desperation coming off Whitney's shills lately? The woman is clearly hard up for money. Someone's gotta pay those lawyer bills, honey!

February 23 – 7:38 p.m.
Big Hick Energy: At least she's barely posting about the kids now. I don't trust any of these influencers' recommendations. It's all lies.

February 23 – 7:42 p.m.
Smug Takes: Duh, people. These influencers are, for the most part, simply producing ads. Some of them are more creative at how they execute it, but at the end of the day, this is their job. They're here to make money, not be your friend.

CHAPTER 30

MIA

The last place Mia wanted to be right now was at a party. But when your best friend, who supported you through the second worst year of your life (and your first, four years before), turns fifteen and throws a big bash, you have to be there. Especially after you stupidly accused her of selling stories about you to tabloid websites. After Mia had come to her senses, she apologized profusely for her accusations. (And now she was convinced that Olivia Banks was the culprit.)

Mia could tell that Camila still hadn't fully forgiven her, but she knew she would soon. That was the kind of friend she was. And tonight was Camila's night.

Standing off to the side of the banquet hall, Mia wished she had been brave enough to invite Alex as her date. But she hadn't been. Even though they still texted every day, she hadn't had the nerve to ask him about Sloane. But it didn't matter. She was here to celebrate her best friend.

She watched the birthday girl dance with her cousins, who had come in from El Paso, her smile big enough to light up the world. Camila had gotten her wish: She was decked out in a magenta one-shoulder dress with a fitted bodice and a high-low skirt that stopped right above her knees in front and flared out in ruffles all the way down to the floor in the back. A sparkly band at her waist drew the eye to the tiniest part of her, while strappy silver heels made her look three inches taller than normal. The pièce de résistance was a shimmering diamond tiara perched on top of her head, her flowing waves artfully styled below it. She looked like a princess. A badass one.

Even though she wasn't exactly in the party mood, Mia loved seeing Camila, Eva, and Omar in their element, surrounded by friends and family. Eva looked like a queen on her throne as she sat at a table in the front of the room, people lining up to talk to her and see how she was doing. Omar, meanwhile, never left the dance floor. She was pretty sure he was having as much fun partying with his friends as his daughter was with hers. Maybe more.

Omar caught Mia's eye, pointed at her, and shimmied her way.

"Wanna dance?" he yelled over the pounding music.

She laughed as he wiggled his shoulders at her. "No thanks." She shook her head at him. "I'm good here."

"You know where to find me if you change your mind!" Sweat beaded on his forehead, Omar pushed back his hair, grinned at her, and ran back into the crowd.

A hand beckoned to her in her peripheral vision. Turning, she saw Eva waving her over. Walking to Eva's table, Mia sat down next to her.

Eva looked at her warmly. "I realized I never told you how beautiful you look tonight."

Mia ducked her head, her cheeks starting to heat. She'd used some of the allowance her mom sent to buy her first little black dress. Knee-length with a tulle skirt and subtle sparkles at the neckline, it set off her crimson hair, which Camila had helped her style into loose waves. She'd also let Camila do her makeup, including winged eyeliner. Mia actually thought she looked pretty—too bad Alex wasn't here to see her. She felt more like herself tonight than in the photo shoots for her mom, where they put her in brightly colored outfits and caked makeup on her face.

"Thank you. You look beautiful too," Mia said. And Eva did. She was wearing a silver maxi dress and a gorgeous beaded headscarf to cover her thinning hair. She looked positively regal.

"Thanks, Pepita." Eva reached up and patted her headscarf. "I may start wearing this every day."

Hearing her nickname reminded Mia of the one flaw in her Olivia Banks theory—she had no idea how the mean girl would know about Eva's silly pet name for her.

Before they could chat any more, a gentle hand landed on Eva's shoulder. It was a short, stocky woman with thick white hair to her shoulders and deep brown eyes. "How are you doing, mija?" she asked Eva.

"Hanging in there, Tía." After kissing the elderly woman on both cheeks, Eva turned to Mia. "This is my sweet aunt Consuela, who drove all the way from McAllen to see her great-niece celebrate her big day. Tía, this is Mia, Camila's best friend."

After taking Mia's hand and patting it softly, Consuela smoothed her purple dress and matching gauzy jacket and sat down on the other side of Eva. "You look really good for someone on chemo," she said.

Mia sucked in a breath, but Eva threw her head back and laughed.

"Oh, honey. That's not what I meant," said the woman.

Wiping the tears from her eyes, Eva smiled at her aunt, who had a horrified look on her face. "No, no, no. That made me laugh. I hope I look good for someone on chemo. They usually don't look great."

"What I meant is that you look healthy and beautiful."

"Thank you, sweet Tía."

Her aunt lowered her voice. "Is the prognosis good?"

"Yes," Eva replied. Though Mia could tell by the thin smile plastered on her face that the last thing she wanted to be talking about right now was cancer.

Consuela reached over and patted Eva's arm. "Good. We need you around here."

Eva looked out at Omar and Camila dancing and laughing, her eyes shiny. "I'm gonna stick around as long as I can," she said.

The song that was playing, some hip-hop tune that made Mia's ears throb, came to an end, and the DJ lowered the music so he could make an announcement.

"Ladies and gentlemen, it's time for the speech portion of the night. First up: Mr. Omar Garcia!"

The crowd cheered as Omar hurried to the center of the dance floor, and the DJ handed him a microphone.

"First off, thank you all for being here. It means a lot to all of us after a rough few months." Omar made eye contact with Eva and winked. Eva reached over and placed her hand on Mia's. "But I'm pleased to report that Eva and I are happy and healthy and thrilled to be celebrating our awesome fifteen-year-old daughter, Camila!" The crowd whooped as Camila feigned a curtsy.

Mia knew her bestie was having the time of her life. Earlier in the night, as they were getting dressed, Camila had said, "I love this."

"What?" Mia asked from her perch in front of the full-length mirror, where she sat cross-legged, trying to put on mascara without looking like a raccoon.

Camila was standing behind her, expertly applying bronzer. "Parties. Dressing up. Attention."

Shaking her head, Mia marveled at how different they were. But she was glad her friend was happy on her big day.

Omar looked ready to burst with pride for his daughter. "And now the guest of honor would like to say a few words. And then we're all in for a treat—she's going to dance!"

The crowd cheered as Omar gave Camila a kiss on the cheek before handing her the mic. His love for her was written all over his face.

Looking completely in her element, Camila smiled and took in all the cheers and "happy birthday"s being shouted at her. "Echoing my dad, thank you all for being here. I've dreamed of this day for years, and this is so much more fun than I even imagined." She laughed, throwing her head back exactly like Eva had done minutes ago. "I also want to thank my wonderful parents for giving me this party. I know not everyone is so lucky to have amazing parents like you."

Mia's breath caught in her throat. Camila wasn't speaking specifically about her mom—was she? She slouched down in her seat. Everyone knew Mia's family was in turmoil. She looked over at Eva, who had her head bowed. It was true, the Garcias were wonderful. Mia tried to concentrate on that.

Taking a deep breath, she turned her attention back to the dance floor, where Camila had taken her place for her big dance number. The music started and Camila threw her arms into the air. Mia was in awe of her best friend, who looked as comfortable dancing in front of the audience as Jennifer Lopez herself.

Mia turned to Eva to praise her daughter's awesomeness, and that's when she noticed Eva had slumped to the side.

When she placed her hand on Eva's arm, she realized the woman was warm and clammy.

"Eva?" she said, shaking her gently. "Eva?" She stood this time, trying to get Omar's attention.

The movement must have alerted Consuela to a problem, because she turned, saw Eva limp in her chair, and screamed.

The music cut off instantly, and Camila, seeing the commotion, cried out, "Mom!"

Omar ran to their table. He patted his wife's cheek as he cradled her in his arms. "Wake up, my love." Eva's eyes briefly opened before fluttering closed again.

Laying Eva on the floor, Omar turned to look right at Mia. "Call 911."

She nodded, scrambling to pull her cell phone out of the tiny silver clutch Camila had let her borrow.

The ambulance arrived in a matter of minutes, sirens blaring. By the time two EMTs entered the ballroom with a stretcher, Eva was awake and alert, though Omar wouldn't let her sit up. Although she was conscious and no longer woozy, she said she had some pain around her chemo port. Once the

EMTs heard the word "chemo," they insisted on bringing her to the hospital to get checked out.

"You can never be too careful, ma'am," one of them said.

The party was over as the crowd awkwardly watched Eva get wheeled out on the stretcher—something Eva clearly hated. Mia and Camila held on to either side of the stretcher as the EMTs pushed Eva out into the warm, clear night and swiftly loaded her into the ambulance.

Omar planted a kiss on Eva's hand before the EMTs closed the doors. "We'll be right behind you. See you at the hospital."

After making the rounds to say goodbye to their friends and family, Omar and Camila silently and stiffly walked with Mia to the car. The drive to the hospital took less than ten minutes, but it felt like an eternity.

"I'm so sorry your party ended this way," Mia whispered to Camila at a stoplight.

"I don't care about the party," Camila said through sniffles. "I just want my mom to be okay."

"She's going to be fine," Omar said from the driver's seat. But Mia noticed he hit the gas the second the light turned green.

As they entered the ER room where Eva was resting, Mia was struck by how small she looked. The strong, vibrant woman she so admired had shrunken down in size and spirit. Her face was contorted in pain, even as she slept. It was so hard to see Eva like this. She could only imagine how Camila was feeling.

Mia turned to her friend and grabbed her hand. Camila looked at her gratefully. They both stood there, frozen, unsure of what to do in the quiet room, where only beeping machines punctuated the silence.

"Mija, you can sit on her bed and hold her hand," Omar said quietly. "I bet she'd like that."

Camila stared at him for a moment, hesitating, before dropping Mia's hand and walking to her mother's bedside. Instead of sitting next to her mom, she crawled into bed with her, clinging to her arm silently. Camila's sparkling magenta dress was the only color in the stark white hospital room.

"What did the doctors say?" Mia asked Omar quietly.

"She's run-down from the chemo. Probably has a small infection. They are pumping her full of antibiotics and fluids, and then she should be fine to come home."

"Good." She shuffled her feet, looking around the room. Mia didn't know what else to say or do. But she knew she needed to move. "I'm going to get something from the vending machine. Anyone want some M&M's? Pringles? Peanuts?"

Omar smiled, shaking his head. Camila didn't even bother responding.

Mia turned and headed out into the hallway, feeling disoriented by the white walls, random doors, and busy nurses. This was the first time she'd been in the emergency room since the day her father died.

Turning right, she headed toward the pinging sounds of the elevators, and then hooked a left, spotting the waiting room. *The vending machines have to be around here somewhere.* She finally found them, hidden in the corner.

When she opened her clutch, Mia was relieved to see a few singles that she must have slipped in without realizing it. Pulling out a dollar, she inserted it into the machine. *Salty or sweet?* Honestly, she wasn't even hungry. But she had to get out of that room. Finally, she hit A5, watching as a bag of Cheez-Its fell to the bottom of the machine.

Grabbing the little red bag, she fed another dollar into the soda machine next to the vending machine and selected a Coke. *Salty and sweet,* she thought as she heard the satisfying clunk of the can as it rolled down to the opening for her to grab it.

Pleased with her snack, she headed back to the elevator, which whisked her down to the lobby. Pushing through the glass double doors, Mia took a seat on a bench right outside. It was past midnight now, but the February weather was muggy. She chewed on a Cheez-It and washed it down with a sip of Coke, reaching into the bag again and again. Chew, sip, chew, sip. The caffeine, salt, and sugar calmed her. It was a relief to be outside and away from all the emotions and pain in Eva's room.

The sound of sirens wailed in the distance, coming closer each second. Mia's skin turned clammy, but she couldn't make herself move from the bench, even when an ambulance sped around the corner, heading toward the ER bay.

The ambulance squealed to a stop twenty feet from her, and two EMTs jumped out, running around the vehicle to open its back doors. Mia started to shake as they unloaded a stretcher occupied by an elderly man with an oxygen mask obscuring his face.

Watching the EMTs whisk the man through the double doors and into the emergency depot, Mia wanted to jump out of her skin. Had he had a heart attack, like her dad?

Would he survive? Her hands shook as she reached for another Cheez-It before dropping it back into the bag. Her appetite had disappeared.

Silence had replaced the scream of the sirens. Mia stared down at her trembling hands. She'd been saying she wanted to be a doctor for years, but how could she be a cardiologist if the sight of an ambulance made her shaky? Would sparing other families the pain her family had felt after her dad died so suddenly overwhelm her every day? And if she didn't go to med school and become a cardiologist, did that mean she'd failed her father?

Her phone beeped, pulling her from her thoughts. It was Camila.

> Dad says we should call an Uber and
> go home to get some sleep.

> Ok. Be right up.

Her legs were wobbly as she walked back inside the hospital. Bracing herself against the wall of the thankfully empty elevator, Mia took deep breaths. She needed to be strong for Camila right now.

Back in the hospital room, she found her best friend sitting up in Eva's bed, but Eva was still asleep.

Mia's face dropped.

"She's fine, out for the night." Omar gave her a tired smile. "You girls need some rest too."

Camila gave her dad a hug. "We'll see you tomorrow, okay?"

Omar nodded and waved goodbye before sinking down in the armchair next to Eva's bed. Mia guessed that was where he'd be sleeping tonight.

Nurses smiled at their festive dresses as they walked to the elevator in silence.

"I get it now," Camila said as the elevator doors closed and the machine heaved its way down to the lobby.

Mia glanced at her, confusion on her face. "You get what?"

Camila looked down at her hands. "I don't like this kind of attention. All those people staring at us and whispering about something so sad, so private." She looked up at Mia, pain in her eyes. "This kind of attention is bad."

Nodding, Mia put her arm around Camila's shoulders and squeezed. This kind of attention—the attention you never asked for—was bad. It felt good to finally be understood by one of the most important people in her life.

CHAPTER 31
WHITNEY

After driving six hours straight with only one quick stop to get gas and use the restroom, Whitney pulled up to the hotel she'd booked just outside of her hometown. She opened her car door and stretched her legs, relishing the feel of her muscles releasing some of the tension that had been plaguing her for hours.

She climbed out of the car, grabbed her luggage out of the back, shut the trunk—and was smacked in the face with a gust of wind and dust. Shielding her eyes with her arm, she hurried toward the lobby doors as she waited for the gust to dissipate. In the years since she'd been back home, she'd forgotten about the dust. It was so thick in the panhandle that particles creeped under closed windows unless the seams were covered with wet towels.

Once inside, Whitney pulled a tissue out of her handbag and dabbed at her face. The clean white square turned beige with grime wherever she touched. She couldn't show up dirty to visit her own mother in the hospital. She wished she could shower, but there was no time. Brendan was supposed to be here any minute.

After checking in and bringing her bags to her room,

Whitney changed into a nicer outfit and did her best to remove any stray dirt particles from her hair and face.

She'd stepped out of the elevator in the lobby when she
saw Brendan pull up in a tiny sports car that used to be red
but was now mostly rust.

"Sis!" Brendan jumped out of the car when he saw her.
"How are you doing, stranger?" He opened his arms for a hug.

As she sank into his burly chest, Whitney marveled at the
fact that her baby brother had matured into a grown man
in the years since she last saw him in person. Now twenty-
nine, he'd filled out and gotten even more handsome, if that
was possible. She was almost relieved to see his backward
baseball cap, dirty ripped jeans, and Grateful Dead T-shirt.
In her black slacks and ruffled polka-dot blouse, she looked
like she was visiting the queen next to him. Maybe she didn't
need to shower after all.

"It's so good to see you," her brother said as they pulled
apart. "I wish Rosie could have come with you."

"I know. I talked to her last night. She feels terrible she
couldn't come see Mom."

Brendan turned to open the passenger door for her. "Well,
it's a long flight from Australia."

Whitney climbed into the car. "I forgot about the dust,"
she said. "I feel dirty already."

Brendan laughed as he slid into the driver's seat. "Yeah,
the dust sucks, but the sunsets make up for it."

"True." The pastel sunsets out here were worth writing
songs about.

Once they were buckled in, Brendan sped out of the hotel's parking lot and got on the highway, heading to the hospital that currently housed their mother.

Looking over at her baby brother's profile, she couldn't imagine that he cared about influencers. Maybe, by some miraculous chance, he hadn't heard about the lawsuit.

"So. How's Mom doing?" she asked.

"Still a tough old broad." Brendan grinned as he glanced at her out of the corner of his eye.

"Seriously, though."

Brendan focused back on the road. "The surgery went well, and they've gotten her up and walking already. They're gonna move her to the rehab care unit in a few days, and they said she'll be there for about a month."

After Brendan's initial call, Whitney had learned that their mother had fallen in the morning while making a second cup of coffee.

"Any idea how she fell?"

Brendan's face tensed. "I think she'd had too much to drink."

"It was ten in the morning!"

"She was either still drunk or started drinking as soon as she woke up."

"Jesus." When they were kids—and her mother was actually home—Whitney could remember her having a beer every now and then, but drinking so much that she fell? That wasn't the mom she remembered. "Wait. How did she get alcohol?"

Whitney watched as her brother's face turned as guilty as a dog who stole a sandwich off the counter. "Brendan!"

"What?" He shrugged. "I think she's bored. Since Dad died and she moved into that place, she doesn't have anything to do except watch *Judge Judy* and sip gin and tonics."

"They have outings and activities like bingo and painting." Whitney could hear the indignation in her voice. She'd picked the retirement community herself, so she knew all the fun things they offered. The reviews said it was very nice. She hadn't had time to visit before moving her mom there, but she'd done her research. And she didn't see Brendan or her other siblings stepping up to make anything happen.

Brendan gently elbowed her. "It's a nice place, sis. But Mom's used to working all day, every day. I think she's depressed."

"Aren't we all." Whitney looked out the little car's window, watching the scenery go by. If you could call brown, flat dirt as far as the eye could see "scenery." She'd also forgotten how brown this town was. The houses, the buildings, and even the billboards were shades of walnut, tan, and copper.

"So." Brendan slowed down at a red light. They were about five minutes from the hospital now. "What's going on with the lawsuit?"

Whitney sighed. *So much for that miraculous chance.* Fumbling to pull a water bottle out of her bag, she took a swig. "You know about that?"

"Yep. We do have the internet out here, ya know." Brendan gave her a pointed look. "But don't worry. I haven't told anyone else."

"Thanks." Whitney was relieved her mother didn't know her "successful" daughter was a fraud. "The trial is set for next month. And I haven't seen Mia in months. It's awful."

"That sucks. I miss that goober." The last time he'd seen Mia she had been a sweet sixth grader. "How's work?"

Whitney let out a bitter laugh as she flashed back to the disastrous photo shoot at the kids' boutique. "I don't know how to answer that right now. Everyone hates me, yet I'm still making money."

Brendan was quiet as he turned into the hospital parking lot and pulled into the first available spot. Turning the car off, he looked at her. "Thank you again for sending me that cash a few months back. I appreciate it, especially since you've been under so much pressure."

Whitney fought to keep tears from flooding her eyes. "Thanks. It's been rough."

"I can imagine." Brendan chuckled as he got out of the car. "Actually, I can't imagine. Because I have no kids or responsibilities."

Whitney shook her head and smiled as her baby brother put his arm around her shoulders. "You should get some. It's fun."

They were both laughing as they walked through the parking lot, but Whitney's smile faded when they entered the hospital. The nerves built as Brendan checked his phone and they waited in silence for the elevator. She knew her mother would make a comment about how long it had been since Whitney had visited her.

Brendan led her to their mother's room on the fourth floor. A whiff of hospital-grade antiseptic wafted through the air, burning her nose and bringing her right back to the emergency room the day Michael died. Would she ever associate a hospital with anything other than death?

She willed her stomach to quit rolling as Brendan pushed open a door with quiet voices behind it. Inside, they found their mother, along with their sister Stephanie, holding her four-month-old baby, and Stephanie's husband, David.

"So it took breaking my hip for you to actually come home, huh?" her mom said when she saw them.

"Hi, Mom." Whitney strolled up to the bed as Brendan hugged Stephanie. Her mother wasn't a hugger, so Whitney placed her hand on the bed's rail. "How are you feeling?"

A hardworking Texas woman through and through with short gray hair and rough leathery skin, Sandy looked older and more frail than the last time Whitney had seen her. Though she knew it was her fault for not coming to visit more. The years always seemed to speed by.

"Okay," her mom said. "They're taking good care of me here."

Whitney winced. She wondered if her mother expected to move in with one of her children, like her friend Alice had. Not that she'd want to go to Austin. She knew her mother would never forgive her for leaving home, not after how hard her parents worked to support her and her siblings growing up. And she'd never admit she was proud of how hard Whitney worked either, the career she'd built, how now she supported herself and all of them. Her mother was too stubborn for that. But she knew her mother was proud of her, even though she never told her.

"How are my grandbabies?"

Whitney gritted her teeth. What was she supposed to say? Her daughter hated her and her family was falling apart? To avoid answering, she turned to her sister with outstretched arms. "Looks like you've got a grandbaby right here."

"It's so good to see you." Stephanie gave her a hug. "This is Amelia." She tilted the baby so Whitney could see her.

"She's gorgeous," Whitney breathed as the baby looked up at her with big blue eyes. "Can I hold her?"

"Of course." Stephanie beamed with pride as she placed the baby in her sister's arms.

"Hello, little one," Whitney said as she started to sway in that instinctive way that adults do while holding a baby. Her chest was tight as she ran her finger over the baby's tiny hands and smooth, soft skin. Why had she waited so long to come home? She should have been here when Amelia was born. She'd let the guilt of leaving all those years ago prevent her from getting to know her siblings as adults now.

Whitney smiled at Stephanie, her eyes bright. "She's perfect. Being a mother looks good on you." She remembered when her sister refused to eat anything besides mac 'n' cheese, and now she had a baby of her own.

Amelia's eyes fluttered shut as Whitney swayed. "Hey, I've still got it," she whispered.

Holding this baby in her arms made her flash back to when she'd had Mia. She'd been twenty-two years old and so in love with her brand-new baby and her husband. That time in her life had been wonderful. Idyllic even. Before the twins rocked her world. Before Michael died, taking a part of her with him. Before her blog and social media blew up. Before Mason was born. Before the lawsuit. Back when life was simple.

"To answer your question, Mom, your other grandkids aren't babies anymore." She kept her answer vague, even though the guilt was crushing her throat. "But everyone is doing well. Busy, busy."

"Good. Sure would like to see them." Her mother picked at a string on the blanket covering her.

"I know. I'll have to plan a trip this summer." Whitney handed Amelia back to Stephanie. She sat down in the chair next to her mom's bed, smoothed her hair, and put on a false smile. "You look great! Brendan said they are going to move you to rehab soon. Is that the plan?"

With that, Whitney went into first-daughter mode. She sent Brendan, Stephanie, and David down to the cafeteria to grab something to eat. Then she picked up her mother's room, refilled her water cup, and ordered her lunch. When the nurse came in to check on Sandy, Whitney asked her all about the care plan and what her mother would need at rehab.

Once everyone was back from lunch and her mom looked ready for a nap, Whitney had Brendan take her to their mom's place to pack her a suitcase. She'd bring that over tomorrow. Then they stopped by their brother Tom's house to say hi to him and his family. It was a whirlwind.

By the time Brendan brought Whitney to her hotel for the night, she was exhausted. She called Judith once she was settled in her room and had taken that shower.

"How's your mom?" Judith asked.

"She's okay, though she looks frail. They have her up and around, but I can tell it's hard for her to be so dependent on other people." Whitney paused. "How are the kids? Have you heard from Mia at all? It feels weird that I'm out of town and she doesn't even know."

"The kids are fine. And I did hear from Mia. Camila had her quinceañera last night. Eva passed out in the middle of the party, and they had to go to the hospital."

Whitney gulped. "That's terrible." She ached to be home with her daughter at that moment, to shield her from yet another health crisis.

"Eva has an infection but should be fine. Mia said she and Camila were so tired they slept in their party dresses."

"What a nightmare. I hope Eva recovers quickly."

They chatted a bit more before saying their goodbyes. Whitney snuggled into her fluffy hotel bed. This should be a mother's dream—a night of blissful sleep all alone—but she couldn't turn off her brain. All she could think about was Mia and her mother. How had she lost touch with the two most important women in her life?

For the next three hours, Whitney flipped through TV channels, watching a few minutes of one show here and bits and pieces of a movie there. Nothing held her attention very long.

She needed to see her mother. To reconnect. To tell her she missed her and appreciated everything she'd done for her growing up. And possibly get any tips she had for raising teenagers.

Throwing on shoes, Whitney left the hotel in the middle of the night. She didn't know if she could get into the hospital, but she was going to try.

On the short drive to the hospital, all she could think about was Mia. She didn't want her relationship with her daughter to end up like the one she had with her mother. Cold. Distant. They didn't understand each other, so they didn't bother trying. In twenty years, if she was as disconnected to her daughter as she was to her mother, Whitney would not be able to stand it. She had to repair their relationship. As soon as possible.

The hospital lobby was quiet other than a few personnel milling about. Heading straight to the elevator, Whitney did her best to pretend like she was supposed to be there in the middle of the night. When the elevator dinged open on the fourth floor, she dashed down the empty hallway to her mother's room.

Opening the door, she saw the room was dark, other than a soft light coming from a crack in the bathroom door. The quiet was punctuated by her mother's soft snores.

"Mom?" she whispered.

"Whitney?" Her mom sounded confused. "Is everything okay?"

"I couldn't sleep." Shutting the door softly behind her, Whitney made her way to the chair next to the bed.

"Oh." Her mother fumbled to turn on the bedside light. Waking someone who recently broke a hip wasn't Whitney's best idea ever.

"I messed up." She leaned forward, placing her elbows on her mother's bed.

"What do you mean?" Sandy pressed the button to prop her bed up.

"I'm sorry for not staying in better touch. And for keeping the kids away from here for too long." Whitney paused, considering how much she wanted to reveal about the trial. "And I've messed up with Mia. We've been fighting. A lot."

Reaching over to pat her hand, Sandy chuckled. "Mia's a teenager. That's normal."

Whitney stayed quiet. She knew her mom couldn't know how bad things had gotten.

"My only advice is to listen to her. Like I wish I'd listened to you."

Whitney blinked in surprise. "What do you mean?"

"Do you remember that time you waited up for me to get home from work?" Sandy asked. "It was midnight, and you sat me down and told me you didn't want to babysit your brothers and sister anymore. You said it wasn't fair and you didn't have time to study or hang out with your friends."

Whitney had no recollection of that. She must have blocked it out.

"I told you no—that our family didn't work if you didn't help out." Sandy shook her head. "You were so mad at me, as you should have been. You were my kid, not my childcare. But I was too focused on myself and my own problems to figure out a better solution. I've been thinking about that a lot these past few years. I regret telling you no every day."

Whitney sucked in a breath. She'd never expected her mother to say something like that to her. Ever. "Oh, Mom."

Her mother cleared her throat. Whitney handed her the water cup, so she could take a sip.

"I used to think that you helping so much with the kids was normal. That it was your duty as the oldest. But now I realize you shouldered too much. You never got to be a kid. And I'm so sorry for that."

The realization that she was doing the same thing to Mia hit Whitney like a punch in the face. She was making her own daughter work against her will, the exact thing that ripped her own family apart. And even worse, she was showing images and revealing tidbits about her kids' lives to millions of people, without even asking for their consent. She realized now that she'd stripped them of any autonomy, just like her own parents had done to her. How had she been so blind?

Her mother had reflected and seen the need to apologize, something Whitney never thought would happen, especially after all this time. And not from her stubborn mother. But she was exactly the same, wasn't she? She'd never told Mia she was sorry. Not for posting photos she didn't like or invading her privacy. Now she realized she should have done what her daughter had asked without even a second thought. Instead, she'd dug her heels in and built a wall between them that she doubted she'd ever scale. Why would she do that? Why was she so stubborn? Mia meant everything to her, and she'd let their relationship disintegrate.

"Whitney?" Her mother looked at her with worried eyes, bringing her back to their conversation. "Is everything okay?"

She blew out a big breath. "Yeah. I just realized I have some changes I need to make."

Her mother leaned back against her pillows, exhaustion on her face. "It's never too late." Her mother placed her hand on top of Whitney's. "Thanks for coming. I've missed you."

"Me too." Whitney watched her mother fall asleep before leaning forward in her chair, resting her arms on the bed.

They stayed like that all night, with Whitney finally falling asleep sitting next to her mother. When she awoke the next morning, she was determined to change her relationship with her daughter—before it was too late.

February 28 – 7:31 p.m.
Ashley Graham Crackers: Um, where in the world is Whitney?? She hasn't posted in days.

February 28 – 7:38 p.m.
Vegan Vampire: I'm seriously worried about her but didn't want to be the first to say it.

February 28 – 8:06 p.m.
Basic Barbie: Me too! I hope everything is okay.

February 28 – 9:02 p.m.
Olivia Mild: She just posted that she's out of town due to a family emergency.

February 28 – 9:05 p.m.
Smug Takes: Now that we know she's safe, can we please get back to our regularly scheduled snarking? I'm getting cavities from all this sweetness.

CHAPTER 32

Mia raised her face to the sun, relishing the warmth on her skin. She was sitting in the grass out front after school, trying to figure out what to do with her afternoon. Camila had a tutoring session and Eva was still recovering from her infection, so Mia was trying to give her space to rest. Mia had nowhere to go. She was a child without a family; a state without a capital; an island. She knew everyone was excited for spring break, but all Mia could think about was the impending trial.

Usually March was her favorite month because it started the countdown to the kite festival. Before her dad died, March 1 was practically a holiday. They'd work all month creating the biggest, most colorful kite they could. The year before he died, they'd built a showstopping red-and-yellow dragon. And in previous years, they'd made a rainbow-colored parrot, an octopus with eight extra-long legs, and a spaceship with an alien sitting on top.

All that work culminated in Mia and her dad flying their kite together on a breezy, blue-sky Austin day for a festival where it felt like the whole city was out in Zilker Park, celebrating the sunshine. They'd run around under fluffy white

clouds, laughing as the kite swooped and soared and sometimes crashed. Her dad would chase after her, yelling, "You've
got it, Mia-bo-bia!" while her mom and the twins watched,
eating sandwiches and chips on a picnic blanket. The day was
always perfect. Her heart hurt just thinking about it.

And that's when she remembered something that had happened with Alex. When they'd first started texting months
ago, he had told her that his mother had nicknamed him
Walter Cronkite after he dressed up like the famous anchor-
man for Halloween in the seventh grade. He'd slicked back
his hair, drawn on a mustache with her dark eyeliner, and
worn his first skinny tie.

Mia had thought that was the cutest story. And then Alex
had asked her if she had any nicknames. She'd told him her
dad had called her Mia-bo-bia. She'd also told him her little
brother called her Mimi . . . and that Eva called her Pepita.

Her breathing turned shallow as thoughts swirled in her
head. It was him. He'd sold those stories about her and her
family and Eva to the gossip site. But why? Why would he
do that to her? She had thought they were friends, or even
something more.

Looking around, she realized the school grounds had
cleared out. The high school was quiet, but she knew Alex
would still be working away in the newspaper office.

She stood up and headed for the doors before she lost her
nerve. Opening the door and poking her head inside, she
looked to her left and then right, checking for the security
guard or worse—one of the Filters. She had zero desire to see
anyone right now. She was on a mission. Focused. In control.
Only shaking slightly.

Climbing the stairs two at a time, Mia was out of breath when she reached the newspaper offices. Taking a moment to compose herself, she took slow breaths, in and out, willing her heartbeat to return to normal.

When she finally stuck her head in the doorway, she found Alex exactly where she'd assumed he would be: sitting in front of his computer, feet up on the desk, drinking a Coke. While in the past Mia wouldn't have been able to stop herself from swooning over his shiny hair, expressive eyebrows, and red Converse, today she felt nothing other than a storm of fury inside her threatening to thunder open at any moment.

She stepped into the room with a wide stance and her fists balled at her sides, trying to take up every inch of space she could. "It was you, wasn't it?"

"Oh, hey." A smile lit up Alex's face when he saw her. He kicked his feet off the desk, bringing them down to the ground. "What was me?"

Striding toward him, she stopped in front of his desk and pressed her shaking hands onto the wood, trying to steady herself.

"You're the one who's been selling the stories about me to that gossip website." Her voice cracked halfway through the sentence, but she ignored it because the shocked look on Alex's face was all the proof she needed. He clearly never expected to get caught.

Alex's face went blank as he stood up and backed away from her. "What are you talking about?"

Mia straightened and put her hands on her hips. "You know what I'm talking about. The *Daily Buzz* stories with lies about my mom going bankrupt and CPS investigating her. And revealing Eva had cancer for no reason." She paused, staring Alex down. A blush was creeping up his neck, over his cheeks, and to the tips of his ears. "Do you know, I actually thought it was Camila who was doing it. Camila! Because she's one of the only people who knows Eva calls me Pepita. I'm ashamed that I thought my best friend in the whole world would do something like that to me."

Mia edged forward, making Alex shrink back until he was pressed against the blackboard. "But then I remembered that I had told one other person about Eva's nickname for me. You. But then I thought—no, that's crazy. Alex is a real journalist who believes in the truth, accuracy, and fairness. He'd never stoop so low as to sell salacious stories about a classmate—better yet, a friend—to a gossip site. He's going to Northwestern on a journalism scholarship! There's no way he'd do this."

Alex's eyes kept sweeping the room, as if he was trying to figure out the best way to get out of this situation.

"But it was you, wasn't it?"

Alex was silent for a moment. Then he shrugged and crossed his arms over his chest. "Fine. It was me."

Even though she'd known he did it, hearing Alex say it out loud made Mia's jaw drop. "Why?"

Alex rolled his eyes, as if he didn't owe her an explanation. "The website's editor in chief promised he'd get me an interview for the *New York Times* internship program next summer. Do you know how competitive that program is?"

She didn't reply.

"They also paid me three hundred dollars a story, and I

needed the money, okay? Northwestern isn't cheap, even on a partial scholarship."

"Wow." Mia shook her head, her mind buzzing. "So the going rate for buying Alex Liang is nine hundred dollars. Good to know."

A flicker of guilt flashed across Alex's face. "Whatever."

"Why does that site even care about me and my mom and Eva?"

"Clicks, Mia. Those stories got lots of clicks. That's all that matters these days."

A bitter taste filled Mia's mouth. How stupid. "Money and internships aside, why would you do this to me? I thought we were friends. I had a crush on you!"

Alex shrugged. "I know you did, Mia. But to me, you were just a source."

The room tilted. She really had imagined their connection, that he might have a crush on her too. What an idiot she was.

But then she remembered all their conversations, all their texts. Hundreds, maybe even thousands, of texts. "Oh, really? That's why I know you used to stutter when you were little, and it took years of speech therapy to get past it. And that your dad wishes you wanted to be something more practical, like a doctor. I know that your mom calls you Walter Cronkite. And you feel like a failure that you only got a partial ride to Northwestern."

That's all it took for the smug smile to be wiped off Alex's face. "I . . . uh . . . only told you those things . . . uh . . . to butter you up to tell me . . . uh . . . your secrets." He looked down at his feet. "Those things aren't even true."

Mia smirked, knowing she had the upper hand. All those things were true. But she could play his game. "If that's the truth, then I'm sure you violated some journalism oath. Maybe I should call Northwestern's journalism school to ask their opinion."

As she watched all the blood drain from Alex's face, Mia felt a surge of power. She headed for the door.

"Wait. Mia . . . you wouldn't do that to a friend, would you?"

She turned to look back at him. "Good thing we're not friends, isn't it?"

* * *

MIA SPEED STOMPED the mile to the Garcias' house, though she had so much adrenaline running through her, she could probably run a marathon. She pounded up the walkway and pushed open the door. She found Camila and Eva in the living room. Eva was lying on the couch, while Camila sat near her feet, about to take a bite of a granola bar.

"Whoa, what happened?" Camila asked. "You have smoke coming out of your ears. Literally."

"It was Alex." Mia walked past Camila's questioning look and sat down on the chair across from them.

"What was Alex?" Camila asked, her snack forgotten in her hand.

Throwing her head back, Mia let out a big exhale. "He was the one who sold the horrible stories about me. About us."

Camila tilted her head, blinked three times, and looked at her mom. "I did *not* see that coming."

Mia turned to look at them with tears pooling in her eyes.

"I'm so sorry." It would be an understatement to say that she felt like the worst friend ever for thinking that Camila would be disloyal to her.

"Oh, Pepita," Eva said. "It's not your fault. You didn't know he was . . . he was . . ."

"A douchebag?" Camila supplied.

Eva gave her a look. "I was going to say 'jerk,' but yes. That."

Mia dropped her head in her hands. The rush she'd felt after confronting him was starting to wear off. "I thought we were friends. But he assured me today that we are not. He said I was nothing but a source."

"Ouch." Camila cringed. "But also, that's a lie."

Mia nodded, looking off into the distance. "The kicker is that he acts like he's going to be the next Ronan Farrow or something. And teachers act like it too! But he's starting off his journalism career showing that he has no morals."

"Bad people get away with a lot of terrible things," Eva said gently.

"I know." Mia looked down at her hands. "You both know how much I hated being in the spotlight. I don't want to be vindictive, but I can't let Alex get away with this, right? He violated the journalistic code to sell those fake stories. I mean, I even thought Camila was the one selling the stories for a while!"

Eva's eyebrows raised, and Camila shook her head.

"Sorry," Mia whispered.

"Quit apologizing, Pepita," Eva said. "Everyone makes mistakes."

Mia didn't think she could ever possibly apologize enough.

And neither could Alex Liang, not that he would. "Is there anything I can do to fight back?"

"I know!" Camila's face glowed. "You can tell your story on social media. Use my feeds, and it'll get around the school pretty quick."

Even though her stomach clenched at the thought of being fodder for her school's gossip mill yet again, Mia had to admit it was a good idea. "Yeah. I'm sick and tired of people telling my story for me. It's time for me to do it for myself."

"Are you sure?" Eva asked, a skeptical look on her face.

"I'm sure." Though her rapid heartbeat and sweaty palms said otherwise. "What do I have to lose?"

That set things into motion. Camila tried to convince her to let her pick her outfit and do her hair and makeup, but Mia told her no. She needed to look like herself for this.

While Mia worked on what she was going to say, Eva and Camila set up the lighting. They didn't have the ring light that her mom swore by, so they turned on all the lights in the dining room, brought in two extra lamps, and hoped for the best.

After an hour of writing, Mia was ready.

"Want me to read it?" Camila asked.

"Nope. I'm good." Mia held tight to the paper she'd written her speech on.

"Are you sure you want to do this?" Eva asked one last time.

"Yes. I have to. For me."

Eva nodded. "Okay, Pepita."

"You go, girl," Camila chimed in.

Mia rewarded her with a big eye roll.

Her hands shook as Camila stood next to her phone, which was set up on a small tripod on the dining room table, her finger poised over the record button. Although Mia was plenty nervous about speaking, Camila had assured her they could keep rerecording until she felt good about it, and then Camila would post everything on her Instagram Stories and TikTok.

"Ready to take it from the top?" Camila asked, effortlessly settling into the role of director as Eva stood behind her looking nervous.

"Yep." Mia took a deep breath in, blew it out, and then rolled her shoulders back.

Camila pointed at her after hitting the record button, signaling her to start. Mia nodded, a shaky smile appearing on her face.

"Hi, everybody. I'm Mia Golden, and you may know me as the girl who sued her influencer mother for violation of privacy." She chuckled nervously. "But what you may not know is that someone has been selling stories about me and my family and my best friend's family to a gossip website. Today, I finally figured out who it was: Alex Liang, the editor in chief of the newspaper at my high school. He admitted to me less than two hours ago that he did it for the money."

Clearing her throat, Mia glanced down at the script she'd written, but she didn't need it.

"Now, I'm no expert, but that seems pretty unethical for someone who claims to be a journalist. And Alex not only claims to be a journalist but has won several journalism awards and got a scholarship to the Medill School of Journalism at Northwestern."

Mia could see her on-fire eyes reflected back at her from Camila's phone.

"I'm not sharing this to shame Alex, though that may be a bonus. I'm doing this because for my whole life someone else has told my story. My mom, the media, Alex. So now it's my turn: those stories that Alex sold and you may have read online are false. But more importantly, I want to remind you that everyone is entitled to a right to privacy, and a right to tell their own story, whether they are two years old or a hundred years old. As my dad used to say, 'You've got to fight for what is right.' He was right, and I'm going to stop sitting on the sidelines. I hope you all will too. Thank you."

Mia watched as Camila hit the stop button. "So what did you think?"

"Absolutely perfect," Camila breathed.

"Agreed." Eva's eyes were bright with tears. "I'm so proud of you for standing up for yourself."

Mia's heart swelled as she looked at these two women who meant so much to her. "Thank you. And good. Because there is no way I'm saying all that again."

"Want to watch it back?" Camila asked.

Mia slowly shook her head. "Nope. Upload it, please."

All three held their breath as they watched Camila work her magic on Instagram and TikTok. "Done. They're posted."

Within a minute, Camila's phone started pinging with notifications. As she started to click them open, Mia stopped her. "Leave it. It doesn't matter." She was sure there were people who agreed with her and plenty who didn't. Either way, she didn't really care what anyone else thought. She was living on her own terms now.

Camila nodded and put her phone in her pocket.

"How do you feel about . . ."—Eva waited for a beat, gaining their attention—"baking cookies?"

Mia grinned. "If they're chocolate chip, I'm in."

"Ditto," Camila said.

"Of course they're chocolate chip." Eva wrapped an arm around each girl and walked them to the kitchen.

CHAPTER 33

WHITNEY

Usually when she left her hometown after a visit, Whitney had to force herself to breathe, in and out, in and out, until she shook off the suffocation that took hold when she was around her family for too long. But as the Texas plains receded in her rearview mirror this time, Whitney's heart was full. Seeing how great her siblings were doing (well, except for Brendan, but she knew he'd get there eventually), meeting baby Amelia, and actually having a real, honest conversation with her mother for the first time in ages had changed everything. This time when she said, "I'll bring the kids to visit soon," she'd meant it.

Now she was heading back to Austin. Back to real life. Back to the lawsuit and impending trial. That realization made her stomach drop. Who would have ever thought she'd feel happier in her old hometown than her new one?

The thing was, it didn't have to be that way. And she knew it. A big change needed to be made, and she was the only one who could do it.

As the highway miles passed under her car wheels, Whitney became more and more determined to restore her relationship with Mia. But how? She tapped her steering wheel to the beat of the Taylor Swift song blasting on the radio. She knew what her daughter wanted: Mia wanted her to quit her social media career altogether. In a perfect world, she'd pull the plug on everything—Instagram, TikTok, her blog. But in a perfect world, Michael would still be alive, and she wouldn't have to worry about paying the mortgage each month.

Whitney pounded the steering wheel. It felt like she was in a Choose Your Own Adventure book, but every decision led to her demise. The situation with Mia was so big, it felt impossible to solve. She knew there was no other job that would allow her to make the kind of money she made as an influencer. So the only choice was cutting expenses. On her last night at home, her brother Tom had pulled her aside and quietly offered to chip in on their mom's rent. While she was grateful for the help, it wouldn't make enough of a dent for her to quit her job. Should she stop paying Rosie's tuition? Whitney cringed. She couldn't do that to her sister. Should she sell the house? The thought of uprooting their whole family again made a lump form in her throat. Whitney couldn't imagine that Mia would want to move when she had only three years left at home.

Oh god, Mia would be gone in three years. Whitney eyes burned. There had to be a way to make this work. One where she could rebuild the trust she'd broken with Mia while keeping her influencing career. Maybe she could be another type of influencer instead? Would her community still follow her if she focused primarily on fashion or beauty? She wasn't particularly interested or talented in either subject, but she could try. Though most of the fashion and beauty influencers she knew posted about their families too. Because that's what their followers wanted.

Her phone rang, breaking her out of her thoughts. She looked around, realizing that hours had passed as her thoughts swirled. The name Tawny flashed on the phone screen.

Whitney hit the speakerphone button. "What's up?"

"Have you seen Mia's video?" Tawny's voice was urgent.

"No. I'm driving home from visiting my family. Should get to Austin in about thirty minutes," Whitney said. "What's Mia's video?"

"Check Camila's TikTok when you get home."

Whitney groaned. "Is it bad?"

"It's . . . interesting."

"Like I-need-to-pull-over-right-now interesting?"

"No. It can wait." Tawny made her promise to drive safely and call after she'd watched the video.

Whitney pressed on the gas, making it home in record time. Her plan was to watch the video in her driveway before the kids got wind that she was there. But she hadn't even put her car in park when Chloe, Charlotte, and Mason ran out the front door to welcome her home. She should have known that a moment to herself wasn't going to happen. And she couldn't deny that she was delighted to see them too.

Whitney gave each one a long hug, brought her bags inside, and thanked Judith—who looked drained to the core—for taking care of the kids for the week. She sent her mother-in-law to her room for a rest and started dinner as the kids jumped around, asking her questions about their grandma Sandy, their aunt and uncles, and their new baby cousin.

The twins had to tell her all about their science project presentations and field trip to a museum, while Mason simply wanted her to hold him. They all hopped around like excited puppies when she pulled out a bag of mini cakes that she'd picked up on the drive home and told them they could eat the treats for dessert.

The whole time she was cooking, eating, doing the dishes, and getting everyone ready for bed, Mia's video was in the back of her mind. But right as she got the kids down for the night and the kitchen cleaned up and was about to head to her office, Judith appeared in the kitchen, rubbing at her eyes.

"I can't believe it. I fell asleep," she said with a yawn.

"I can believe it. My kids are exhausting." Whitney grinned at her. "Let me heat you up some dinner."

"Thank you." Judith settled into a chair at the dining table.

"Thank *you* for watching the kids." Whitney put a cup of hot tea in front of Judith. "I couldn't have left without you. And I really needed to go."

"Was it a good visit?"

"It was. It actually was."

The microwave dinged, and Whitney jumped up to grab Judith's plate of food.

"This looks delicious." Judith rubbed her hands together when she saw the spaghetti Whitney had thrown together, along with a simple salad.

Before she took a bite, Judith gave her a serious look. "I do want to talk to you about something, though."

"Oh no, what? Did something happen to one of the kids at school?"

"No, no. This is about me." Judith took a deep breath. "I realized I was kind of hard on you after that photo shoot."

Whitney shook her head. "It's okay. That shoot was a disaster."

"It's not okay. I've been way too hard on you. And if I'm being honest, I'm sorry about how I treated you before you and Michael got married. Suggesting the prenup and . . . everything. I wanted the best for my son, but I handled it poorly. And I didn't even try to get to know you. Now I know you were exactly what he needed in his life."

"Oh, Judith." She sniffed, dabbing at her eyes. "Where is all this coming from?"

Her mother-in-law shrugged and took another bite of spaghetti. "I'm exhausted after a week of watching the kids, and you've been doing it all by yourself since Michael died. For four years you've been their mother and the sole breadwinner. And you've handled it all with grace and gumption."

Whitney rubbed at her forehead. This was all a lot to process. She sat quietly as Judith ate her dinner. Her exhaustion from the drive mixed with the shock from Judith's apologies made her lightheaded.

Finally, she spoke. "I've been thinking a lot too." She pulled at a thread on the place mat in front of her. "I need to fix everything with Mia. I don't know how yet, but I'm going to figure it out."

Judith nodded. "Good. And I know you will."

After her mother-in-law went up to bed, Whitney headed to her office, finally able to watch the video. Flipping open her laptop, she typed Camila's handle, @SpicyCam, into the TikTok search bar. Mia's beautiful, serious face immediately filled her computer screen. "Hi, everybody. I'm Mia Golden, and you may know me as the girl who sued her influencer mother for violation of privacy."

Whitney hit the pause button. Her hands were shaking. She couldn't believe her daughter had put a video of herself on social media. She didn't know if she could watch the rest. Was this a takedown of her? If it was, it meant that she might be too late to fix things with Mia. She rubbed at her temples, trying to work up the courage to watch the whole video.

Taking a deep breath, Whitney hit the play button and braced herself. But as she listened to her daughter talk, she realized this wasn't about her—this was about Mia. Whitney's jaw dropped as Mia described how some punk named Alex Liang had been selling stories about their family and Camila's family to a tabloid site. *What is wrong with kids these days?* It took everything Whitney had to not pick up the phone and call the boy's family herself.

When the video ended, she hit play again. This time, as she watched her daughter stand up for herself, she was in awe of her maturity and composure. Mia had grown up before Whitney's eyes, and she was only now realizing it. She was incredibly proud of Mia for telling her own story and fighting back against Alex, but she was so sorry she had to do it. Especially because Whitney knew she was the reason. If it hadn't been for her career as an influencer, none of this would have ever happened. No one would have sold stories about their family, because no one would have cared.

Whitney clicked out of TikTok. She felt like she was thinking clearly for the first time in months. It was time for her to do for Mia what she wished her own mother had done for her all those years ago. She needed to listen, really listen. She needed to apologize. And then she needed to make a change.

Whitney could either go on believing forever that being an influencer was the only thing she was capable of doing—and potentially lose her daughter. Or she could take a leap into the unknown and take her career in a completely new direction, one that didn't involve invading her children's privacy. She could believe in herself. Not only could she write, but she was a good salesperson, and clearly she knew how to build a community. Those were valuable skills. Surely there was another way to use them.

Sitting alone in her quiet office, Whitney knew one thing for sure: shutting down her social media and blog was the only way to begin to fix the damage she had done to her relationship with Mia.

As her mother said, "It's never too late."

Now all she needed was the courage to make the first move. To be brave. Like Mia.

She looked at the clock. It was too late to call Tawny, but it was still a reasonable hour in California.

Whitney picked up her phone and dialed.

"Taylor?" she said when her manager answered. "Can you talk?"

March 1 – 6:22 p.m.
Basic Barbie: Did anyone see the video Mia made talking about some guy at her school selling stories about her to a gossip site? That poor girl can't catch a break.

March 1 – 6:25 p.m.
Ashley Graham Crackers: That is horrifying. These influencer kids are going to need so much therapy later in life.

March 1 – 6:33 p.m.
Smug Takes: If you don't like the way influencers share their children, unfollow them. Or at the very least, stop clicking on their links. That will at least slow the money train down.

March 1 – 6:49 p.m.
Retail Therapy & Rainbows: But I love following influencers! It's my guilty pleasure.

CHAPTER 34

MIA

Thanks for the ride." Mia jumped out of the Garcias' car and shut the door behind her.

"No problem. Just call when you're done." Omar waved and pulled away from the curb.

She was back at Caleb's office for yet another prep session. They'd been practicing what she would say if she was questioned by her mother's lawyer on the stand for a few hours a night for the past week. Caleb said he wasn't sure that he wanted or needed her to take the stand and testify against her mom, but he wanted Mia to be ready, just in case.

The receptionist was on a phone call, but she smiled at Mia and waved her into Caleb's office.

Mia opened the door and stumbled when she found Caleb already meeting with someone. A woman with long auburn hair sat in the chair across from him.

"Oh, uh, sorry," Mia stammered, stopping in her tracks.

The woman turned and looked at her.

"Mom?"

"Hi, sweetheart." Her mom stood up. Dressed in jeans, a navy "I Love Austin So Much" T-shirt, and sneakers, she almost looked like her pre-influencer self.

"What's going on?" Mia turned to look at Caleb, her eyes wide.

Caleb gave her a big smile and motioned for her to sit down. "Come in. There have been some developments in your case."

Her face was on fire as she sat down in the chair next to her mother, leaning slightly away. She looked at her lawyer with confused eyes. "What developments in the case?"

"Mia, your mom has something to tell you." Caleb nodded at Whitney.

Her mom cleared her throat. "I'm settling the case."

Mia's heart thumped in overdrive as her mom's words sank in. "What does that mean?" Her voice was practically a whisper.

"That means your mother has agreed to all your terms," Caleb said. "She's going to pay you and your siblings for the work you've all done for her through the years. She's removing all the photos you want removed, and she's not going to use you or your siblings as content anymore."

Mia shook her head, trying to stop the ringing in her ears. She'd gotten everything she'd wanted. How? Why?

She finally looked at her mother but didn't smile. "Why now?"

Caleb stood up. "Why don't I let you two talk? I need to get all the paperwork ready anyway." He paused to squeeze Mia's shoulder as he left his office.

Once they were alone, her mom gave her a shaky smile. At least Mia wasn't the only one who was nervous.

"Before I explain, I first want to apologize to you. I handled the pictures from Dad's funeral and the bathtub photos—

and really everything—all wrong. I was so mad at you for filing the lawsuit, but I never should have put you in that position to begin with. I'm so sorry."

Mia stared down at her hands. Her mother was saying everything she had wanted her to say. This didn't feel real.

She suddenly had an overwhelming urge to bite her cuticles, but before she could bring her hand to her mouth, her mom reached over and covered Mia's hand with her own. It felt better than she wanted to admit.

Mia pulled her hand away and watched her mom's face fall. "Why did you change your mind now, after all this time?"

Whitney sighed. "Lots of reasons. For one, there was your video."

Mia's mouth dropped open. "You know about that?"

"I do. Your video was incredible. I'm so proud of you for standing up for yourself. And I know your dad would have been proud too."

Feeling slightly dazed, Mia squeezed her eyes shut.

Her mom kept talking. "And for another, both your grandmas apologized to me for things that happened a long time ago—"

Mia's eyes flew open. "About what?"

Whitney paused. "I promise I'll tell you about it later. But the point is that they made me see it's never too late to apologize if you wrong someone, and I *wronged* you. You asked me to protect your privacy, your father's privacy, your siblings' privacy, and I refused. I thought it would ruin my career and torpedo our lifestyle, but those things happened anyway. And honestly, I realized losing sponsors and followers didn't matter. What ripped my heart out was losing you."

She looked at her daughter with a sad smile and lifted one shoulder in a half-hearted shrug. "I can't lose you, Mia."

That made her heart start to soften. The truth was, Mia couldn't lose her mother either. She loved her and wanted them to be close again too. And her mom was saying all the right stuff. Maybe things really would be different now.

"What about your influencer career?" Mia asked quietly, controlling her voice.

"I'm shutting it down."

Mia dropped back in her chair. "What?"

Whitney wiggled her fingers in the air. "Surprise."

"But what about money?"

"I was worried about that too, but Taylor gave me the idea to offer my social media expertise, as she called it, to the companies I've worked with as an influencer. I stayed up all night putting together a proposal and sent it out. I've already booked two clients."

"That's amazing."

A blush spread across her mom's cheeks. "Thanks. I don't know if I'll ever make the amount of money I made as an influencer, but I'm going to try my hardest." Whitney cleared her throat. "We're also going to have to watch our spending. And we may have to sell the house. But I'll try my best to stay in the same school district."

"Okay." Mia didn't even know what to say at this point. It had only been a few minutes, but everything was different. No more fighting. No more trial. She could move back home again.

"You know, after I posted that video, I told Camila I wasn't going to read the comments."

Her mom raised her eyebrows. "Smart move."

"But I couldn't help myself."

"I know that feeling. Were the comments nice or rude?"

"Mostly nice. So many people gave me encouragement and shared their own stories. You know, lots of other teenagers don't like the things their parents share about them on social media."

Whitney nodded. "I believe it. How did that make you feel?"

"It made me feel really good. Like there were a lot more people like me than I knew. It was like a . . ."

"Community?"

"Yeah." Mia bit her lip. "It made me kind of understand why you started blogging and sharing on social media."

"That's how it started for me too, and it honestly helped me a lot after your dad died." Her mom's voice was warm and gentle. "I'm glad you can see why I did it, but it was never supposed to be at your expense. That's not worth it to me."

A smile took over Mia's face. She still couldn't believe her mom was saying all this. It was like she completely understood Mia's point of view now.

"If we're sharing all our secrets today, I have another one." Mia folded her arms over her chest. "It's something I haven't told anyone: I don't think I want to be a doctor."

"Really?" There was surprise in her mother's voice but not judgment. "What made you change your mind?"

"I hate hospitals. I get anxious every time I'm in one and flash right back to the day Dad died."

"Truthfully, I'm not the biggest fan of hospitals anymore either."

"It's been really hard watching Eva go through chemo too. I don't know if I have the strength to see pain and suffering every day."

"Oh, sweetie." Whitney stood and moved in front of Mia, pulling her up for a hug. "I'm so proud of you for being mature enough to realize your old dream no longer fits."

Mia fell into her mother's arms. "But if I don't become a cardiologist"—her sobs broke up her words—"I feel like . . . like I failed . . . like I failed Dad."

Whitney wrapped her arms around Mia, tutting softly. "How could you ever think that?"

Mia sniffled, pressing her face against her mom's shirt, exactly like she used to when she was a toddler. "I worry his life, and death, meant nothing."

"Of course your father's life meant something." Whitney smoothed Mia's hair, threading her fingers through the red strands. Mia had missed that.

"Your father created you, and Chloe, and Charlotte, and Mason. You are the loves of his life and his legacy. You don't have to become a doctor for him. I know for a fact all he wanted was for his children to be happy. That's what every parent wants. The good ones, anyway."

"Yeah?" Mia sniffled.

"Yes." Her mother nodded. "I promise."

They pulled apart when there was a light tap on the door. It was Caleb. "Everything okay in here?" he asked.

Mia wiped at her eyes. "Everything's great."

"Wonderful." Caleb held up a stack of papers. "Are you ready to start some paperwork?"

Mia grabbed her mom's hand. "We're ready."

CHAPTER 35
WHITNEY

It had been ten days since she told Mia she was pulling the plug on her blog and social media accounts. It took Whitney that long to get everything organized. First, she'd had a long talk with Taylor, who took her decision as well as could be expected. Then she'd drafted an email to all the brands she had ever worked with, letting them know she was calling it quits. At the same time, Taylor combed through Whitney's finances, making sure she'd received payment for every sponsored post or ad campaign she'd ever done.

And she'd had a lot of time to reflect. Every parent believed they would do the right thing for their children, but when push came to shove, Whitney had done the wrong thing. And she hadn't been doing the wrong thing for only six months. It had been years, actually. All because she'd been so scared she couldn't hack it any other way. That she couldn't make enough of a living to sustain them at a regular job. And because she loved the attention and admiration she got from her "fans." She'd been scared and selfish long enough. Now she was ready to change.

Every time she felt anxious about shutting down her social media channels and the blog, she'd watch Mia's video. (She'd saved it in case Mia ever needed a reminder of her moxie.) Seeing her fifteen-year-old daughter stand up to someone who had lied to her, who'd sold her story, who'd looked at her as a commodity and not as a person, reignited the fire in her belly and recharged her resolve. Whitney had heard the boy had been kicked off the newspaper—by his classmates, no less—and his scholarship to Northwestern was under review. Turned out, selling made-up stories about a source for money to tabloid websites violated the morality clause in his scholarship. She'd heard through the gossip mill that his parents were furious.

But Whitney had done the exact same thing to her daughter—and her other kids too. She'd viewed them as props, not people. Not all the time, but enough to have been a problem. It was the thought of someone else doing it to Mia that made Whitney finally see how wrong it was.

Whitney was beyond proud of how Mia had defended herself. Making that video took guts. Far more guts than she'd had at that age.

She looked at her watch. Mia should be home any minute.

Whitney could hear Mason and the twins in the kitchen with Judith making brownies. Her mother-in-law was staying with them a bit longer, until Whitney got her sea legs with her new job. Judith was also going to help her sell this house. After Whitney discussed it with the kids, they'd decided to downsize every way they could. Mia and the twins had said they were fine with moving, as long as they could stay at the same schools. Besides, they all needed a fresh start in a home that didn't have photos all over the internet.

Mia had mentioned getting a job to help support the family too. Whitney told her absolutely not. She had worked enough for this family over the years to last a lifetime. Mia needed to enjoy these last years being a kid, to have time to figure out who she was and what made her happy. But then Mia announced she was interested in studying law after getting a small peek at how court cases go through the system. She'd even scored an internship with Caleb for the summer. That Whitney had been okay with—as long as Mia saved most of the money she made for college. Whitney couldn't wait to see what was in store for her brilliant daughter.

"Hey, Mom." Mia strolled into her office eating a brownie, like it was the most natural thing in the world and just weeks earlier they hadn't been in the middle of a legal battle.

Whitney grinned at her daughter. "Hey, yourself." Excitement and contentment competed inside her. "Do you have a second? I want to show you something."

"For sure." Mia pulled up a chair next to her.

"I wrote this today."

Mia leaned toward Whitney's laptop, read for a moment, and then looked at her mom with her eyebrows raised. "Whoa. This is happening today?"

"Yep. I'm ready."

Mia nodded, and then turned back to the screen to read the goodbye Whitney had written to her followers.

After eight years, it's time for me to bid adieu to my blog and social media accounts. I'm sure you all know why, but let me say this publicly: I've long said my family comes first, but my actions showed that was not true. It's time for me to change that. Thank you all for sticking with me through the many ups and downs of my life. Your support has meant the world to me.

Xo, Whitney

"It's perfect," Mia said. "Short and sweet."

"Exactly." She could have written some self-serving post about the 2,500 photos on Instagram and 356 pages of content on her blog that summed up her career—and family—for the past eight years. But this wasn't about her anymore. This was about her kids, especially Mia.

"Will you do the honors?" Whitney asked Mia, whose eyes lit up.

Within seconds of uploading the statement to Instagram, Whitney's account was flooded with comments, mentions, and DMs.

Please say it isn't true!

Noooooo! Whitney, don't go!

But I wanted to watch Mason grow up!

Who will I turn to for parenting advice now?

It gave her a little thrill to see all the nice comments, even though it shouldn't. She knew the hateful ones would be rolling in soon enough. But Whitney would be lying if she said she wouldn't miss the community she had built. Even if the "community" was mainly made up of people she'd never met. (She'd also reached out to Jane Mumford to give her a heads-up that she was shutting things down—and made her promise to stay in touch.)

"What about the blog?" Mia asked.

"I already archived all the content," Whitney said. She'd exported everything, like WordPress recommended, but she doubted she'd ever look at it again.

She didn't tell Mia her finger had shook as it hovered over the red "DELETE THIS SITE" button. "This action CAN-NOT be undone," the site helpfully reminded her. *That's kind of the idea*, she'd thought. Exhaling a deep breath, she'd pushed the button, smiling as the screen went black.

WordPress had a final message for her: "At this point, any-one who attempts to visit your site will see a message stating your site is no longer available and has been deleted by the author."

That's right. Deleted by the author. This was her choice, and Whitney knew without a doubt it was the correct one.

She shut her laptop and looked at Mia. "You know what sounds good right about now?"

"What?"

"A walk. It's gorgeous out."

Mia leaped to her feet. "I'll go with you."

Her heart danced in her chest as her daughter reached over and took hold of her hand. Whitney marveled at how much things had changed in such a short amount of time.

They walked out the front door and into a perfect spring

afternoon. Online, her career as an influencer was over. But in the real world, the sun was shining, birds were chirping, there was a light breeze, and life went on.

Whitney waved at a neighbor who was collecting letters from her mailbox, and Mia pointed at a deer nibbling grass in a lawn down the street.

"How'd your biology test go?"

"It went okay." Mia shrugged. "I'm not worried about it."

Whitney smiled. "Good."

They turned the corner, not knowing where they were headed or how long they'd be gone. But Whitney was fine with that. She didn't know exactly what the future held, but one thing was certain: she'd have her children by her side. Offline.

March 12 – 4:36 p.m.

Retail Therapy & Rainbows: Wow. I can't believe Whitney actually left the internet. Good for her. Family is more important.

March 12 – 4:38 p.m.

Moose Willis: Bye, Felicia!

March 12 – 4:42 p.m.

Smug Takes: I'm not buying it. She loves the spotlight way too much. She won't be able to stay away for long.

March 12 – 4:48 p.m.

The Good Karen: I say bravo. Clearly she learned something about the right to privacy. Now if only all these other influencer moms would follow suit.

March 12 – 5:03 p.m.

Smug Takes: Mark my words: She'll be back.

ACKNOWLEDGMENTS

In 2009, I interviewed health and fitness bloggers for *Self* magazine—almost all of whom have since built large followings on Instagram. Back then, no one knew how popular and pervasive influencer culture would become. Over the past fifteen years, as my life has changed, I have turned to influencers for their content about weddings, interior design, and raising children. And as a magazine editor, I've watched as they've competed with publications as trusted sources.

I had the idea for this book in 2020. Like it did for many moms who were home with their kids during the pandemic, social media became a lifeline for me while I cared for kids who needed to be fed, schooled, and entertained all day, every day. I saw influencers post their family's routines, homes, meals, and even cancer diagnoses and deaths. For many of us, social media became both a memory book and a way to process the intense event we were going through. That time period made me think deeply about how parents use social media, and what it means for this generation of kids, like my own, who never got to choose whether or not they wanted to be featured on it. I hope *Hate Follow* starts a bigger conversation about children and social media.

Thank you to my agent, Rachelle Gardner, for understanding

this book and seeing its potential from the beginning. And my deepest thanks to my editors: Asanté Simons, who gave this book a home at William Morrow and championed it from the start, and Tessa James, who got the book to the finish line. Working with everyone at William Morrow has been wonderful, including art director Ploy Siripant, who along with artist Laurence Bentz created the cover of my dreams; copy editor Stephanie Evans, who caught timeline errors and typos; and the stellar marketing and publicity team: Jessica Cozzi, Deanna Bailey, Danielle Bartlett, Eliza Rosenberry, and Amelia Wood.

One of the great pleasures of writing fiction for me has been all the wonderful people I've met along the way. First and foremost, my amazing writing squad: Hadley Leggett, Amy Neff, and Lauren Parvizi. Thank you for the writing (and life) encouragement, the Zoom calls, the retreats, the millions of texts, and so much more. You are my people.

Thank you to my Austin writing cohort, Debra Doliner, Caroline Freedman, and Lexi Riemer, for the meetups and support. (And to Chandler Baker and Alex Kiester for introducing us!) And to Lacy Phillips, Natalie Kikić, Elizabeth Brooks, Beth McNeil, and Sarah Munn for the early reads and excellent notes. (And to Bianca Marais for connecting us!) I've also met many lovely writers through the Women's Fiction Writers Association and Writers' League of Texas, including Kate Taggart and Sara Kocek, who did a fantastic developmental edit on this book.

To KJ Dell'Antonia: I will always be grateful that we got paired together through the WFWA Mentor Program—and that you read my whole book when you didn't have to! Your feedback was invaluable.

Thank you to my friends who have read my work, listened to me talk about this book, and supported me through the ups and downs of publishing, including Meg Mulloy, Tula Karras, Erin Howard, Ashley Womble, Rennie Dyball, Connie Fennewald, Bonnie Lang, Celeste Pustka, and Camille Bartley.

I leaned on many experts for this book, including Allison Korn, who answered my legal questions; Natalie Dale for medical advice; and Lucy Cottrill and Julia Lentz, who read portions of Mia's story and answered questions about high school. Any mistakes are my own.

To my first and most loving reader, my mom: Thank you for reading all my drafts and for always seeing the best in me. And to my dad, who always roots for me and inspired two specific parts of this book—stinky fish and the half beard. I knew you'd get a kick out of both.

To my husband, Ray: I am genuinely so lucky to have found a life partner who does so much for me and our family. Thank you for the delicious meals, enthusiastic grocery shopping, and adventures you take the kids on so I can write. This book couldn't have happened without you.

And to my children, M and K: People have long told me that I should write a book, but it wasn't until you were born that I found my voice and tapped into my heart. Thank you for the cuddles, cuteness, and daily inspiration. (Just promise you won't ever sue me, okay?) Love, Mom